Praise for
Tracy Brogan

"Heart, humor and characters you'll love—Tracy Brogan is the next great voice in contemporary romance."

— *New York Times* bestselling author Kristan Higgins

"Tracy Brogan is my go-to, laugh-out-loud remedy for a stressful day."

—Kieran Kramer, *USA Today* bestselling author of *Sweet Talk Me*

"With trademark humor, lovely, poignant touches, and a sexy-as-sin hero, *The Best Medicine* is Tracy Brogan at her finest. Charming, witty and fun."

—Kimberly Kincaid, author of *Turn Up the Heat*
(*A Pine Mountain Novel*)

Love Me Sweet

A BELL HARBOR NOVEL

Other Titles by Tracy Brogan

Crazy Little Thing
Highland Surrender
Hold on My Heart
The Best Medicine

Love Me Sweet

A BELL HARBOR NOVEL

Tracy Brogan

Montlake
Romance

Published by Montlake Romance, Seattle

www.apub.com

Amazon, the Amazon logo, and Montlake are trademarks of Amazon.com, Inc., or its affiliates.

ISBN-13: 9781477819630
ISBN-10: 1477819630

Cover design by Mumtaz Mustafa

Library of Congress Control Number: 2014912701

Printed in the United States of America

For Meredith.
Thank you . . . thank you very much.

Chapter 1

FOR A SUN-KISSED CALIFORNIA GIRL like Delaney Masterson, frostbitten Bell Harbor was a ridiculous place to hide, which—naturally—made it the perfect place to hide. No one would look for her here. Not in this off-the-beaten-path lakeside town tucked somewhere between Central Nowheresville and Eastern Neverbeentheresburg. Certainly not in this teetering, tottering Victorian house with its lavender siding and crooked roof. Especially in the dead of winter.

It was January, after all.

In Michigan.

Seriously, in all her life she'd never seen so much snow. No wonder the whole damn state was shaped like a mitten.

"I'll take it," Delaney said, peering down at the fluffy-haired blonde by her side. Donna Beckett—her new landlord, as of that very instant.

The two of them were standing inside a sparsely furnished living room, having spent the last twenty minutes looking around eight hundred square feet of uninspired, shag-carpeted rental property. This was no plush palace. No urban loft. The ad on craigslist had been overly generous when listing the amenities, but it did have two bedrooms upstairs, a functional—if dangerously outdated—kitchen, a few pieces of plaid furniture, and it at least appeared to be clean. Clean-ish. Better than the last six places Delaney had looked at. None of those other houses were remotely acceptable—unless she'd been looking for something run-down, too small, or possibly haunted, which she wasn't.

Here the smells of bleach and deodorizer mingled in the air, possibly masking an underlying aroma of crud, but the weather outside was frightful, like swirling, twirling snownado kind of frightful, and she was tired of looking for a place to live. The Bell Harbor Hotel was too expensive. She was on a strict budget now, and her money would only last for so long. And besides that, the hotel was crowded with far too many people who might recognize her. This house would have to be fine. It needed to be fine.

"Do you offer a month-to-month lease?" Delaney asked, adjusting the temples of her black-framed reading glasses. They were too big and kept slipping down her nose. She should have tried them on before buying them, but she'd been in a hurry at the store and grabbed the thickest, ugliest ones she could find. She'd grabbed a baseball hat and a box of hair color too. L'Oreal's Utterly Forgettable Brown, #257. It wasn't much of a disguise, but she'd worry about that later. So far Mrs. Beckett hadn't shown any signs of recognizing her, which was a relief. Maybe this town was so small they didn't have Internet.

Or cable.

Or tabloid magazines.

Or any sort of social media whatsoever, because Delaney's face had been plastered all over the place recently. Impossible to miss.

Rotten paparazzi.

The petite landlady ran both palms down the front of her well-worn gray sweatshirt. It had the image of some kind of aquatic mammal on it. A walrus? Or a manatee? It was hard to see thanks to the thick reading glasses, but whatever it was, it wasn't attractive. Delaney knew fashion, but it didn't take an expert stylist to know that big, old shirts with big, old blobs on the front were not flattering in any way, on any shape or form.

"I'd prefer a twelve-month lease," Mrs. Beckett answered, tugging at the banded hem of the sweatshirt and making the manatee shimmy a little. "But I suppose we could shorten it to six. Would six months work for you?"

Six months. Delaney wasn't certain she'd be staying six weeks, much less half the year. Given her current set of circumstances, she couldn't plan that far ahead, but she suspected a month-to-month place would be hard to find in the middle of Snowmageddon, and this little shack did have a certain charm to it. Maybe it was the lacy scrolled woodwork in the corner of the doorways or the thick crown molding. It was cute and cozy in its own antiquated way. And Lord knew Delaney Masterson could use a little cute and cozy right about now, because she knew opulent and extravagant came with a huge emotional price tag.

"Six months is OK, I guess." She adjusted her fake glasses once more.

The landlady nodded. "Excellent. I have the leasing papers in my car. I'll just need your driver's license, a security deposit, and the first month's rent."

Driver's license? Delaney's heart plummeted faster than the sales of her dad's last CD. She didn't want to show her driver's license to Donna Beckett. She didn't want to show it to anyone. She pressed a thumbnail against her bottom lip, stalling for time.

"Right. OK. Here's the thing, Mrs. Beckett. My wallet got stolen last week so I don't have my identification with me right now. But how about if I pay you six months' rent up front, in cash, and we call it good?"

It was a risk. Delaney might have to move out at a moment's notice, and then she'd be out that extra money, but Mrs. Beckett's expression lit up like a marquee when Delaney said *cash*. Everybody loved cash, and if spending a little extra now meant keeping her ID tucked deep inside the Louis Vuitton backpack currently slung over her shoulder, then it was worth it.

"Six months . . . *in cash*? When would you want to move in?" Mrs. Beckett's voice was breathy now, livelier than it had been before. Yes, cash was definitely the way to go.

Delaney gestured toward the window. "Today. Now. All of my stuff is in the car." Outside in the driveway sat the rusted yellow Volkswagen she'd bought a week ago from Ed's Used Car Lot in Encino. Nine hundred bucks. Cash. No questions asked, making it worth every penny, but not a penny more.

"All your stuff is in that little thing?" Mrs. Beckett's pale brows knit as she squinted past the icy window glass at the aging vehicle. Herbie the Love Bug it was not. And that wasn't really *all* of Delaney's stuff. It was about one one-millionth of her stuff, but it was all she'd managed to jam into her suitcase on her way out of town.

Delaney forced a smile, dialing it up to *extra bright*, a trick she'd learned from her supermodel mother. If you act perky enough, people believe you're trustworthy. "I travel light."

"I should say so. Where are you from?" Mrs. Beckett returned her gaze to Delaney's face.

Delaney tugged down the brim of her baseball cap.

"Um, Miami."

It was the first location that popped into her head, but she wasn't from Miami. Of course she wasn't. She wasn't even from Florida. That was a stupid answer. Delaney tried to smile bigger to mask her mistake but her lips wouldn't stretch any farther.

Donna Beckett scratched her head, giving her short hair a little extra pouf on one side. "Miami? My goodness. Why would you leave sunny Miami to come up here in this terrible weather?"

That was an excellent question, and it needed a logical answer, but the truth was far from logical. Even Delaney realized that. She'd come here on a whim, an emotionally charged reaction sorely lacking in strategy. Still, she should have said she was from Fargo or Minneapolis or someplace just as cold and snowy as it was here. Like Siberia or the South Pole. Duplicity was not a skill Delaney had mastered. Maybe it would get easier with practice.

"I heard there was good skiing around here," she answered.

Mrs. Beckett nodded. "Sure, I guess. Although for even better skiing, you'll want to head up north."

Up north? Seriously? How much farther north could she go before she hit the Canadian border? Sure, she was on the run and hiding out, but things hadn't gotten so dire she needed to leave the country.

Yet.

"Great. I'll keep that in mind. Up north," Delaney said. "So do we have a deal?" She stuck out her hand for a shake. This had to work.

Mrs. Beckett's gaze moved from the outstretched hand to Delaney's face, peering intently. There seemed to be some indecision going on in the landlady's mind. Delaney hiccupped. She did that when she was nervous.

"Six months *in cash*?" the landlady asked again.

"Cash," Delaney answered, adding a jaunty little tilt of her head with the next hiccup, and patting the backpack. "Unfortunately my checkbook and debit cards were stolen along with my wallet, but the good news is I stopped at the bank before leaving home and got some money."

Yes. She had, and it hadn't been easy. Turns out banks weren't very enthusiastic about giving customers their money *back*. Especially customers who wanted thousands of dollars, and double especially when they wanted it in tens and twenties.

"How did you get money from the bank with no identification?" Twin creases of suspicion deepened between Mrs. Beckett's brows, but Delaney gave a fast roll of her shoulders, a subtle shrug meant to evoke nonchalance—a nonchalance she certainly didn't feel—and the lies just kept on rolling out.

"Oh, that was no problem. They know me at the bank. In fact, I used to work there. When I was in college. In Miami. I worked at the bank in Miami during college."

Delaney nodded, agreeing with herself and hoping the power of repetition and suggestion was on her side. Like a Jedi mind trick. *These are not the droids you're looking for.* Still, a bank teller? In Miami? She'd never been a bank teller. And she'd never finished college either. She was a celebrity stylist in Beverly Hills, just like her two sisters, and occasionally she helped out in their mother's luxury soaps boutique.

Delaney adjusted the backpack on her shoulder, feeling the strap gnaw into her skin. Thousands of dollars in paper money was physically heavy, and heavier still when you considered the possibility that you might be making the biggest mistake of your whole, stupid, irrelevant twenty-seven-year life.

Mrs. Beckett wiped her palms again and glanced at the backpack. "Well, I suppose if you pay it all up front, it would be OK, but I will need you to sign a lease before you bring anything in. And I'd still like a copy of your driver's license just as soon as you have it."

Relief washed over Delaney at the apparent ease of this transaction. She was in, and she could stall on producing a license indefinitely. With any luck, by the time she finally offered it to the landlady, she'd have the woman thoroughly convinced she was not *that* Delaney Masterson.

"Sure thing. No problem." Hiccup.

Mrs. Beckett smiled. "I guess we have a deal, then, but I should mention that my husband, Carl, will be doing some repairs over here in the next few days. He needs to fix the leaky showerhead in the bathroom. And the back door doesn't always lock. You need to give it a little extra tug, not that you have to worry much about locking doors in this town. Bell Harbor is the safest place around."

Safest place around? Good. Delaney sincerely hoped that was true. She also hoped it was a place where people minded their own business and wouldn't butt into hers. Privacy was what she craved above all else. The chance to be completely and totally unobserved, with no one snapping a photo or sifting through her trash. It was time for her to fade into the mist like . . . well, like mist.

Fifteen minutes later Delaney scrawled an illegible signature on the leasing contract in front of her. She and Mrs. Beckett had moved into the linoleum-floored kitchen and were now seated at the square dinette table. Its dingy white-and-gray-speckled top was surrounded by a scarred metal rim. The chairs were metal too, with cracked red seat cushions. Old enough to be retro but so dinged up they just looked old.

Delaney slid the papers back to her new landlord, her pulse thrumming right under her skin. "Here you go, Mrs. Beckett."

"Oh, you can call me Donna," she said, picking up the lease agreement and bringing it close to her face. Her eyes narrowed, her gaze directed at the spot where Delaney had signed. Donna's cheeks flushed a little, and the paper crackled as she gripped it tighter.

Delaney held her breath. This jig might be up. Her fingers tapped restlessly on her thighs as she wondered if she should have just thrown herself on the mercy of this manatee-loving woman and admitted who she was.

Five seconds stretched into an endless ten.

At last Donna chuckled and shook her head. "This is awkward. I should have brought my reading glasses because I can't quite make out your signature and I'm afraid I never asked your name. Does this say . . . Elaine Masters?"

Elaine Masters?

Delaney's heart skipped a beat. The jig was still firmly in place—and here was her chance. Her chance to remain anonymous. Her chance to create a whole new *her*, even if it was only temporary. She'd never thought of using an alias, but the idea was brilliant. Irresistible.

The decision took no longer than a blink.

"Yes, it does," she said, offering up the first genuine smile she'd shared with anyone in weeks. "My name is Elaine Masters."

———————

For an adventure-show cameraman like Grant Connelly, home was a campsite near the Ucayali River in Peru, or at the base of an active volcano like Tinakula, or maybe some ramshackle motel in Katmandu if he decided to splurge on having a solid roof over his head, but now it was time to head home to Bell Harbor because his younger brother was about to do something irretrievably stupid.

"Stupid," Grant murmured.

Assistant producer Jake Simmons didn't bother to look Grant's way. Instead he leaned closer to the video monitor in front of them and adjusted a few dials. The two men were inside a makeshift editing room, their office for the past two months, although it was really nothing more than an oversized canvas tent full of high-tech equipment powered by a big-ass generator—a generator that had been a bitch and a half to haul through the Philippine jungle to their current location. Jake tapped the monitor with his index finger, pointing at the image of a man dangling over a rocky precipice several yards from where they sat.

"Who's stupid?" Jake asked. "Surely you're not referring to the star of *One Man, One Planet*, are you?" His voice was commercial-grade enthusiasm, but Grant knew he shared the same low opinion of the man on-screen. Blake Rockstone. Their idiot boss.

Blake turned his face toward the camera lens as if he could hear their criticism. He couldn't, of course. He was too far away and too busy pretending to be in a precarious predicament. Exaggerated facial expressions and clever camera angles made it look as if he were high in the air, when in reality, a mere six feet separated him from a soft, mossy landing. Six feet and a protective harness hidden under his clothes, the gutless coward.

One man, one planet?

Hardly. More like one mammoth ego supported by dozens of highly skilled but invisible men. Lately everything about this show had become fake, from the dangerous situations right down to the survival skills of the star. Blake Rockstone was no daredevil. He wasn't a great outdoorsman either. Shit, he wasn't even a happy camper.

And two nights ago he'd slept with Grant's girlfriend.

Make that *ex*-girlfriend.

"That horse's ass couldn't start a campfire with two blow torches and a gallon of gas," Grant muttered, "but in this case, I'm talking about my brother." He held up a smudged, tattered envelope, ivory cardstock—now bent, spindled, and mutilated after its journey all the way from Bell Harbor, Michigan, to their camp at the base of Mount Pinatubo. It had taken more than a month to get there, judging from the date stamp, and how the thing had found its way to him in the Philippines was a mystery, but it was the contents he found the most surprising.

"What's that?" Jake asked, his gaze flicking over Grant like a mosquito before returning to the monitor.

"I'll show you what it is." Grant tugged the card from the envelope, adding another tear in his haste. He'd read the thing fifteen times in as many minutes but it still hadn't sunk in.

"Evelyn Marjorie Rhoades and Tyler Robert Connelly cordially request the honor of your presence at their wedding as they join together in holy matrimony." Grant flung the invitation down like pocket aces on the table in front of the monitor. "Who the hell is Evelyn Marjorie Rhoades? The last time I talked to my brother, he wasn't even dating anyone."

Jake picked up the invitation and looked it over like it was a jungle leaf waiting to be classified. "Married, huh? When's the last time you talked to him?"

Grant stood up and walked to the boundary of the tent, looking out into dense foliage. It was late afternoon and hot as hell, even for the dry season, but it wasn't the weather making him sweat. It was the hollow realization that his brother's life was heading in a direction the complete opposite of his own.

"I don't know. Three months ago? Maybe four? I know for sure I talked to him in June when we were still in New Zealand."

Jake arched one sandy-colored eyebrow and counted on his fingers. "June? Dude, it's January. That was six months ago."

Grant turned back around to face him. "Six months? Yeah, OK, so I haven't talked to him in a while, but he never said anything about her then, and now all of a sudden he's getting married? That's the stupidest thing I ever heard."

A monumentally stupid thing—and a move straight out of

their mother's playbook. Marry first, get acquainted afterward. To hell with the consequences. She was on her third marriage now but he'd thought Tyler had better sense.

"You think marriage is stupid?" Jake's chuckle was slightly patronizing but Grant ignored that.

"It is if you're twenty-seven years old and have never left Bell Harbor. My brother is still a kid."

"Hey, I resent that. I'm twenty-seven, you know." Jake took off his safari hat and wiped the perspiration from his forehead, but he didn't sound resentful. He sounded amused, which only added to Grant's irritation. He took off his own hat, running a hand through his shaggy brown hair, making it stand on end.

"That's my point exactly, Jake. You're traveling, having adventures, living a life. *And* you're smart enough to stay single. You see what I'm saying?"

Jake's sudden laughter split through the clearing, causing a bar-bellied cuckoo shrike to flap its wings and squawk in annoyance. "I'm single *because* I travel all the time, dumbass. You don't realize how lucky you are to have Miranda."

Grant opened his mouth to explain he wasn't lucky at all. Miranda had her own agenda, her own reasons for joining this show that had nothing to do with him, but he swallowed the words. He didn't want to talk about her right now. Not even to Jake, his closest friend and frequent partner in crime.

Jake looked back at the wedding invitation, turning it this way and that. "Anyway, this is kind of a fancy invite. Maybe this Evelyn chick is rich."

Grant stuffed both fists into the deep pockets of his cargo pants. "I seriously doubt that. She must be pregnant. Why else get married in such a hurry?" His poor, dumb, irresponsible brother.

Jake shook his head. "You're a real romantic guy, you know that, Grant? Maybe you should get a job on one of those reality dating shows."

Grant's snort wasn't subtle. "You know as well as I do there is no *reality* in reality television."

Jake turned back to the monitor. "Probably not, but I'd sure as hell rather work on a set with twenty-five hot bachelorettes than hang out in the jungle with you for the rest of my life. No offense."

Grant's mood lightened. Jake might be on to something. "No offense taken. I suppose I'd rather live in a house full of beautiful women than follow this asshat around too." He pointed to the video monitor where Blake Rockstone had dropped from the rope and was pretending to wrestle a fifteen-foot python near the edge of a lake. The thing was totally fake. Made of rubber. They'd ordered it from Amazon. "But even so," Grant added, "there's a big difference between hanging out with a bunch of women and actually marrying one."

Jake handed back the invitation. "I had no idea you were so averse to the concept of wedlock. What does Miranda think of that?"

Grant felt all the muscles in his shoulders seize up. No, he didn't want to talk about this now, but it was evidently unavoidable. There were only thirty-five people in this camp, after all, and the news would get out soon enough. In fact, he was surprised it wasn't already public knowledge.

"Miranda has jumped ship," Grant said.

She hadn't just jumped ship, though. She'd jumped from his boat into Blake's. Of all the insults, losing a woman to that Eddie Bauer mannequin was a real kick in the groin.

Jake's eyes widened. "What do you mean?"

Grant reached up and tried to squeeze the knot of tension out of his shoulder. "Blake offered her a better deal and she took it.

He says he'll make her the cohost of the show, which apparently comes with a broad range of job requirements."

Jake leaned closer. "Are you kidding me? She's with Blake now?"

"Well, last night after dark, she moved all of her stuff from my tent into his. So, yeah, I guess she is. He's a big star, you know. I'm just the cinematographer. Guess being with him in front of the camera is better than being with me behind it. I was just a stepping stone on her path to fame."

Jake's face flushed, his voice lowered. "I'm sorry, bro. That's lousy."

It was lousy. His relationship with Miranda had always been more about convenience than true love, but still, he had cared about her, and she'd used him. On a humiliation scale ranging from having your fly unzipped to showing up at a bar mitzvah buck-ass naked, well, this left him feeling kind of naked. He'd be damned if he let anyone know how this left him stinging, though. He wouldn't give her the satisfaction of showing his wounds.

"Well, what Miranda lacks in sensitivity she makes up for in ambition. There's not much opportunity in a place like this for a woman like her. I guess she had to take her shot."

Not much opportunity for him in a place like this either. He'd been thinking about that quite a bit lately, even before this debacle with Blake and Miranda. Grant was director of photography and coproducer of *One Man, One Planet*. He was at the top of his game professionally, but his income and reputation depended on creating a quality show, and lately Blake had been phoning it in. What had started out a few years ago as riveting television full of majestic photography and wild adventures had been reduced to close-ups of Blake eating beetles secretly made of sugar, and sound bites aimed at the lowest common intellectual denominator. They'd gone commercial, and Grant's integrity was taking a hit. He didn't like that. He had bigger goals for his career. And for his life.

Grant picked up the wedding invitation and read it once more. Maybe it was time for him to move on to a new phase too, just like Miranda had. Just like his brother was doing.

No. Not maybe. Definitely.

The decision was spontaneous, but he knew in his gut it was the right call.

"I'm going home," he said as much to the jungle as to Jake.

"For the wedding?"

"Nope. For good. I'm quitting."

Jake knocked over a canvas chair as he took a giant step closer. "Quitting? Because of Miranda? Don't do it, bro. You can't leave me in the jungle with Blake. You'd miss this."

Grant stepped out from the shade of the tent into the bright sunshine. Overhead the sky was a rich, cloudless blue. The air was noisy with the clicks and chatter of the jungle, heavy with the sweet scent of sampaguita jasmine.

"It's not about her. Not really. It's about a lot of other things. I will miss this, but I haven't seen my family in ages, you know? My grandfather deeded that house to me last year when he died and I haven't even been back to see it yet. Remember? We were filming in Cambodia so I missed the funeral?"

Jake stepped into the sunlight next to him. "Then go home for a vacation, visit with your family, but don't quit."

Grant looked up to the peak of Mount Pinatubo. "You know how, when you get to the top of a mountain, you enjoy the view for about five minutes before you start looking around for the next summit? That's where I'm at, Jake. I need a new challenge."

Jake scratched his head. "OK, I get that, but everything you've ever said about Bell Harbor is that it's a dead-end town with nothing to offer, so why go back there now?"

"I don't know. I probably won't stay for long, but it's a good place to regroup, maybe rescue my brother from throwing his life away." He smirked at Jake.

He was mostly kidding about rescuing Tyler. Mostly. If his brother wanted to waste his future in that tiny town, it wasn't Grant's problem. In fact, he'd made it a policy to not let family drama pull him back to Michigan. His job was all-consuming, sometimes even dangerous, but it was still easier than negotiating Connelly family politics. Even so, he did miss them. And back in Bell Harbor he could make some new plans. He had lots of connections in this business, and with just a few phone calls he could probably work out a deal better than what he had now. Maybe even produce his own show where he could be the boss. He had some ideas.

So . . . what the hell?

It looked like Grant Connelly was going home.

Chapter 2

DELANEY DIDN'T REALIZE SHE'D LEFT the lights on in the kitchen when she'd gone to Gibson's grocery store, but there they were, glowing brightly through the window. Good thing too, since apparently around here it got dark at dinnertime. She pulled two overloaded grocery bags from the passenger seat of her car and hurried inside, nudging the back door of the house closed with her hip. She set the bags on the yellowed Formica countertop and halted in her tracks, snow dropping from her boots.

Slung over one of the dinged-up dinette chairs was a coat. A man's coat, by the looks of it. Black, bulky, and definitely not new. And a pair of weather-beaten boots too. One was sitting upright in the middle of the linoleum floor, and the other lay on its side in the hallway as if the wearer had taken them off while still walking.

She heard the shower upstairs turn on, accompanied by a cheery whistle, and her curiosity melted with the snow.

At last, the long-lost Carl had come to do his chores. Thank goodness too, because she'd been here for four days and that leaky shower was full-bore water torture. She'd taken to counting the drip, drip, drips as she lay in her lumpy bed. Last night she'd gotten to three hundred ninety-seven before she'd finally drifted off to sleep and dreamt she'd moved into an enormous clock.

Delaney slid her arms from her coat and turned to hang it up on the hook by the door. A glowing pocket caught her gaze, and the telltale buzz of vibration sounded in her ears. Her phone was in that pocket but she had no intention of answering it. She'd turned off the ringer sometime during her drive through Utah after every single family member had called to implore her to return home where she belonged. She wasn't going back to Beverly Hills, though. Not yet. Not until everyone in the media had moved on to a new scandal and forgotten all about hers.

Still, from habit, she pulled the phone out to see who was calling, and Melody's face appeared. Her middle sister. Her tenacious middle sister who'd called sixty-three times since Delaney had left home over a week ago. Melody was quite possibly the only thing more annoying to Delaney at the moment than that leaky showerhead, and she'd never give up. Frustrated, Delaney tapped the phone's surface *really hard*, but the effort was unsatisfying. "I don't want to talk, Mel. I'm fine but I don't feel like talking, OK?"

"Michigan?" Melody's voice was anything but melodious. "What the hell are you doing in Michigan?"

Delaney looked out the window as if her sister might be poised on her front step, ready to storm in, followed by the flashing cameras. "What makes you think I'm in Michigan?"

"You have a location finder on your phone, moron. It was pretty easy. I've known where you've been this whole time."

"Shit." That was a distinct disadvantage of trying to hide in this digital world. Delaney might need to buy a new phone and get off the family plan. "Who else knows I'm here?"

"Nobody, just me, but seriously, how did you end up in Michigan?" Melody's voice mellowed and Delaney could picture her sister just then, lying in the big hammock on their back deck, soaking up the warm sun. Delaney hadn't been warm since Nevada.

She straightened her shoulders as if Melody could see. "Michigan has its appeal. *Condé Nast Traveler* said it was gorgeous here. Apparently the sand dunes and beaches are magnificent, although I haven't seen any yet. So far everything is just piles of snow."

Melody paused on the other end. "You went to Michigan because of its beautiful beaches? In January?"

That may have been a flaw in Delaney's plan but she wasn't going to admit to it. "I wanted to get a good parking space. So, what's it going to cost me for you to keep this a secret?" Everyone in her family had a price. Even her, and she was willing to pay for her privacy.

"I don't know yet," Melody answered. "For starters, how about you tell me what you're hoping to accomplish with this stunt. Mom is climbing the walls, you know, and she's taking it out on all of us. And what am I supposed to tell people who ask where you are? Everyone is getting worried because you're not answering your calls."

Delaney pulled a box of cereal from the grocery bag and put it in the cabinet. "Tell everyone I'm at a spa. And it's not a stunt. I just needed to get away from the rabid media for a while and be on my own. Tell Mom not to worry. I'm fine."

"I'm sure she'll be glad to hear that, Lane, but what she also wants to know is when the hell you'll be back. She can't keep putting off our production people, you know. We have a show to make and they're all pretty eager to talk to you. You're the girl of the hour, you know."

Delaney couldn't quite name the tone in her sister's voice. It was a fine line between derision, amusement, and envy.

"I bet they are. Can't they just read the tabloids like everybody else?"

"The tabs are just recycling the same stuff over and over. Our producers want to see your reaction to all of this. They want to know what really went down." Then she giggled. "Oh, sorry."

What had gone down was Delaney.

"Thanks, Mel. That's very sensitive of you."

"I know. It just slipped out. Oh! Shit. Sorry. Again." She didn't sound sorry. Not in the least. "But listen, Lane," her sister continued, "this story is money in the bank, but only if you come home and tell your side of it."

"I don't want to tell my side. I just want everyone to mind their own business." She plunked a box of crackers on the shelf next to the cereal.

"Nobody in Beverly Hills minds their own business, and besides, you signed a contract to do a second season, remember? The producers are expecting you here."

"So they can sue me if they want to. If you, Mom, Dad, and Roxanne want to parade around in front of the TV cameras and yank all the skeletons from our closets, be my guest. I'm done with it. One year was enough for me. The whole show was supposed to be about Dad anyway. Why are they so interested in us?" Delaney reached into the grocery bag and pulled out a bottle of wine. She wished it had a screw top so she could open it right now and guzzle it straight from the rim.

"Hmm, let's think," Melody answered. "Fifty-six-year-old rocker trying to make a musical comeback versus his three hot daughters. Who do you think is going to make for better reality television?"

"But the show was supposed to be about Dad's career."

The eye roll was implied in Melody's tone. "No it wasn't. The show was always supposed to be about us. Why do you think they named it *Pop Rocks*? He's not a *Pop* without us daughters. Geez. No wonder they never call you the smart one."

They never did call her the smart one.

And it pissed her off.

Everybody thought Roxanne was the smart one. Melody was the musical one. Go figure. And Delaney? Well, somebody had to be cast as the ditzy baby of the family. The unpredictable wild child. That wasn't her, though. She wasn't *that* wild, and she wasn't *that* ditzy, but carefully selected editing from the first season had certainly painted her that way. And then of course there was The Scandal.

"I don't want to do the show anymore. I've had enough . . . exposure. It was sort of fun the first season but then Boyd went and ruined everything. He completely humiliated me."

Boyd—as in Boydell Hampton—the preacher's son with the baby face and the mile-wide naughty streak. The kind of guy who talked poetically about being a missionary but who was really far more interested in exploring the missionary position. And every other position he could think of. Their fling had been as brief and fiery as one of his daddy's sermons, but that had been ages ago. She didn't even remember who had broken up with whom. First they were together, then they weren't, but she hadn't thought of him in ages.

Not until last month when Mount Lascivious erupted by way of a grainy, low-quality video. She didn't know he'd ever recorded them in the act, but there she was, her head bobbing up and down over Boydell Hampton's junk. Somehow that video had found its way into the media machine—the machine that regularly fed and shred celebrities' lives with remorseless impunity—and the next thing she knew, headlines like "Delaney Masterson Masters the

Son of a Minister" popped up and waved around as frantically as Boyd's erection.

In the last four weeks, Delaney's name had become every late-night comedian's favorite punch line.

Melody's voice over the phone was determined and calm. "We can sue him, Lane. The lawyers are looking into it. Tony thinks we have a strong case."

"No!" Delaney gasped. She opened a drawer, looking for a corkscrew. That wine wasn't going to open itself. "I don't want Tony the lawyer looking into it. I don't want to go to court. That will only keep this in the news that much longer."

"So you're just going to do nothing but sit on your ass inside some igloo in Michigan? That's crazy."

"No, I'm not just sitting on my ass. I've decided to use this time to better myself."

"Better yourself?" If disbelief had a ringtone, it sounded just like that.

Delaney's jaw tightened. "Yes, I had a lot of time to think about things while I was driving across the country, and I realized I don't know how to do much other than *accessorize*. So, if I'm going to have all this time to myself, I should make the most of it, maybe try to develop some skills that are outside of my comfort zone."

"Like what?"

"Well, for starters, I'm learning how to knit."

Melody's burst of laughter was not encouraging. "Knitting? That's outside your comfort zone, you crazy risk taker?"

"Shut up. You're missing my point. I just want to try some new things, and maybe find a way to offer something useful and tangible to the world. I found a place online where I can donate knitted baby hats for newborns."

Delaney could have run a 5K in the time it took for her sister to respond.

"You're knitting . . . baby hats?"

"Yes."

"Girl, you have lost your frickin' mind. I'm calling Mom's psychiatrist."

"I haven't lost my mind. Maybe I've finally found it, and now I understand that I should be doing something to contribute to the greater good."

Her sister's laughter turned into a sniff of impatience. "OK, then. How about you contribute to the greater good of our family and come home? We need you here. You're the best one on the show."

"That's ridiculous. Of course I'm not the best one." Was she? The best one?

"Yes you are, Lane. You're the funniest and we need you or the ratings will tank."

"Did Mom tell you to say that?" Delaney loved her parents, but emotional manipulation was Ginsu sharp at the Masterson household, and this television show had brought out their most desperate qualities. Everyone but her seemed determined to stake their claim in the public's consciousness.

"No, she didn't," Melody answered. "This is coming from me. So just think about that, OK? This isn't just about you. It's about the whole family."

The whole family? Really? How had things turned so topsy-turvy that the whole family was relying on her? The ditzy baby of the family? The one with the sex tape? Her father was Jesse Masterson, eighties pop icon with three platinum records to his name. Her mother was Nicole Westgate, a Victoria's Secret model turned luxury-soap maker, and Delaney's sisters were both better looking and far more stylish than she was. They didn't need her to make *Pop Rocks* a successful show. She just wanted to go back to being anonymous. But she had signed a contract. Her failure to show up for filming could impact them all.

She pulled open another drawer. *Corkscrew. Corkscrew. Please let there be a corkscrew.*

"OK, I'll keep that in mind, Mel. But in the meantime, promise not to tell anyone where I am? Please? I need this time."

Melody's sigh was emphatic. "Fine. And for what it's worth, if I see Boyd Hampton on the street, I'm going kick him in the groin so hard his nuts pop out of his nostrils."

Delaney's laughter was loud inside the diminutive kitchen. She'd needed that laugh. "Please do, and then ask him why the hell he did this to me after all this time. I haven't seen him in five years."

"Well, that's no mystery. He did it because your fame is exploding. He wants his slice of your fifteen minutes, and the tabloids probably offered him a ridiculous amount of money for that tape. But you know, if you went on TV, you could ask him yourself. I'm sure he'll be watching."

Delaney yanked open the final drawer. *Yes! A corkscrew.* "Nice try, Mel. I'm not going to talk about this in public. Ever. Not ever in the whole future of everness." She could not feel more decisive about anything in her life. And she needed to end this phone call, because opening the wine required both hands. "Listen, I really do have to go because my landlord is upstairs fixing the shower and I want to go see what's taking him so long. I'll call you in a couple of days."

They said their final good-byes and Delaney poured herself a glass of merlot—into a jelly jar, because that's what she'd found in the cupboard. Sometimes function was more important than style.

Upstairs, the water continued to run and Carl had begun to sing. Loudly. Well, actually *sing* was kind of a strong word.

Caterwauling was more accurate. Like he was trying to wash a wounded pelican down the drain. An unpleasant sound. How long did it take to swap out a faulty showerhead, anyway? She splashed a little more wine into her jelly jar and brought it with her to the stairs.

A sock lay on the first step. Another one five steps higher. Carl certainly had made himself at home. At the top of the creaky steps was a heap of something beige that most definitely had not been there when she'd left. She picked it up, careful not to spill wine on it.

It was a sweater, one of those thick cable-knit sweaters that only fishermen wore. A queasy sort of churning started low in her gut. Something here wasn't right. She dropped the sweater back onto the shag carpet and took another few steps, pausing outside the bathroom.

The shower ran. Carl caterwauled.

But . . . the caterwauling . . . gurgled. And the water didn't sound as if it was spraying right down the drain. It sounded . . . like . . . like splashing.

Splashing?

Delaney put her hand on the wooden door and gave it a nudge. It opened a few inches and bumped up against something heavy. She nudged harder and spied a big black duffel bag sitting on the floor. With a final shove, the door flew open. And so did her mouth.

She hadn't meant to scream so loud.

Heck, she hadn't meant to scream at all, but that crazy old dude wasn't *fixing* her shower. That crazy old dude was *in* her shower! What the hell? The jelly jar slipped from her shocked fingers and shattered against the black-and-white tile floor, splintering into a thousand sparkly fragments. Wine spewed. Her scream echoed off the baby-blue walls, then so did his.

He yelled back, in obvious surprise, and flailed around behind the frosted glass, arms reaching, body twisting.

Delaney snatched up her pink blow-dryer from the counter and pointed it like a gun. The shower door flew open with a clang of glass and metal. And there stood a man.

A totally naked, totally shocked man.

Brandishing a loofah on a stick.

"What the hell?" he shouted. "Who are you?"

"Who am I?" she screeched. "Who do you think I am, you crazy fuck? What the hell are you doing in my shower?"

Her pulse beat like bongos, erratic and hollow. He was a big guy. A big naked guy, muscular and dripping wet. Her eyes dropped down. She couldn't help it.

Carl was not at all what she expected. Donna Beckett must have a whole lotta something fabulous hiding under that manatee sweatshirt because this guy was hot. And half Donna's age.

"Hey!" he shouted, following her gaze. He dropped the loofah and grabbed a paperback novel from the top of the toilet tank. He opened it and covered himself. Sudsy water ran down his arm. "Who *are* you?"

"I'm De . . . Elaine. Elaine Masters." Her cheeks burned hot, and not from the steam he'd built up in that shower. She forced her eyes back to his. "I'm your tenant."

"My . . . my what?" He brushed a bubble of shampoo away from his hazel eyes with a nicely muscled forearm.

"I moved in a few days ago. Didn't Donna tell you?"

He was staring at her as if she were a rabid dog in need of outmaneuvering, but at the mention of Donna's name, a look of subtle comprehension seemed to pass over him. "*Donna* rented this place to you?"

"Yes."

Crazy Naked Man had the nerve to offer up a chuckle and a hint of lazy smile. He swiped more water away from his face with one hand while holding the book firmly in place with the other. That was her book. She'd just about gotten to the good part and now the pages were drenched and pressed up against his . . . *hiccup*.

"OK, sweetheart, we seem to have a little situation here," Naked Man said, "but let me finish this shower, and as soon as I'm dried off we can straighten everything out, OK? Put the blow-dryer down before you electrocute us both."

Sweetheart? Her ire officially surpassed her surprise and she forgot about her ruined book. "Don't you *OK sweetheart* me, you jackass. Get out now or I call the police." That was a lie. She couldn't call the police. If she did, her name would be front and center in the news again. Not to mention that little matter of a fraudulent signature on her lease. But he didn't need to know that.

"I'm soapy," he said impatiently, as if that should explain everything.

She waved the blow-dryer, aiming at his chest. That very fine chest. "I don't care if you're Dopey, Sneezy, and Doc. Your wife rented this place to me and you need to get out of my shower."

She thought there might be dimples under that scruffy facial hair. Hard to tell, though, because that little bit of smirk was now gone.

"Donna's not my wife. She's my mother. And this house isn't hers to rent. It's mine."

———

Eight thousand miles. That's how far Grant had traveled to get to this shower.

Seventy-two hours ago he'd been in the hot, sticky jungle having an even hotter, stickier argument with Blake Rockstone—his idiot boss who was none too happy to hear that his coproducer and director of photography was quitting in the middle of a shoot, but maybe Blake should have thought of that before stealing Grant's girl. The fight ended in a stalemate with Blake threatening to sue him for breach of contract. Too bad Grant couldn't countersue Blake just for being a douche bag.

After that, Grant had boarded a rickety plane of questionable flight-preparedness in Pampanga, and spent the next horrendous twenty-four hours sardined between two Japanese businessmen, one who snored and drooled like a Saint Bernard, and one who wanted to rest his bald head on Grant's shoulder.

Twelve hours ago he'd landed in Chicago only to discover his flight to Bell Harbor was canceled because of a blizzard. He managed to score a ride home with a church group generous enough to offer him a spot on their school bus, and spent the final leg of his journey being Saved. So right about now, all he wanted was a long, hot shower and a long, deep sleep.

Meaning that whoever this pissed-off brunette was, whatever deal she'd arranged with his flaky mother, they could talk about it after he'd scrubbed the jungle from his skin and rinsed the shampoo from his hair.

"What do you mean it belongs to you? It can't belong to you. I just rented it," said the girl, aiming that pink blow-dryer right at his heart.

If he wasn't so damn exhausted, he might find that funny. She was holding the thing as if it would protect her. It was a *blow-dryer*! He nodded at it. "What do you plan to do with that thing, honey? Style me to death?"

"That's it. I'm calling the police." She took a step backward, one foot landing in the hallway.

"Wait! Wait. Just wait a second." The knot of tension he'd carried for days, which had only just begun to wear away, came back with a blunt blow to the sternum. That's all he needed. The police showing up here before his family even knew he was home. He'd meant to call ahead, but he'd kind of wanted to surprise them. Plus phone reception being what it was over the Pacific Ocean, he hadn't bothered to try. All things considered, that may have been an oversight on his part. "Please let me rinse off, OK? Calling the cops will just waste everybody's time, and if Mickey Pinkerton is still the sheriff, he won't make it out here until Tuesday anyway."

"Then I'm calling your mother."

"No!" His voice came out in a burst and the girl's big blue eyes went bigger still. "Look, please, don't call my mother. Just. Wait. OK? I'm at a serious disadvantage here, don't you think? So if you could demonstrate just a little bit of patience, I'd really appreciate that. No one in my family told me they'd rented my house. I thought my brother was living here."

"That's pretty hard to believe." She backed up farther as if preparing to bolt.

"I've been out of the country. And my mother is . . . unreliable." That was the nicest way he could think of to say his mother was a walking disaster in a polyester tracksuit. She was unpredictable, shortsighted, and lacked both impulse control and problem-solving skills. He loved her, of course. She was still his mother, but he'd figured out it was a lot easier to love her if he hardly ever saw her.

The brunette looked him up and down once more, her perusal so thorough he felt partially vulnerable and partially turned on. He might have sucked in his gut just then, when her bright gaze slipped over it. She was cute, and she was blushing. He hadn't seen a woman blush in a very long time. The paperback in his hand twitched and he pressed it against himself a little more firmly. This would be an inopportune moment for an erection.

She set the blow-dryer down on the white countertop and crossed her arms. "What's your name?"

"Grant."

Her chin tilted. "Grant what?"

"Grant Connelly."

"Ah-hah!" She scooped up the blow-dryer with both hands and pointed it at his chest again. "That's not my landlady's last name! Who are you really?" she demanded. Her face scrunched up in what he could only assume was her meanest expression, but it wasn't remotely effective. She had the face of a homecoming queen, all sparkly eyed and rosy cheeked. In those tight jeans and big red sweater, and the bouncy ponytail on the top of her head, she was about as menacing as a ladybug.

He shook his head, once, slowly. "She got remarried. Donna Beckett is my mother's name. Is that who you rented this house from?"

The woman paused. Her doubtful expression fell away and she set down the blow-dryer again, gently, with a slight air of embarrassment. "Yes."

The surge of adrenaline he'd felt at her entrance burned away, and now Grant was more fatigued than ever. He hadn't had a decent night's sleep since finding out about Miranda and Blake, and the last few days of travel had been hell in a bucket. He just wanted to dry off and find a bed. "OK, so can I please finish this shower and talk to you when I have some clothes on?"

She paused, looking skeptical once more.

Her gaze slid back to his groin.

"You've ruined my book." She pressed a thumbnail against her lip, and he silently reminded himself that flaunting his physical state of interest would probably not work in his favor at the moment. But he couldn't resist. If she was going to keep staring, he'd give her something to look at.

"This book?" He lifted it chest high and smiled as both of her hands slapped over her eyes with a smack so loud the sound bounced off the walls of the bathroom.

"Oh my gosh, yes, that book. Never mind. Put it back. Put it back." She turned away and waved a hand at him, refusing to look.

Wow. She *was* a homecoming queen. She would've fit right in on that church bus he'd come home on. He looked at the soaking-wet paperback. The cover had a bare-chested man holding up a great big sword. Nothing phallic about that. "*The Chieftain?* Hmm, looks racy. Don't worry. It'll dry."

She gave a single shake of her head. "Trust me. It's ruined. So . . . I guess . . . I guess I'll just wait for you in the kitchen. But if you're not downstairs in ten minutes, I'm calling your mother. And the police."

Chapter 3

DELANEY HEARD HIS FOOTSTEPS ON the stairs a full twenty minutes later. She'd picked up the phone five times to call Donna Beckett since leaving that bathroom, but she hadn't because he'd asked her not to. She was polite that way, plus she was still hoping to settle this situation calmly and quietly. The fewer people involved in her business, the better. Sure, this guy could be a prison escapee, a drug dealing, car thieving ax murderer, or some kind of deranged sociopath—or all of the above—but his story seemed plausible enough, and he didn't really *look* like a deranged sociopath. Not that she had much experience in the deranged sociopath department. Then again, maybe she did. She *had* grown up in Beverly Hills, after all.

He came around the corner of the living room dressed in well-worn jeans and a white T-shirt. A swirly tattoo of initials was dark against his bicep. She'd missed seeing that when he was in the shower, what with all his other manly business capturing her attention.

"Took you long enough," she said.

"I had to clean up all the glass. Apparently somebody dropped something in the bathroom." Without glancing her way, he paused near the thermostat to adjust the dial.

"Hey! What do you think you're doing?" She picked up the phone again. Maybe she *would* call his mother.

Now he looked at her. In this light his eyes weren't so much hazel as they were green, but either way, they were trained on her, and she wished they weren't.

"I'm turning up the heat. It's freezing in here," he said.

"No, I have to pay for that heat. Turn it back down and put on a sweater. And some socks. Better yet, put on your coat and boots and go someplace else. What did you say your name was?"

"Grant Connelly." He walked past her and into the kitchen.

She turned to watch his movements. "OK, Grant Connelly. You're showered, dried off, and dressed. So now you need to ska-doosh right on out of this house. The house which I have rented and paid for."

He looked over his shoulder at her as he put his hand on the refrigerator door handle. "Do you have any food?"

"What?"

"Food. You know? Something to eat?" His wet hair was messy, as if he'd shaken like a dog to get the water out but hadn't bothered with a comb, and the scraggly beard looked like more a case of lost razor than style decision. Clearly he was not trying to impress anyone.

"Yes, I have food, but it's mine," she said.

His smirk was sly and crinkled the corners of those eyes, whatever color they might be. "If it's in my fridge, then I should get to eat some of it, don't you think? I can't go anywhere on an empty stomach."

A puff of relief escaped from her lungs. Go anywhere? Good. He was planning to leave, and she then could have this place back to herself. That's all she wanted. To be left alone.

"There's peanut butter and jelly," she said.

"Peanut butter and jelly?" The smile turned dubious and he looked her over more carefully. "How old are you?"

First rule of celebrity was never admit your age. "How is that any of your business?"

"I just want to make sure I'm not harboring a runaway sixteen-year-old."

Delaney crossed her arms and all but stomped her fuzzy-slippered foot—which would not have helped prove her maturity, so she refrained.

"I'm well beyond sixteen. I just happen to like peanut butter and jelly. So how about I make you a sandwich while you get your things together and then you can lea—" Another thought interrupted the first. "Where's your car?"

He shook his head and opened the refrigerator. As if he owned the place. "I don't have one. The church bus dropped me off."

"The church bus?" Oh, no. Not another preacher's son. She would've rather he'd been dropped off by an alien spacecraft.

"Yep. Church bus. Hallelujah and amen." He did the Jesus woot-woot with both hands, then pulled an apple from the top shelf. He really wasn't catching on to the whole *get-your-ass-out-of-here* vibe she was sending. He seemed to be more in the *make-yourself-at-home* mode.

"Well, if you don't have a car, then we should call you a cab. It's getting late, and in case I haven't mentioned it, I'd like you to leave." The sooner she could get him gone, the sooner she could start to breathe again. He didn't seem like the tabloid-reading kind of guy, so there wasn't much chance of him recognizing her, but it was unnerving to have a total stranger in her house. Or his house. Landlady's son or not, she didn't know anything about him.

Except for what he looked like naked.

She did know all about that. Hiccup.

"Yeah, about leaving." He set the apple on the counter and ran both hands through his wet hair, slicking it back a little. It looked good that way. Sexy, which Delaney so did not need to notice. Her lungs went whump as her knees went goosh.

He took a step toward her. "See, my family doesn't know I'm back in town yet. I was hoping to surprise them, but it's too late to do that tonight, so I think I'll just crash here and call my mother in the morning. In the meantime," his voice dropped and his mossy-eyed gaze met hers, "how about if I make that sandwich for myself and you can entertain me with a story about why you have a backpack full of cash sitting in the closet."

All her blood seemed to clot in place, leaving her queasy and breathless. She leaned back, as if she could physically evade the question. "You went into my closet?"

One light brown brow lifted and he crossed his thick arms. "Technically it's my closet. Where'd you get that money?"

Damn it. She'd had a lot more control over the situation when he'd been naked and soaking wet. A man without his pants was a man willing to negotiate, but right now she was the one exposed and vulnerable. She took a big, deep breath. "The money is mine, and I don't owe you any explanation. That was totally unethical of you to go through my things."

He shrugged, broad shoulders flexing under white cotton. "It was an accident, but maybe we should call those police now and we can both talk to them."

He was bluffing. What a bluffer!

Delaney straightened up and stood her ground. "Why would you call the police just because I have my own money? This is none of your business, you know."

He tilted his head. "Probably not, but I think I'd sleep a little easier if I knew you weren't some mobster's girlfriend who helped herself to all the loot in the casino safe."

Her fisted hands went to her hips. "Do I look like a mobster's girlfriend?"

Well, that was a stupid thing to ask. She didn't want him studying her face that way. She may as well pull out the latest edition of *Us* magazine and show him her picture, although since arriving in Bell Harbor she'd given herself long bangs with a pair of dull scissors and dyed her normally highlighted hair a nondescript brown. With no makeup, she looked a lot different than those stock photos tabloid magazines used for covers. Still, she wished she'd put on her fake glasses. She pulled her new bangs down and over to the side as if that might hide her identity while Mr. Plain White Tee stared. Evaluating. Scrutinizing.

"No. You don't look like a mobster's girlfriend," he finally said, "but I'm trying to figure out why somebody with that much cash on hand would be renting this old house in Bell Harbor."

What the hell was she supposed to say to that?

Of all the houses in all the towns, she had to go and rent a place that wasn't really up for rent to begin with, and one that came with a man inside. That was some shit luck. Almost as shitty as having her old boyfriend sell their sex tape to the tabloids. What had she done in a previous life to deserve this particular situation?

Time to dial up the perky. "Look, I swear the money is mine. I just . . . I wanted a change of scenery so I took all my money out of the bank and decided to do a little traveling, have a little adventure for myself."

Wait. Shoot. That was probably a foolish thing to admit. If he had a mind to, he could make her and her money disappear, and no one in her family would ever know what had become of her. Damn it. There sure was a steep learning curve to being on the lam. For instance, is that even what they called it anymore? On the lam? Well, whatever it was called, she wasn't proving to be very good at it.

Grant picked up the apple and shined it on his shirt, right over that muscular torso. "You're looking for adventure? In Bell Harbor? In the middle of winter?" He sounded doubtful, and with good reason.

Delaney tossed her ponytail in what she hoped was a convincingly carefree manner. "I heard you have good skiing here. But listen, if you can get my rent money back from your mother, I will gladly go elsewhere."

That wasn't entirely true. She'd go elsewhere all right, but she wouldn't be glad about it. None of the other places she'd looked at had been remotely acceptable, and with her luck, if she went back to the hotel, she'd get snowed in and end up like Jack Nicholson in *The Shining*. Leaving town wasn't much of an option right now either. There was sixteen feet of snow in every direction, and she was driving a frickin' Volkswagen Beetle. She'd nearly ended up in the ditch on the way home from the grocery store.

Grant continued to stare, until the pressure nearly broke her. Maybe she should offer up the famous Masterson smile. It had worked in convincing his mother, but something told Delaney that Grant Connelly was a little sharper in the intellect department than Donna was. So she waited, silent, while his body seemed to fill the space in front of her. The scent of one of her mother's trademark soaps emanated from his skin. Ginger peachy. Most certainly not his usual fragrance, and the idea of him using her bath bar made those knees of hers wobble again. Not the time to be weak limbed. She crossed her arms and tried to look determined. Certain. Not guilty. The money was hers, after all. That was the only thing that really mattered here. He didn't need to know all the details about why she'd left Beverly Hills.

His sigh, when it came, was full of resignation. "You swear to me you're not some runaway Girl Scout who took all the cookie money?"

She held up three fingers in what she hoped was the Girl Scout salute. "I swear."

———————•———————

This chick was no Girl Scout, and anybody on the move with that much cash had to have a story, but he was just too damn tired to care. He hadn't even meant to find that bag. He'd gone into the first bedroom and opened the closet just to throw in his own stuff, and there it was, a backpack, unzipped and gaping wide with banded stacks of money inside. If she was a thief, she wasn't very good at hiding it.

He scrubbed a hand across his whiskered jaw and resigned himself to wondering. Whatever her situation was, it wasn't his problem. Tomorrow he'd go see his mother and the rest of his family. He'd get the girl's deposit back and send her on her way. He turned back to the kitchen counter. "Fine. Whatever. Where's the bread?"

"That's it?" Her voice squeaked in surprise, and then she hiccupped.

"That's it for now. I told you, all I want is food and sleep. I'll get your deposit back for you tomorrow and you can find another place, because you can't stay here."

"Deposit and six months' rent," she said.

"What?"

"I gave your mother a security deposit and six months' rent, so she'll have to give it all back. In cash."

A dull thudding began inside his skull, like the pounding of a Kayumanggi drum. Historically, things involving his mother did not go smoothly, and this had catastrophe written all over it. He turned back around, hoping maybe the girl would be gone. That maybe he was asleep and he'd dreamt up this whole thing. But no. There she was, all innocent looking, which meant she was anything but. "Please tell me you didn't pay my mother in *cash*."

She frowned, delicate as an angry kitten. This chick was too cute for his own good, but at the moment, his mother's gambling habit was the primary issue. Donna liked the slots, but they didn't like her. If she had fifty bucks in her pocket, the only safe bet was that she'd lost it, and six months' rent was a lot of scratch to donate to the Four Eagles Casino.

"Yes, I paid her in cash."

"How much did you give her?"

"Six thousand dollars."

He smacked his palm against his forehead. "When did you pay her?"

"Four days ago. The day I moved in. Why?"

Four days. Damn it. If he'd called ahead, none of this would be happening. If he'd let his family know he was coming home as soon as he'd gotten the invitation from Tyler, this place would've been empty and waiting for him. Just him. The sweet brunette and her backpack full of bills would have kept on going instead of moving into his closets and barging into his bathroom. But he hadn't called. He'd wanted to surprise them, and instead, he was the one surprised, and now he'd be stuck with this woman, because unless things had changed since the last time he talked to Tyler, there was no way in hell his mother would still have that rent money.

"What's your name again?" He couldn't remember for the pounding in his skull, and since she was leaning toward this side of hot, thinking of her as The Girl Scout seemed kind of raunchy.

Her hesitation was subtle but her unease was clearly growing. "Elaine Masters. From Miami. So how is it that you own this house but didn't know your own mother had rented it out?"

"My grandfather died last year and left this place to me, but this is the first chance I've had to come home. Work keeps me out of the country most of the time. Last I'd heard, my brother was living here." He started looking for the bread again, more to give himself something to do. He'd be able to think more clearly if he wasn't gazing into those baby blues of hers. And right now he needed to *think*. And pray his mother hadn't gambled away that money.

"What kind of work?" She stepped forward and opened a cabinet, pointing at the bread.

He took it with a nod of silent thanks as he pulled the loaf from the shelf. "Cinematography."

She slammed the cabinet door so hard the hinges rattled. "Cinematography? You mean, like, a videographer?"

He hadn't said arms dealer or evil scientist, but her instant scowl suggested he had. "Yeah, sort of. Ever heard of *One Man, One Planet*?"

"Yes." Her answer was clipped, her lips pressed into a tight line after she spoke.

He pointed at his chest with his thumb. "Director of photography and coproducer until a few days ago when I quit."

It felt good to say that. He'd quit. Not because he was running away from the mess of Blake and Miranda, but because he wanted to move forward toward his own plans.

"Do you spend much time in LA?" She sounded more like she was asking if he'd ever been *convicted*, or just arrested.

"Not if I can help it. I don't like Los Angeles."

"Why?"

He took two slices of bread from the bag and set them on a plate. "It's soulless. I spent a lot of time there when I was first starting out but the fake got to me pretty quickly. Glad to put that town in my rearview mirror."

The wind howled outside, a lonely moan that rattled the windows. A draft from under the door wafted across his bare feet, and he tried to recall the last time he'd been cold. Blake didn't like to shiver on camera, so they tended to shoot where it was warm, and Grant had forgotten what a winter in Bell Harbor was like. Now he was starting to remember why he'd avoided them.

"So now you're back in Bell Harbor to do what? Stay? Pass through?"

Clearly his motives were suspect to this woman, but why, he could not imagine. He wasn't the one traveling around with stacks of cash stuffed into a bag.

"I'm here for a while. Like I said, I just quit my job, so things are a little up in the air for me." He found the peanut butter in another cabinet and went back to the refrigerator for the jelly. Elaine had retreated to the edge of the kitchen, eyeing him with a new wariness. It made him feel as if he was being unreasonable, and wrong somehow. But this situation wasn't his fault. Then again, it wasn't hers either. This problem was Donna's.

"Look," he said as he spread some jelly on the bread, "I'm a nice guy, and I'm a tired guy. I'm going to eat this sandwich and go to bed. If you want to spend the night here, that's fine. Or you can go to a hotel. Either way, I'll try to get your money back tomorrow. OK?"

He hadn't counted the stacks in that backpack, but there was certainly enough to keep her comfortable someplace besides his house, still he wasn't some asshole who'd insist she leave tonight, especially in this brutal weather. He glanced up at her and thought he saw her dash away a tear, but she blinked fast and looked out the window as if evaluating her options.

Under the circumstances, he guessed her distress made sense. That was her money they were talking about. And although *he* knew she was safe from him, *she* didn't know that. He knew he wouldn't kick her out with no place to go either, but she didn't.

A burdensome sense of chivalry overcame him—brought on by his extreme fatigue and hunger, no doubt, because although he *was* a nice guy, he wasn't *that* nice. He wanted her gone. Still, he had to make the offer. "Not exactly Miami out there, huh? All things considered, I suppose if you want me to stay someplace else, I could. And I guess I should call my mother."

Chapter 4

"THERE HE IS! OH, CARL, come and say hello. You remember my oldest son, Grant, of course. And this is Elaine. She's renting the house."

It was nearly nine o'clock in the evening when Delaney and Grant arrived at his mother's house. A couple of black Labrador retrievers bounced around and barked as if they'd never before seen people, and Donna was equally aflutter, her cheeks stained pink as she hugged Grant so enthusiastically his breath came out in an amplified gasp.

"OK, Mom. Glad to see you too," he said, smiling and patting her on the back as if reminding her to let him go.

Donna's manatee sweatshirt had been replaced by a peach-colored cardigan that did nothing for her complexion, and Delaney started to mentally make her over. It was a hazard of her job as a stylist, constantly re-dressing people in her mind. Grant's mother had been pretty once. Delaney could see that in her delicate bone structure and the color of her eyes. With a just little effort, this landlady might even be attractive.

Delaney could not say the same for the house, however. This place needed a complete overhaul. It was faux–Swiss chalet on the outside, but inside it was Early American tacky. Cheap ginger-colored paneling, rust-and-avocado plaid upholstery on a gargantuan sofa, and salmon-colored shag carpet, circa 1975. Family photos in mismatched frames hung on every spare inch of wall, and where there were not pictures, there were stuffed and mounted animal heads. Deer, rams, rabbits, and something that looked very much like a garden-variety billy goat. Somebody around here liked to shoot stuff. Awesome. If the conversation about her money went south, Delaney just might end up on the wall.

"I can't believe you're here," Donna said to Grant. "You could've knocked me over with a two-by-four when I heard your voice on the phone!" She tugged his arm, leading them into the lemon-yellow kitchen. A big pine table filled much of the room, and a wilted poinsettia sat in the center. Leftover from Christmas, no doubt, although from the looks of it, Christmas five years earlier.

"We didn't even know if you'd make it to the wedding," Donna continued. "Your brother said he'd tried to call you weeks ago but couldn't get through. Oh, he'll be so glad to see you."

Grant looked around the house as if taking in all the knickknackery of his childhood home, and Delaney found herself wondering just how long it had been since he'd been back to Bell Harbor. Judging from his mother's behavior, it had been quite a while.

"I've been pretty deep in the jungle, Mom," Grant answered. "Not much cell reception when you're thirty miles from the nearest tower."

"Oh, yes. Of course. Now let me look at you." Donna cupped his face with both hands. He was a good head taller so she had to reach up. It was a sweet moment, mother and son, and Delaney felt like an intruder, but Grant had been pretty insistent she come along. Probably so that as soon as she got her money, she'd leave.

"Look at that face," Donna said, smiling, turning his head one way and then the other. "Oh, my, how I've missed that face. Except for the beard, you look just like your father."

Grant caught her hands with his own and moved them away.

Probably because his mother seemed just on the verge of pinching his cheeks. "It's nice to be home, Mom. You look good."

"Oh." She reached up and fluffed her short blonde hair. "You're sweet. Isn't he sweet, Carl?"

Delaney turned to find a tall, lanky, white-haired man leaning against the counter, wearing a fuzzy blue bathrobe over black-and-red flannel pajama pants. He lifted a can of soda by way of a greeting. "Nice to see you again, kid. Sure has been a while. Can I interest anyone in a sloe gin fizz?"

"Oh, Carl, don't be so silly. No one likes those." Donna waved her hand, shushing him.

He cocked a white eyebrow. "Amaretto sour, then? Phil Collins?"

"It's a Tom Collins," Donna said, then turned back to her son and Delaney. "How about coffee?"

Delaney stole a glance at Grant. Was she supposed to stay? Take the money and run? What was the etiquette here? One thing she did know was that she had a deplorable lack of options overall. If the house really belonged to him, the contract she'd signed was null and void. Which was made doubly irrelevant by the fact that she was pretending to be something, and someone, she was not. But the money was legally hers and they were obligated to return it.

"Coffee, sure," Grant said. He pulled out a scarred wooden chair for Delaney. OK. She was supposed to stay. At least for a while longer.

Donna's hands smoothed the front of the peach cardigan. "So, I see you two have met, obviously. That must have been a bit . . . interesting."

"You could say that," Grant said, sitting down next to Delaney. "Did it occur to you to tell me you were planning to rent my house?"

Donna's cheeks flushed. "We tried to tell you, honey, but it was so hard to get ahold of you. You could call more often, you know."

Carl sat down on the other side of Delaney. "Have you ever tried a sloe gin fizz? They're delicious."

"Not now, Carl," Donna said, resting a hand on his shoulder before turning to fuss with the coffee pot. "Anyway, we tried to tell you, Grant, but the point is, you didn't know. So I guess you'll have to find another place to stay for a while. Your sisters are coming home for the wedding, and of course my sister Tina will be arriving soon, but I suppose you could sleep on our couch."

He didn't look too happy about that suggestion.

Delaney hiccupped.

"Or," Grant said slowly, "we could give Elaine her rent money back and she can find a different place to live. I'm for that option. So please tell me you still have it."

His mother seemed very focused on those coffee filters all of a sudden, and a pressure began to build inside Delaney's lungs, as if she'd lounged for too long inside a steam bath.

"Have what?" Donna asked.

"Her rent money."

His mother turned around slowly. "Not exactly."

"What does *not exactly* mean?" he asked.

"It means no. I don't have it. I spent it."

The pressure expanded and Delaney's next hiccup was actually painful. Of course this woman had spent her money. Because why should this current streak of bad luck stop now?

"All of it?" Grant's voice took on an edge. "You spent six months of rent money in just four days? How? At the casino?"

"No." Donna looked indignant, then chagrined. "Well, yes. A little of it, but not all of it. There have been wedding expenses, you know. Plus I wanted to get Tyler and Evie something really nice as a gift. Your brother has done so much for Carl and me, you just have no idea. Of course you wouldn't because you're never around.

But everyone keeps telling me I have to pay for things and not just take them, so this time I used real money. It's a wonderful present. Tyler and Evie are going to love it." She took a big breath and plucked a coffee filter from the stack. "But yes, the money is gone."

Delaney clenched her fists under the table. Gone, gone, gone. The money was gone and so was all her hope for a fast resolution to this latest dilemma. Every dollar she had left was in her backpack, and although it was certainly enough to keep her head above water for a few months or maybe more, being out six grand was a big dent in her finances.

Grant wiped both hands across his face, pressing his fingers against his temples for a full five seconds. Delaney looked at Carl.

He mouthed the words, "Sloe gin fizz?"

She shook her head but wondered if she should say yes. She could use a drink right about now.

Grant let his arms fall to the table with a thump, and he sighed. "OK, Mom. Then we can just return whatever you bought them and get a refund from the store, because Elaine needs her money back. She needs to find another place."

Yes, she did need to find another place, and she did need that money back. Maybe the paparazzi's interest in The Scandal would wane soon, but until it did, going home to Beverly Hills was not on Delaney's list of viable options.

Donna's face flushed a rosy shade of *I'm in trouble* as she popped the filter into the coffeemaker. "Return the gift? Well, I don't really expect we can return it."

A muscle twitched in Grant's jaw, and his fingers drummed on the table. "Can't return it? Why? Is it monogrammed?"

"No, but it might be branded."

"Branded? What the hell did you buy them?"

Donna opened the can of coffee and scooped up some grounds. "A cow."

Grant's mouth dropped open in tandem with Delaney's but he recovered slightly faster while she was still trying to breathe.

"A cow?" he said.

"Yes. A cow." Donna turned and faced them squarely. "Evie is always talking about how unhealthy meat products are these days, what with all the hormones and bad feed and all that. And my friend, Dody Baker, she said she'd recently bought herself a cow that gets fed only fresh green grass and it gets to live on a farm until its time comes. A happy cow. And I thought, what a nice present."

"A cow," said Carl, pulling a cigarette from the pack on the table. "This is news to me. Or should I say *moos*?"

"You take that nasty smoke outside, Carl," Donna said.

He nodded and lit the cigarette anyway.

Grant leaned forward toward his mother and splayed his hands out on the tabletop. "OK, so how much did the cow cost?"

Donna avoided his stare and put another scoop of coffee in the maker, snapping the lid shut. "Well I couldn't just buy them the cow without getting them the freezer too. That's really where the money went. In the freezer."

"That's what I call cold cash," Carl murmured to no one in particular.

Delaney might have laughed if she hadn't been so transfixed by the oddity of it all. If anyone needed a reality show, it was these people.

"You bought them a cow and a freezer." Grant's voice was flat. He didn't sound all that shocked, but Delaney thought a slaughtered cow and a freezer to keep it in was quite possibly the grisliest wedding present ever. Maybe it was a Midwestern thing.

"Does Tyler know that's what you bought them?" Grant continued.

"Of course not. I want it to be a surprise. So don't you tell him either." She turned to fill the coffee pot with tap water, talking even as her back was to them. "You know, this is partly your own fault, Grant. The house only belongs to you because your grandfather's dying wish was that you'd move back home and rejoin this family. But you didn't do that, did you? No. You just kept gallivanting around the globe and shunning us."

Grant popped back in his chair as if he'd been cuffed on the chin. His cheeks flushed. At least the little bit Delaney could see above the facial scruff. There were broad currents of family history here, and it piqued her curiosity, but at the moment she was just a spectator.

"I wasn't gallivanting, Mom. I was working. And I wasn't shunning anyone either."

Donna turned back so fast that water splashed from the pot. "The hell you weren't. You've been mad at me ever since the day I married Hank. Don't think I don't know that."

Hank? Who the hell was Hank? Delaney stole another glance at Carl.

He blew smoke from the corner of his mouth without moving his top lip. "Hank, second husband. I'm number three. Third time's a charm." He nodded at Delaney, looking for her agreement. She smiled weakly, because really, what else could she do? She shouldn't be here right now. She had more than enough of her own family drama to contend with. She didn't need to be a part of this one. She just wanted her money.

Grant sighed beside her. "Mom, this isn't the time for that discussion. Right now we have to figure out where to get the money to pay back Elaine and get her out of my house." Grant's gaze passed from his mother to Carl. "I don't suppose you have any money?"

Carl shook his head, not looking the least bit concerned. "Nope, sorry, kid, but I'd be happy to make you a beverage. I find that most problems are more easily solved after everyone has enjoyed a cocktail."

Delaney felt inclined to agree but decided to keep her mouth shut. If only she'd done that with Boyd she wouldn't be in this mess now.

"Do you have any money, Grant?" Donna stepped forward, ignoring her husband and apparently forgiving her son for the shunning and the gallivanting. She put her hand on Grant's arm. "Maybe you could pay Elaine and then I could pay you."

He shook his head. "I don't have an extra six grand lying around, Mom. Most of my cash is tied up in a work project right now, and until Blake decides to stop being an asshole, I can't get my hands on any of it. He wants to sue me for breach of contract."

His mother pulled her hand back and pressed it to her heart, but her sigh wasn't despondent. It was full of infatuation instead. "Oh, that Blake Rockstone. What a fella."

"Did you not just hear me say he wants to sue me, Mom? He's an asshole."

Delaney had only seen Grant's TV show once or twice, and she'd thought the host was about as engaging as a Styrofoam cup. He had the same overprocessed quality too. She recognized Botox when she saw it, and he'd had plenty.

"Please don't use profanity in my home, young man," Donna scolded. "That's a quarter in the swear jar for you."

Grant ran a hand through his hair, messing it up even more than it had been before. "Add it to my tab. In the meantime, give me the information you have on the cow and the freezer and I'll see what I can do about getting a refund."

Donna shook her head. "You'll do no such thing. That's my gift to Tyler and Evie."

Exasperation finally filled his voice and stretched it thin. "Mom, I'm sure that Ty and this Evelyn person will understand the circumstances."

His mother came forward and pulled out the angry-mom finger point, waving her hand so close to his nose she nearly touched it. "No, you don't understand, Mr. Smarty-Pants. That house sat empty for months after your grandfather died with no word from you at all. Tyler didn't want to live there but he did, just so he could do the upkeep on the place in case you came home. He cut the grass and shoveled the snow, and he even painted the whole inside. We would have asked you about it, but you never return calls. Half the time, you don't answer e-mails. You're next to impossible to get ahold of, and it didn't make sense to leave it sitting empty, so I rented it." His mother stood back up and crossed her arms, defiant, satisfied she'd made her point. "I took this nice young lady's money in good faith and promised her she'd have a place to live for six months. So you'll just have to find yourself someplace else to go until her lease is up. Maybe that'll teach you to call your mother once in a while."

"That went well," Elaine said as they climbed back into her little piece of shit Volkswagen that he could hardly fit his legs into. It was dark and cold, just like his mood.

Grant didn't respond. His ears were still ringing from the shellacking he'd just received from his mother. Apparently there was some resentment built up there, but what did she expect from him? She'd married Hank just months after Grant's father had died, and Hank, that SOB, had made it perfectly clear there was no room in the house for Grant after that. So he'd left.

Then Hank took off, and Carl showed up. Grant was busy working by then and trips home were harder to schedule. He'd been back a handful of times over the years and hadn't intended to stay gone for so long, or be so unavailable, but every opportunity to come back to Bell Harbor had gotten trumped by a new assignment. He didn't get to the top of the heap by saying no to job opportunities. Bad timing and logistics had kept him away from his grandfather's funeral, but he'd been in Phnom Penh. He couldn't have gotten home even if he'd wanted to. And sure, maybe he had been a little careless about keeping in touch, but his mother didn't need to rip on him about that in front of a total stranger.

"So . . . yeah," Elaine added when he said nothing. She turned the ignition key and the engine reluctantly coughed to life. "We seem to have a situation here. What do you suggest we do about that?"

He clenched his fists inside his gloves.

Shit.

Shit. Shit. Shit.

What could he suggest?

He couldn't just evict her. This problem was not Elaine's fault, and even if she did have a backpack full of money, she was still out six months' rent. What if she took them to court? That's all he needed. Her suing him right along with Blake. What a huge pain in the ass that would be. Somehow he had to pay her back, or find one of them another place to stay.

Grant pushed his hair back from his eyes. He was in serious need of a trim. He also needed a suit for his brother's wedding. And a car. And groceries. And some decent winter clothes. And about fifteen hours of uninterrupted sleep. Now he understood why babies cried when they got too tired. He was miserable. He should have stayed in the fucking jungle. Civilization was too complicated.

"OK, so look," he finally said as Elaine slowly backed out of the long, snow-covered driveway, "here's the thing. I'm going to be busy with family stuff for the next few days or so. You probably figured out my brother is getting married soon. So I can try to find a place to stay, or you can look around, or go back to the hotel, but in the meantime . . ."

His voice dwindled away. It was a crazy idea. A crazy, stupid idea. They were complete strangers, after all, but he'd lived in enough cramped cabins and campsites to know that living in close quarters wasn't that big of a deal. Not for him, anyway. If he was able to ignore Miranda in twenty-five square feet of jungle clearing, he could certainly handle himself around this girl.

"In the meantime, what?" she asked.

"We could both stay at the house."

"You want to live together?" The car lurched to a halt as she plowed into a snowbank and got them stuck.

"Just for a couple of days until I can figure something else out. I mean, you can move out whenever you decide to, but the truth is your rent money is gone and I don't have it to give back to you. I might in a week or so but not right now."

"Don't you have friends you could go stay with? Or live with your mother?" she asked, punching the gas pedal and digging the tires farther down into the snow.

Figures a Miami native wouldn't know how to rock a car out of a snowbank.

"Straighten the wheel and tap the brake while you accelerate."

"What?"

"Trust me. It'll adjust the torque on the tires and give you better traction. And don't floor it. Just give it a little bit of gas."

Three more tries and they were out of the snowbank and slip-sliding down the icy road.

"And no, I'm not staying with my mother and Carl, and I don't have friends to stay with either. Not around here. In case you didn't catch on to what my mother was saying, I haven't really kept in touch with the old Bell Harbor gang."

"Can't you stay at a hotel?"

He rubbed a glove over his chin. "I could, I guess, but I have to be honest . . . I don't want to. That house is mine, so in spite of what my mother said, your lease is no good. If I stay at a hotel, that's money wasted I can't get back. It's money wasted for you too, really. But if we stay together, eventually, I'll get your full six months' rent back. That's actually a pretty good deal for you, don't you think? You can stay there rent-free until one of us comes up with a better solution."

Elaine was silent as the car's wipers scraped icy particles across the windshield. It was snowing again, in big clumps. The wind whipped around as she white-knuckled their way to the next road. Terrible driving weather. Terrible weather for just about anything other than sitting next to a roaring fireplace with a beer in one hand and remote in the other. That's what he wanted. A fire, a drink, and a ball game. Or better yet, a big, soft bed.

Finally Elaine sighed. "I'm not interested in having a roommate."

"Honestly, neither am I, but I'm making you a good offer. You've got a heck of a lot more money than I do at the moment—"

"That money," she interrupted him, then stopped and pressed her lips together for a moment. Then her voice went low. "That money has to last me for a while. It's all I have."

It's all she had? It looked like plenty, but there was a lot this girl *wasn't* telling him, and no matter what her financial situation was, his family still owed her six grand.

"Listen, I want to get you your money back, and I don't want to be a jerk about this, but I don't have the time to figure out another place to go right now. Tyler is getting married this weekend, so if we could just share for like, four days, maybe five, then I can figure something else out. But right now I'm going on hour thirty-eight with no sleep and I just want a place to lie down. Stay or go, but give me some time to work out an alternative."

Her sigh was quiet, a puff of white against the cold air inside the car. The pause hung in the air next to it.

"OK," she finally answered. "I guess that would be OK. Maybe. But just for a couple of days, and then you have to leave, or get me my rent back. Agreed?"

A warmth passed over him. It was a surprising sensation. What was that? Relief?

Sure, because if she stayed, then he didn't have to feel guilty about kicking her out, and if *he* stayed, he didn't have to bother finding another place in the next hour. It was all about taking the path of least resistance. This was the easiest thing, and it would work. For the short term, anyway. She wouldn't take up much room and didn't seem to be much of a talker.

"Agreed," he said.

This could work.

Or . . . it might be a terrible mistake.

Chapter 5

GRANT CONNELLY HAD MADE A terrible mistake. Elaine Masters was quiet, sure, and he appreciated that. Most women he knew were interested in sharing all the details of their lives, the more insignificant the better, but his housemate was just the opposite. She said almost nothing. In the past day and a half, she'd read, murmured into her phone, and did something with knitting needles and yarn which in no way produced anything recognizable and was typically followed by her mumbled cursing and the sound of something soft being tossed into the trash basket.

None of that bothered him, though.

What bothered him was the yoga.

The yoga that she'd been doing for over an hour now, wearing a miniscule top and clingy pants. He tried not to watch her but the house just wasn't that big. Unless he was in the bathroom or his bedroom, he could see her. The stretching and the balancing and the arching. Heaven help him, the arching! She was as bendy as a pole dancer and ten times sexier because she seemed so unaware of it.

"Are those my panties?" Her voice broke into his illicit thoughts.

He'd come into the living room to say a pair of her underpants had accidentally ended up with his laundry, then he'd gotten stupidly distracted by her ass. It wasn't his fault, though. He'd walked in and there it was, perky and round and way up in the air. Come on. What was he supposed to do except appreciate the view?

She stood up and he glanced down at his hand where his thumb was rubbing absently over the silky pink material. God damn it. She was going to think he was a pervert.

He cleared his throat. "Um, I guess so. They were in the dryer, and they sure as hell aren't mine." He held them out, dangling the lacy bit on his fingertip, and she snatched them from his hand.

"Thanks. Are you heading out?" She nodded at the coat he had draped over his arm.

"What? Oh, yeah. I'm meeting my brother for lunch."

She glanced out the window at the blowing snow. "Is he picking you up?"

"No, I was going to walk. It's not that far."

She pressed a thumb against her lower lip. She did that a lot, and he wished she wouldn't, because all it did was draw his attention to her mouth. As if he needed another reason to notice her mouth. It was lush and distracting, and every time he looked at it he wondered what she'd taste like. He'd dreamt about her last night, and that was *before* he'd seen the yoga.

Maybe he'd just been in the jungle for too long, or maybe he was feeling latent rebound effects from being emasculated by Miranda. Women didn't normally affect him this way. Oh, he appreciated them for sure, but he'd never had to work too hard to capture one's notice. He'd never much cared if he succeeded or not either. Miranda hadn't broken his heart, she'd only wounded his pride. But something about Elaine Masters was pulling him in deep, and it was clear she wanted none of it.

This morning he'd accidentally bumped up against her in the kitchen and she'd looked ready to castrate him with a cleaver. She was closed for business, no doubt about that, and it was probably for the best. She carried a secret along with that bag full of money, and whatever it was, an ex-husband or something just this side of illegal, he didn't want to be a part of it no matter how flexible and bendy she was.

"Do you want to take my car?" she said, seemingly oblivious to his inner turmoil. "It's about twenty degrees below zero out there."

He pulled on his coat. "Are you sure? I might not be back for a couple of hours."

Elaine gave a tight smile. "It doesn't matter. I'm not going anywhere, but if you could fill up my tank, that would be nice."

A frat-boy joke about filling up her tank popped into his mind, but since she'd just caught him ogling her ass and fondling her panties, he decided to keep that to himself.

"Yeah, sure. Absolutely. And thanks," he said.

"No problem. Keys are on the counter. Have fun with your brother." With that, she walked away, ponytail swinging, spandex clinging, backside round and perfect.

Damn. Elaine Masters was about the cutest thing Grant had ever laid eyes on. He needed to get that rent money back to her, like, yesterday, before his emotions went and did something irretrievably stupid.

He picked up the keys and headed out the door.

Bell Harbor had changed since the last time he'd been home. All the tacky little mom-and-pop stores he remembered had been replaced with art studios, bistro-style cafés, and upscale antique shops. It seemed the world had found its way to Main Street while Grant had been busy avoiding it.

His little brother had changed too. Somewhere along the line, he'd filled out and turned into a man.

"Geez, Ty, look at you, all grown up," Grant said as they moved in for a clumsy embrace and thumped each other on the back.

His brother's smile was still the same, though, and similar to his own. "Yeah, six years will do that to a guy," he answered as they sat down.

Grant pulled off his coat. "Six years. Hasn't been that long, has it?"

"Since the last time you've been back? Yeah." Tyler's voice was neutral, and Grant unexpectedly had the sensation of running into an old acquaintance at the airport rather than his own brother. They'd shared a childhood, but few things in their adult lives overlapped. Time lost its meaning in the jungle but obviously it had marched on back at home.

He looked around, taking in the view. The restaurant was small, with a relaxing, homey interior, the dark walls and heavy wood furniture giving it a rustic feel. Big windows looked out over the street where snow continued to pile up. "So, this place is called Jasper's, huh?" Grant said. "Does that have anything to do with Jasper Baker from Bell Harbor High?"

Tyler's blond hair was cut short, and his eyes were the same bright blue as their mother's. "What do you think? How many Jaspers do you know?"

"One."

"Guess that's your answer, then."

They both laughed, sounding like each other, and Grant felt hope they'd find common ground. He'd missed his brother, he just hadn't realized how much until that moment.

"Jasper opened this place a couple of years ago," Tyler said, signaling for the waitress. "I even worked here last summer."

The waitress came over, and they ordered drinks.

"You worked here?" Grant said after the server walked away. "You're still an EMT though, right?" He hadn't missed *every* detail, had he?

"Yes, and now I'm studying to be a paramedic. I started that in September."

"Wow, sounds like you've been busy since I talked to you last. Where'd you find time to get engaged?" The question was supposed to sound casual, but Tyler's expression tightened up.

"Everything with Evie was easy. When you know, you just know."

"Like Mom knew with Hank?"

Tyler's smile fell away completely and Grant wanted to rewind. God, sometimes he had the meanest mouth.

"This is nothing like that, Grant. I hated Hank as much you did. Mom made a mistake and she knows that now, but she was scared."

"Scared? Of what?"

Lines of frustration formed across his brother's forehead. "Is it really that hard to figure out? She was scared of being a single mom with five kids to feed. You and I probably could've managed all right, but Aimee, Wendy, and Scotty were still little kids."

Grant's other brother and sisters. They'd been young when he left, all freckles and knobby knees. At first there'd been lots of letters from them written in dark, clumsy pencil, but those had dwindled as they got older. Then he had trouble remembering things like birthdays. He'd sent presents, sometimes. When he thought of it. But he'd fallen out of the habit of wondering about the things, and the people, he'd left back in Bell Harbor. Work was easier than family, but his mother had reminded him last night that he'd missed a lot. His brother was about to remind him too. He could sense it coming and the realization made him feel lonely and old. And then it made him feel defensive.

"Four months, Ty. Four months after Dad dies and she brings that jackass into our house? Into Dad's house. Grandpa would've helped her. I would've helped."

Tyler leaned back and crossed his arms. "Helped? You mean the same way you helped when Hank left and took all the money? Or how about when she lost her job? Or when Scotty got arrested?"

Grant felt sucker-punched in the solar plexus. He hadn't known about any of those things happening, but what hurt worse was that his brother didn't sound angry so much as he sounded resigned. As if his expectations of Grant were so low, they'd become nonexistent. His involvement in the family had become superfluous. A rolling sense of unease rose up and he swallowed it down. Maybe that's what all those unanswered phone calls were about. Shit. Maybe he *was* a lousy son, and a lousy brother. No wonder his mother had been so pissed at him last night. "When did Mom lose her job?"

"About three years ago. Now she's working at Gibson's grocery store."

"I didn't know that. When did Scotty get arrested?"

"A while ago but it's all handled. I took care of things, and now he's doing great at Fort Jackson. All he ever wanted to be was a soldier like Dad, so they're kicking his ass but he loves it."

The waitress brought their drinks and Grant took a big swallow. To wash down the size-eleven foot he'd put in his mouth. "Scotty's a soldier now. I guess I have been gone a long time. Maybe I should've checked in a little more often, huh?" He tried to make a joke of it, but it fell flat.

"It would've been nice." Tyler's mouth said *nice*, but his tone said *you're a dickhead*. And all of a sudden, Grant felt like one. The world he'd left behind hadn't frozen in place. Everyone had changed, grown up, suffered through turmoil, and he'd missed it all. Maybe somewhere down deep, that had been deliberate.

"I'm here now. Does that count for anything?"

Tyler paused. The frown lines eased a bit. "It *is* nice to see you. I wasn't sure you'd make it to the wedding."

Grant felt some relief at the change in tone. "I would've come sooner but I didn't get the invitation until about a week ago, and as you can imagine, it's a bit of a hike from the Philippines. Mom said you tried to call me, though. I never got a message."

Tyler took a drink and set the glass down firmly. "I never tried to call."

That foot in his mouth went and kicked him in the throat. "You didn't?"

"No. I didn't figure you'd care that much."

Grant's jaw dropped, and the foot kicked him again. "Not care? My brother is getting married and you think I wouldn't care? It's not as if I've stopped being part of the family. Right?" It shouldn't have been a question. It should have been a declaration, but at this moment, he wasn't so sure. "Look, I know I've been shitty about keeping in touch, but that doesn't mean I don't care about you guys. I've just been busy working."

His brother nodded, as if Grant's words were of only moderate interest, but a curve started to form around Tyler's lips.

"Well, like I said. It's nice to see you. Aimee calls you Bigfoot, by the way."

"Bigfoot?"

"Yeah, you know, like a mythical creature that people say they've seen in the wild but no one knows for sure if it's real. That's you to them."

"Great." God, was there anyone in his family who was actually *happy* to see him?

"Just thought you should be prepared. If you're thinking there's going to be some kind of a big parade to welcome you home, you might be a little disappointed."

Apparently Grant had died without knowing it, and had come back as a punching bag. His brother was throwing hook after hook, and it was starting to piss him off. Eight thousand miles. That's how far he'd come, and for this? If he'd wanted to get treated like shit, he could've stayed in the jungle with Miranda and Blake.

"Wow. Guess I'm wondering why you invited me at all."

Tyler rolled his shoulders. "My fiancée insisted on it. Her parents had a fight that lasted twenty-three years, and she said if they could work through that, then you and I should be able to figure this out, if we put in a little effort. You interested?"

Was that an olive branch his brother was waving in his direction or a spear about to skewer him?

"Well, considering the fact that I didn't even know we *had* a problem, I guess, yeah. I'm interested. I quit my job to be here, you know." That wasn't precisely true. He'd quit because he'd wanted to quit, but Tyler was flinging a lot of crap his way and he needed to fling some back.

"Mom said you quit because Blake Rockstone is an asshole."

Grant chuckled at his own expense. "He is. But apparently so am I, so maybe we were a good team." He picked up his drink and took a huge gulp. This was not the reunion he was expecting. It was more like a colonoscopy followed by a tar-and-feathering.

Tyler's grin broadened, also at Grant's expense, but he lifted his glass. "OK, truce. I've said my piece, and I really am glad you're here. I didn't think you'd come, and you've made Evie very happy, and Mom too."

Grant held out his glass, feeling the first hint of genuine warmth since he'd sat down. "How is Mom doing? I mean, really doing? She seemed mostly OK when I went to the house."

"She is OK. She's not allowed in Mason's jewelry store anymore because she swiped a watch from there last fall. I think Scotty leaving town for basic training had her rattled. But other than that, she's managing."

"She's still gambling, you know."

Tyler cocked an eyebrow. "I said she's managing, I didn't say she was cured. She has a new psychologist that Evie got her set up with, and things are improving. I suspect meds are involved."

"Meds to make you stop stealing?"

Tyler shook his head. "No, antianxiety meds. Apparently it's stress that makes her take stuff, so the more on an even keel things stay in her life, the better she does. Carl balances her out nicely. He's so mellow he's like a walking Xanax."

"Yeah, Carl seems all right." Grant took another drink and flipped open the menu left by the waitress. His gaze scanned the list of items but his mind had moved on to the next topic. "So, let's talk about you, now. Tell me about this woman who swept you off your feet."

Surely this would be the part where Tyler explained about the pregnancy and the obligation, maybe even shared his doubts about building a successful marriage. Only he didn't. Instead, his brother's face lit up like Christmas morning and Grant laughed out loud. Tyler practically had cartoon hearts circling his head.

"Wow. That good, huh?"

"Absolutely. Evie's the best. She's a plastic surgeon, beautiful, funny, a good sport, thank God. We met last summer when she gave me stitches."

"Last summer? So this all moved pretty fast."

Tyler's eyes narrowed again, and Grant lifted his hands in mock self-defense. "Hey, I'm not making a judgment. I'm just saying that's not a very long time to know each other."

"You're totally making a judgment, but go ahead. Once you see her, you'll get it." His voice was mild, almost smug. Was Grant being patronized by his little brother?

"When I see her? Why? Because she's pregnant?"

God! He hadn't meant to say that out loud. Damn it. Now he'd have to wash that other foot down too, but Tyler just shook his head as if Grant was the one to be pitied.

"You're a jackass, and no, she's not pregnant, but we plan to adopt just as soon as we can."

Grant coughed on a sip of his drink. "Adopt? Adopt . . . children?" He continued coughing, choking on his aversion to domestication. Tyler seemed far more amused than concerned by this.

"You all right over there? Need to put your head down?"

Grant took another big, painful swallow of his drink instead. "No, I'm good. It's just a lot of new information all at one time, you know? I mean, my little brother, a husband and a dad? It's not . . . it's just not where I'm at in my life at all."

Tyler's smirk was good-natured. "You should come on in. The water's warm. Maybe you could marry that little roommate Mom has you shacking up with. Carl says she's cute."

It wasn't manly to feel light-headed, but Grant couldn't help it. Maybe it was from the coughing fit. Maybe it wasn't. "She is cute, and she does yoga. Lots of yoga."

———◆———

There was only so much yoga a person could do before it transitioned from being soothingly meditative into being mind-numbingly monotonous. Delaney had passed that point an hour ago. She was antsy as hell stuck inside this claustrophobia-inducing house. The snow was drifting up past the windowsills, blocking what little light there was outside, and the baby hats were proving far trickier to make than the online video suggested. Oh, and her roommate seemed a little too interested in her silk panties.

This morning he'd bumped up against her in the kitchen, pretending to reach for something. Yeah, he was reaching for something all right. Her boob. She'd nearly let him catch it too. In spite of his Scruffy McScruff beard and his unkempt hair, she *had* noticed those tasty bits of his in the shower. But fooling around with Grant, the cinematographer/landlord who wasn't really her landlord but who had the power to kick her out at any moment, was a terrible idea. She was already on the run from the damage Boyd had done. The last thing she needed was a romantic entanglement in Bell Harbor—especially a romantic entanglement with a man who made *videos* for a living. That would be an epic disaster.

She needed her rent money back soon, like tomorrow, or she needed to kiss it good-bye and move on without it, because she couldn't stay here. Grant Connelly might be a little lazy in the grooming department, but he was sexy, in a rustic way. Too sexy, and definitely too available. And if the paparazzi somehow found out she was living here with a man, it would be all over the interwebz in an instant. That would be a disaster on an even grander scale of epicness. So as soon as the weather was decent enough to drive, she was leaving. Not to go back home. She wasn't ready for that, yet, but she'd at least head south toward warmer climates.

Delaney took a long, hot shower, trying to wash her troubles away, then plopped down on her bed wearing an LA Lakers sweatshirt and her pink flamingo pajama pants. Her outfit wasn't stylish but it was comfortable. That was one advantage of hiding from the world and *not* being on a reality show. She could wear whatever the hell she wanted with no fear that one of the two dozen cameras in her house would catch a shot of her scratching her ass in saggy pants.

When she'd agreed to do a season of *Pop Rocks*, she'd had no idea what she was signing on for. Parts of it were fun, of course. The money was definitely nice, along with the invitations to movie premiers and parties, but the complete sacrifice of her privacy was a downside that far outweighed the positive. Maybe she'd feel differently if Boyd hadn't released that video, but the truth was, she didn't like people in her business. She liked privacy, and she wanted hers back.

She opened her laptop and set it on her legs. It took a moment to boot up, but soon she was clicking over the keys, surfing for a new hideaway location. That was another advantage of running away from home. She could go anywhere she wanted.

As long as no one recognized her.

And she could find a place that wasn't too expensive.

And no one needed to see her identification.

And it wasn't so far from here that her rattletrap car would never make it.

Come to think of it, maybe she should just stay in Bell Harbor.

A wave of homesickness passed over, pricking pins into her heart. She set the computer on the bed and took her phone from the nightstand to call her sister.

"Hey, how's the frozen tundra?" Melody asked without saying hello.

"Frozen. How are things there?" She settled in against the pillows.

"Insane as usual. Roxanne says you're just doing this for attention, Mom is putting all her nervous energy into driving us crazy, and Dad says if you come back home, he'll introduce you to George Michael."

"Since when does Dad know George Michael?"

"Since never, he's just trying to trick you. Oh, but I do have some good news. Our producers have agreed to start taping the next season of *Pop Rocks* without you. We're all pretending like you're out scouting locations where Mom can open another soap boutique."

Delaney should feel relieved, but the victory was oddly hollow. "Is anyone buying that story?"

"I don't think so. Rumors abound, but so far no one has suggested that you're cowering inside of an abandoned lighthouse in Michigan knitting baby hats."

"I'm not cowering." She was totally cowering. "But what kind of rumors are we talking about? Stuff that's worse than the truth?"

"Oh, the usual celebrity stuff. That you're in rehab. You're off getting breast implants to show off in the next video. That kind of thing. Sorry, Lane." Her sister had a habit of apologizing for things without actually sounding the least bit sorry. "You might want to shut down your Facebook account, though," Melody added.

"Why? What's on there?" She seized the computer again and her fingers flew over the keyboard, bringing up her page.

"Just stupid stuff," Melody answered. "Mean stuff. It's just the haters being ignorant."

Delaney gasped as she saw the screen. Post after post of comments filled it, some with still shots of Delaney leaning over Boyd's lap. The images were blurry, so blurry you could hardly see her face, and if not for the quarter-sized hummingbird tattoo on her shoulder blade, she might have doubted it was her. But it was her.

Who says it's hard to get a-head in Hollywood?

Why master-bate when you can Master-son?

Delaney Masterson sure knows how to pop rocks off.

"Oh, my God, Mel. These are awful." Delaney's eyes began to water.

"I told you not to look, Lane. Just delete the whole page."

"But even if I delete it, these pictures are still out there." Her lungs felt full of sharp rocks as she tried to breathe. "Why are people so mean?"

"They're just jealous," Melody answered.

"Nobody is jealous of me for having a sex tape."

"No, but they're jealous because of who our parents are and because we have a TV show. People think we have it easy because now we're getting famous. They don't understand the struggle is real."

Delaney set the laptop next to her and punched at the pillow behind her, trying to get comfortable although dread made that impossible. "It's so unfair. We agreed to live our lives out in the open for the sole purpose of entertaining people and then they turn on us."

"I know, but unfortunately, in the absence of any defense from you, the trolls will keep attacking. If you came home, head held high—uh, sorry. I mean, well you know what I mean. Stand up for yourself."

"I am standing up for myself by choosing to not add more fuel to Boyd's infamy. As soon as this is no longer news, I'll come home."

"In that case, you'd better get more yarn, because you'll have plenty of time to make baby hats."

"Don't count on it. Knitting is way harder than it looks, but honestly, even if I wanted to come home, I'm stuck here under an avalanche of sno—"

The lamp next to her bed flickered and went out, leaving her in the gray shadows of the room. "Shoot. My light just burned out. I'll call you back later. I have to figure out if there are any extra light bulbs in this place."

"Do you *know* how to change a light bulb?" Melody's familiar teasing made Delaney more homesick than ever.

"No, but maybe there's an app for that. I'll call you later."

She set the phone back on the table and got off the bed. It was getting dark outside, the sky a hazy, deepening gray. Just light enough to see that it was snowing. Still snowing. Always, always snowing.

Delaney walked into the kitchen and flipped the switch. Nothing. No lights. Somehow she must have blown a fuse. She'd seen the electrical box in the basement when Donna Beckett was showing her around. Hopefully there was an app to explain to her what to do with it, because it was getting darker by the minute.

She opened the door to the dank, cobweb-filled basement, but before her slipper-clad foot hit the first step, the muffler of her decrepit car rumbled outside the kitchen window and relief was like a warm blanket tossed around her shoulders. Grant was back. Feminism notwithstanding, she was clueless when it came to home maintenance, and sending him down into the basement seemed like a much better idea than going down there herself.

She was waiting in the kitchen in the dim light when he stepped inside, and she nearly yelped in surprise. Because the Grant Connelly who walked into her kitchen just then was not the same one who'd left earlier that day. His hair was cut short, very short, and the beard, the Scruffy McScruff rattiness that had been the one thing tempering her temptation, was gone. Completely gone.

What remained was one fine, fine-looking man.

Chapter 6

"HI," HE SAID, STOPPING SHORT when he saw her.

Probably because she was standing right in his way, mouth gaping.

It's not as if she'd never seen a good-looking man before. Of course she had. Beautiful men were everywhere in Beverly Hills, but who would've thought such a remarkable specimen had lurked beneath Grant Connelly's junglemania facial fur?

"You cut your hair."

Grant smiled and Delaney felt her lashes batting in Pavlovian response. There were dimples. Faint ones, but dimples just the same.

"Yes, I did. My brother said I looked like a homeless crackhead. I think it was his way of saying he missed me."

Delaney giggled spontaneously and pressed a thumb to her lip.

He stared at her for a second, then held up both arms. Bags dangled from each. "I bought clothes too, because apparently what I was wearing wasn't acceptable enough to impress his fiancée either." He stepped around her and put the bags on the kitchen table. He reached over and flipped the light switch. Nothing.

"I think I must've blown a fuse or something. The light's out in my bedroom too," Delaney said.

He shook his head. "It's probably not a fuse. Power is out all over town because of this storm. I'll check, though."

He was down the stairs and back up before Delaney had sufficient time to snoop in those bags. She'd seen enough to know that one was a suit, though. A charcoal-gray suit. It was probably for the wedding, and he'd probably look pretty good in it, even though the quality wasn't particularly great. And she should probably stop thinking about how he'd look wearing it, because that was making her just as flustered as she'd been when catching him in the buff in the shower.

He came back into the kitchen. "Yep, power's out. No telling when it'll go back on. Could be a cold night so I guess I'll start a fire."

"A fire? Have you got wood?"

A curve played at the corner of his mouth. "Oh, yeah. I got wood."

The door slammed before she realized what she'd said.

Two trips outside, an old newspaper, and some matches was all it took before the fireplace crackled with flames, and Delaney realized having a rugged outdoorsman as a housemate might be the first lucky break she'd had in a long time. He'd found a couple of lanterns and a few candles in the basement, and now the living room glowed with light and warmth—and hormones bubbling just under the surface, like maple syrup waiting to be tapped.

"Did you have dinner before the power went out?" he asked as Delaney wrapped a blanket around her legs and sat down on the sofa.

"No, did you?"

"Nope. But I'll trade you a beer for a peanut butter sandwich."

"Done."

Just a little friendly barter. Nothing sexual about that.

Two beers and two sandwiches later, she reconsidered. Grant was chatty, and relaxed, funny, and charming as he talked about his travel adventures. He was melting her determination to keep things strictly platonic, and everything he shared made her want to tell him her story. Her *real* story, because the lies were a burden, and that load of insults she'd seen on Facebook was a misery she wanted to unload.

But she didn't tell him. She couldn't. Because she didn't *really* know him, and she couldn't *really* trust him. She'd trusted Boyd and look where that had landed her. And at what point in a new friendship, romantic or otherwise, was it appropriate to mention that one's sexcapades had been caught on film?

Or that you were hiding from the scandal-hungry paparazzi?

Or that your name was now a verb in the urban dictionary?

Yeah, that chick totally Delaney-d me under a Snuggie, bro.

Never.

There was never a good time for that.

"So what made you decide to become a cameraman?" she asked instead.

Grant opened two more beers and handed one to her.

"Is this going to cost me another sandwich?" she asked, taking the bottle from his hand.

"Nope. This one's on the house." He sat back down and pulled a pale green blanket over his own legs. "I didn't set out to become a cameraman, I just sort of lucked into it."

"How so?"

"Well, I left Bell Harbor after my dad died and my mom got remarried. You probably picked up on that back at her house."

Delaney nodded and took a sip of beer.

"Yeah, so I headed to Los Angeles. I had some friends who'd moved out there and I figured I could hang with them for a while.

I got hired by a little TV station, running cables and doing odd jobs and such. One day a guy asked me to hold the camera for a minute, and I haven't set it down since. Moved up the chain, moved around stations, did a few different shows. Just about the time I was getting really sick of LA, this on-location gig came along. Once I'd tasted filming out in the wild like that, there was no going back to a studio. No regrets either. I've seen amazing places, worked with some incredible people." He paused for a moment, contemplating. "Maybe that's why I haven't made it home very often. Up until recently, my job was pretty fun."

"Until recently? What changed?"

He took a slow drink, as if deciding what to share. Maybe she wasn't the only one running away from things.

"I left home at nineteen, and took my first location job at twenty-three. Now I'm thirty-one. That's a long time to be traveling."

That was a long time. She'd been away from home less than three weeks and it felt like forever.

"And not *all* the people were great," he added. He looked over at her then, and she wondered if the candlelight was proving as flattering to her as it was to him, all shadows and glowing planes. He looked bedroomy and delicious. Damn. She needed that electricity to come back on before she did something regrettable.

"Like what people?" she asked. "You mean Blake?"

His gaze dropped to his beer bottle. He nodded and picked at the label. "Yeah, Blake, for starters. He's changed a lot in the last couple of years. I've been with him since the first season, and in the beginning it was great. Either one of us would do anything to get an awesome shot or find the perfect angle. We knew we had to be bold, offer something different to give the show real substance. It was a team effort, but somewhere along the line Blake started to believe his own hype."

"His own hype?" She was very familiar with hype.

"At some point being famous became more important to him than creating a quality product. Now he's just interested in showing off his new veneers and landing sponsorship deals. The show has become about him rather than the adventure, and I can't stand that empty celebrity mentality. If I'm filming something, I want it to be real, have some substance. I want it to count for something. That's why I quit." He tipped his beer to his lips and took a fast swallow, then looked back at her and offered half a smile. "How about you? You must've left a job back in Miami. What do you do?"

What did she do? Um, she did all the stuff he just said he disliked. She spent her days in front of a camera helping her family become famous simply for the sake of being famous, and as a stylist she produced no product, other than image—for other people trying to be famous.

"Um, I work with my family. That's sort of a team effort too."

"Ah, a family business? What kind?"

"Soap." The word popped out, just like a bubble. A soapy, sudsy bubble, and it wasn't a complete lie. She did help her mother make soap once in a while, and they did sell it from a trendy little boutique near Rodeo Drive for sixteen dollars a bar. "We own a soap company. It's really my mom's gig but everybody gets involved."

He nodded. "Interesting. So, why leave the soap business and drive up here in the middle of the worst winter Bell Harbor has seen in fifty years?"

His tone was conversational, but she knew he was thinking about her backpack full of money. Anyone would assume she was running away from something, or someone. She realized that, but it didn't mean she could trust him with her secrets, and given his position on celebrity fame, he wasn't very likely to be sympathetic.

She definitely needed to keep the details of her life a secret. She'd move out in a few days and that would be that.

"I told you before. I just wanted a change of scenery."

He looked around the dark room. "Not much of a view here."

Au contraire. From where she sat, the view was just fine. This short-haired, smooth-faced version of Grant Connelly sitting in the firelight was sexy as hell, even if he was huddled under an old fuzzy blanket. Warmth coiled at the very center of her and she recognized it for what it was. Judgment-impairing lust.

She'd had a boyfriend or two over the last few years, but none worth giving her heart to, so it had been a while since Delaney had felt this, the quickening of her breath, the flutter in her chest. The longing. It could just be her general loneliness talking. Running away from all the comforts of home had left her vulnerable, and needy. Maybe Grant wasn't that fine. Maybe his voice didn't have that melty-chocolate quality after all. Maybe that big hand wrapped around his beer bottle didn't mean anything other than he had big hands. Although she'd seen enough of him to know *that* wasn't the case.

"So tomorrow is the wedding, huh?" she asked. No melty quality to her voice just then. More like a rusty hinge. She cleared her throat. "Doesn't that mean you should be at a rehearsal dinner right now?"

He straightened his legs, his feet moving closer to hers, and picked at the label on the bottle again. "They had the rehearsal last week because of Tyler's work schedule. It was the only time they could arrange it. So, yep, the wedding is tomorrow. I get to face all my relatives together in one big room and find out if the rest of them are as annoyed with me as my mother is."

"Well, she seemed to get over it pretty quickly. I'm sure the rest of them will too."

"Maybe. Want to go with me?" His eyes were back on her, dark but flickering in the romancey firelight. That dastardly, misleading romancey firelight.

Her hiccups started right on cue. "Go with you?" Hiccup.

His smile seemed unexpectedly shy, and that bud of lust deep inside her unfurled.

"Well, you don't know anybody here," he said. "And I thought, you know, you might like to meet some people. I've got two sisters who are about your age, which is . . . how old?"

"Twenty-five," she blurted out. That lie was an easy one and probably not even necessary, but duplicity was becoming a habit.

"My sisters are close to that. Wendy is twenty-two and Aimee is nineteen."

Twenty-two and nineteen. The target demographic for her show, and for every tabloid magazine. His sisters might recognize her, and that wedding reception could be chock-full of another cluster of people who might recognize her too.

"Wouldn't your family think it's kind of strange if I came with you? I mean, I'm just the tenant."

Grant chuckled. "Strange is relative, and my relatives are pretty strange, so I think it would be fine. Actually I know it would be fine because my brother said so."

"You and your brother talked about me?" Hiccup. The idea tingled through her limbs in a most pleasant fashion, which was ironic considering her whole purpose in being in Bell Harbor was so that people would *stop* talking about her. But this was different. Grant wasn't talking about her and The Scandal. She was sure of that because she was certain that at the moment he had no idea who she was.

He had no idea who she was.

That reminder smacked her in the forehead in a most *un*pleasant fashion. He was flirting with her because he knew nothing about her, and if he did, he probably wouldn't have suggested she go mix and mingle with his family.

This is my date. Maybe you've seen her in action? Show them the top of your head, baby. Then they'll recognize you.

Goddamn Boyd and his goddamn video. The whole thing left her heart stinging and sent her fledgling attraction to Grant right back into a tight knot. This is where the lying became even more complicated. She didn't like doing it. She liked Grant too much to lead him astray with more lies, but not enough that she could risk trusting him. She'd liked Boyd all right too, and she'd be an idiot to let two beers, some firelight, and a fuzzy blanket turn into her next sexual misstep.

"Um . . . I don't—" Hiccup. "I don't think that's a good idea." She turned to stare at the fire, but not before watching Grant's expression cool.

He set his empty beer bottle on the coffee table next to the couch. "OK. No big deal if you'd rather not go. I just figured you might want to get out of this house."

"That's nice of you, but . . ." What could she say to explain it?

He shook his head. "No worries. I'm going to get some more wood for the fire." He stood up and tossed his blanket near her feet. It crumpled up and slowly fell to the floor, and she felt like doing the same.

———◆———

Grant pulled on his coat and stepped outside. The wind sliced through him in much the same way Elaine's spontaneous rejection had. He'd thought they'd been having a nice bit of conversation tonight. She was laughing at his best adventure stories, not moving her feet back when his stretched out on the couch near hers, staring at him like she'd never seen a man before. Then he'd invited her to the wedding, and her face looked like he'd offered to show her his rash. Maybe she hated weddings, or maybe she was remembering that she had a husband waiting back in Miami, one who was wondering where the hell his wife and all his cash had gone. If that was the case, then she'd done Grant a favor.

Either way, he'd be glad in the morning. Their situation was already awkward enough, and how much more so could it get? How do you say to a woman, *hey, I'll call you* if you only live six feet down the hall? She was right to turn him down, and he'd really only asked because he was nervous about facing the rest of Bell Harbor alone. It didn't have anything to do with the way her skin glowed bronze in the light of the fire, or the way she tapped the edge of her bottle on her lip for a second before drinking her beer. It didn't have anything to do with the lacy bras she'd left hanging on the towel rod in the bathroom either. None of that had influenced him in the slightest.

He gathered up an armful of wood and looked around to see if any lights were visible in other nearby houses. Someone must have some power, but there was not a flicker anywhere. He was used to pitch-blackness after living so long in inhospitable places, but something about this darkness seemed . . . darker. Maybe it was the cold.

He tromped back inside with a plan to stoke up the fire and make himself a bed on the floor. Elaine could sleep on the couch since their rooms would be ridiculously cold. They could handle this. They were both mature adults.

But he went back to the living room and she was gone.

Chapter 7

DELANEY WAS COLD. COLD, COLD, cold. She'd gotten up during the night and laid clothes on top of the blankets, and even felt her way into the bathroom to grab a few bath towels, but the frigid air cut right through the fabric. This polar vortex business was not for sissies. With numb fingers she reached out and snatched her phone from the nightstand to check the time. Seven o'clock in the morning and still dark as midnight outside her windows.

She heard a muffled thunk and a clunk. Either Grant was putting wood on the fire or a frozen raccoon had just fallen off the roof. A scrape of the fireplace screen told her no raccoons were in danger at the moment, but she might be—in danger of going into the other room and apologizing for leaving the way she had last night. What was with her and running away lately? All he'd done was very politely invite her to go to a wedding, and she'd panicked.

She slid from under the covers and picked up the red plastic flashlight next to her bed. Flipping it on, she checked her reflection in the mirror on her wall. Not good. She looked like a ghoul in the harsh lighting, with her dark hair hanging down and her breath lingering around her face like she was exhaling poison. One look at her like this and Grant would retract that invitation anyway.

She pulled the top blanket off her bed, letting all the clothes and towels fall to the floor, and wrapped herself up like a blue fleece mummy. Then she waddled like a penguin into the other room. She was all kinds of gorgeous right now.

Grant was back lying on the couch, taking up the entire length of it, but moved when he saw her.

"Oh, don't get up. You're fine." She sat down on the brown rug with her back against the old, tweedy couch and her feet reaching out toward the brick fireplace. "How'd you sleep?"

He stretched back out. "Not bad. This sofa is pretty miserable but I've slept on worse. You?"

"Not great. According to the weather on my phone it's twelve below zero outside, but it feels like forty below in my room."

"You could've had the couch." The implication was in his tone. You could have had the couch if you'd stuck around.

"Thanks, but since it's technically your house, I thought you should have the warmest spot to sleep. When do you think the power might come back on?"

"No telling."

They watched the fire for a few minutes, not talking, just listening to the wood hiss and crackle. The smoke was rough and hurt Delaney's nose, but at least this spot was warm. She reached her hands toward it, trying to thaw out her fingers.

"I didn't mean to put you on the spot last night," he finally said quietly. "I only invited you because I thought you might want a break from whatever it is you're doing with those knitting needles. And honestly, I thought you might provide a nice buffer between me and my family."

She looked back at him. "A buffer?"

He nodded and scratched at his chin where new whiskers had created a shadow. His eyes were dark in this dim light. "Yeah, a buffer since everyone is mad at me for doing such a crappy job at keeping in touch. I should have known they'd miss me because I'm pretty awesome, but I figured if you were there, maybe they'd go easier on me." He lifted his brows optimistically, silently asking again.

Delaney felt a smile rise from down deep. This kind of emotional manipulation was familiar. Her mother would like him. Not that she'd ever meet him. "So you were planning to use me as a human shield?" Delaney asked.

His own smile was sheepish, and adorable. "Sort of. I could have explained that better to you last night but you pulled a Houdini act and disappeared."

So maybe she'd been imagining his romantic interest last night, or maybe, like her, things felt a little different in the light of day—even when the light of day was still dark out. Either way, she'd had some time to think about things while lying in her meat locker of a bedroom listening to the shower drip. Whatever his intent, she couldn't stay holed up in this house for six months. She'd go cuckoo and end up scribbling frantic little notes to herself and muttering at imaginary lint balls in the corners. She did need to get out, and getting out meant seeing people, conversing with them, and establishing her cover. This wedding could be the perfect venue. If she could convince his family that she was Elaine Masters from Miami, pretty soon she'd have everyone else convinced too, and that would make her life in Bell Harbor much, much simpler.

"So, let me get this straight," she said. "You're not afraid to scale Mount McKinley or swim in shark-infested waters, but you're scared of getting another scolding from your mother?"

"Maybe. I know that sounds kind of . . ."

"Pathetic? Childish? Cowardly? Sad?"

"Wow, I was going to say . . . sensitive, but OK, I get your point." His smile warmed her up faster and hotter than the fireplace could.

Delaney Masterson had made a series of questionable judgment calls in her life, and this one might land right at the top, but . . . what the hell? "All right," she said. "I'll go."

Although much of Bell Harbor had changed with the times, St. Aloysius Church of the Immaculate Conception hadn't. The fragrance of candle wax, varnish, and incense filled Grant's nose, triggering memory upon memory as he walked into the church vestibule with Elaine. He'd gone to school here, been an altar boy with Tyler, snuck sips of communion wine, and confessed to Father Lawrence all the unholy, impure, wonderful thoughts he'd had about Mary Elizabeth Boyer every time she wore her gym uniform.

In his defense, Mary Elizabeth had been the most voluptuous girl in the ninth grade, and he suspected she knew very well what happened to the boys every time she bent over to pick up a badminton birdie. His body reacted to the memory in much the same way it had when he was fifteen.

Damn. He needed to get laid, and soon, if walking into a church made him this horny.

He could just hear Father Lawrence's required penance. "Say three Our Fathers, two Hail Marys, and keep your hands off yourself."

Yeah. He was doomed.

"About time you got here," Tyler called out from a doorway to the left. "Come on in here."

"Brother of the groom. Oh, I love it! This has got to be the other brother of the groom," said a singsongy voice from the left, and Grant turned to see a dark-haired man with a sharp-edged goatee bearing down on them. He wore a navy-blue suit with a pink rose in the lapel.

Grant halted in his steps and Elaine bumped into the back of him.

Tyler chuckled. "Yes, Fontaine, this is my older brother, Grant. He's just arrived from the jungle."

"Wooooooo, the jungle?" Fontaine tapped his fingertips together. "Hello, Tarzan. How delightfully primitive."

"Grant, this is Fontaine, our wedding planner."

"Wedding planner?" His brother had a wedding planner?

The dark-haired man preened. "Why, yes. I'm an interior designer by trade, and a professional organizer, but I love a good party too." He gazed up at Grant. "I guess you could say I'm a *Jacques* of all trades." And then he giggled.

Grant looked at Tyler.

"Fontaine is a good friend of Evie's," Tyler said by way of explanation. Because a Connelly man having a wedding planner required an explanation.

"Nice to meet you, Fontaine. This is Elaine." Grant plucked her out from behind him, tugging on her arm as Goatee Man gave her the once-over. "Oh, honey, delighted, I'm sure." He turned back to Tyler. "Now you, mister, off with your pants. We need to get you into that tux. Lickety-split."

"Wait!" Another voice joined the conversation, and they all turned as a petite redhead rushed forward. She wore jeans and a white sweatshirt that said *Bride*, and when she smiled, Grant understood. Tyler was right. Now that he'd seen his future sister-in-law, the marriage thing made some sense. She was stunning.

He snuck a sideways peek at Elaine. She was beautiful too, especially in the firelight or with her hair up in a high ponytail when she did yoga, but at the moment, her dark-framed glasses hid those gorgeous blue eyes and made her look a little bookish, and the bulky sweater she was wearing hid all her wonderful curves. Not that it mattered how she looked. She wasn't his date. Just his human shield. He needed to remember that.

In a few hours, he'd see some of his old Bell Harbor pals, and maybe a few old girlfriends too. Surely one of his old flames would be interested in a brief reunion of nudity? If he could release a little tension, he could think about things with Elaine more objectively. A tactical orgasm. That's what he needed. Then he'd stop fantasizing about all those lacy bras she'd left back in his bathroom. She really needed to dry those someplace else. It had taken him fifteen minutes to take a leak this morning because the damn things were hanging up right where he—and his dick—could see them. It twitched in his slacks. His dick had a great memory.

The bride moved forward and wrapped an arm around Tyler's waist.

"Shoo, shoo, shoo!" Fontaine exclaimed, flicking his hands at her. "The bride and groom are not supposed to see each other before the wedding. Don't you know anything?"

Evie laughed. "You realize that incredibly antiquated custom was just so grooms of arranged marriages couldn't change their minds once they saw the bride, right?" She turned back to Tyler. "Oh, no. You're not going to change your mind now, are you?"

He shook his head. "Not a chance."

Evie was short, five foot two at the most, but there was nothing small about her energy. Grant reached out his hand to introduce himself and she stepped past it to embrace him instead, bumping into the camera bag he had slung over his shoulder.

"You must be Grant. We're so glad you're here. You win the prize for having traveled the farthest."

If she was faking her enthusiasm about meeting him, she did a convincing job. Maybe she'd had lots of practice with his brother. Faking it. Or maybe she was sincere. She didn't have the same reasons to be mad at Grant like the rest of the family did.

"I'm glad I could be here too. Thanks for making sure I got an invitation."

He tossed a glance at his brother, but Tyler beamed like a man about to marry the girl of his dreams.

"And you must be Arlene, right?" The bride turned to his housemate and gave her a fast hug too.

"Um, it's Elaine," she answered, pushing her glasses against the bridge of her nose.

"Oh, yes. Elaine. Forgive me. I'm terrible with names, but thanks so much for coming."

"Thanks for letting me crash your wedding. It's freezing at my house."

"That explains the sweater," Fontaine murmured.

Evie smiled bigger. "It's freezing at our house too. We're incredibly lucky that the church and reception hall have decent generators. Serves us right for getting hitched in January I guess, but this was the only time Scotty was available. Thank goodness that with all this bad weather, his plane still arrived on time. Anyway, I have to go get dressed. Elaine, feel free to come hang out with the ladies if the guys get too obnoxious for you." She lifted on her tiptoes and kissed Tyler's cheek.

"See you at the altar, right?"

"I'll be the guy in the tux," Tyler answered.

Grant watched his brother's serene face as she walked away and wished he'd unpacked his camera. It was a moment to capture.

Fontaine sighed. "Isn't she lovely? You two are so gorgeous you should have your own action figures. I'd play with you all day long."

Tyler chuckled, and Grant felt a wave of nostalgia for his little brother who was grown up and about to get married.

The day went on and was full of sweet, sentimental moments, one right after the other. Grant pulled out his camera and tried to capture it all. His brother Scotty, proud and patriotic in his military uniform, sharing a story with their sisters, who had both grown into beautiful young women. Tyler looking nervous but eager as he buttoned his tuxedo jacket before the ceremony. Their mother in a pale green dress, her arm laced through Carl's as they walked into the church. Friends and family, everyone smiling. It was a good old-fashioned Bell Harbor lovefest.

A collective emotion pulsed through the congregation as Tyler and Evie said their vows, clear and certain, followed by a happy group sigh as the bride and groom shared their first kiss as husband and wife. Grant's chest swelled with pride, but he couldn't claim it because he'd missed the evolution of this relationship. He'd missed his siblings growing up, their hardships and their triumphs. By his own design, he'd checked out of the family.

Even today, his camera created a distance, as if he were watching it all from afar, but for the first time in a long time, he wanted to be in the thick of it. Not on the sidelines but right in the middle. Years worth of homesickness plowed into him like a rhino, and suddenly, desperately, he wanted back in.

Chapter 8

THE MOST ANONYMOUS GIRL AT a wedding reception is often the one in thick glasses, and tonight, that was Delaney Masterson. No one paid her the least bit of attention. Not the guests, not the servers, not even the wedding photographer. They were all polite, of course. Cordial, friendly, but for the most part, she was invisible—and she couldn't have been happier about it. For the first time since *Pop Rocks* had debuted, she was out in public and completely free from observation. No entertainment reporters, no paparazzi, no fans, no haters. Tonight she was in heaven. Pure, *nobody-knows-me* heaven. It was liberating to shed the costume of reality star, and in the strangest way, she felt more honest tonight than she had in a long time.

Grant introduced her to people as simply Elaine, and no one seemed to question it. Why would they? Under what circumstances would the daughter of rock star Jesse Masterson and supermodel Nicole Westgate show up at a wedding in Bell Harbor in the middle of winter? She wouldn't. But Elaine Masters might.

It didn't hurt that the drinks were flowing freely, or that everyone, from the bride's elegant best friend Hilary right down to the elderly woman in a plaid taffeta dress collecting names for the guest book, was focused on the newlyweds. Tyler and Evie were adorable, and so obviously in love Delaney found herself sniffling with emotion on more than one occasion.

Now here they were at dinner, with Grant in the suit that looked every bit as good as she'd imagined it would, and her in the plainest, beigest sweater she owned, and a brown skirt. She was woefully underdressed—on purpose. She hadn't brought many fancy clothes from home, and even if she had, it wouldn't be much of a disguise if she showed up for the wedding in a three-thousand-dollar Dior dress. She couldn't have afforded that dress on her own, of course, but being a stylist had some nice perks. Namely expensive hand-me-downs.

The meal was nearly over when the toasts began. She got sniffly again as Scotty, the youngest Connelly brother, stood up and talked about meeting his sister-in-law for the first time, and how he'd known right away that Tyler's life would never be the same.

"This is my brother," he said of the groom at the end of his speech. "He's taught me a lot about how to be a good man. He's kept me out of trouble, and he lets me beat him at tennis once in a while. So, although I'm the best man tonight, I think everybody here knows Tyler is the best man every day, and he's definitely the best man for Evie."

Delaney stole a sideways glance at Grant as everyone in the room clapped and then clinked their glasses before drinking. The dining tables were small and only the best man and maid of honor were sitting with the bride and groom, which meant *this* Connelly brother was relegated to sitting with Donna and Carl. His expression as he gazed at Tyler and Scotty was unreadable, and his ever-present camera sat untouched on the table. Something made her reach over and squeeze his wrist. He was the oldest. It should have been him standing up there as best man, but he smiled at her and she wondered if she was overthinking things. She pulled her hand back into her own lap.

———

"So what's it been like living with my brother?" Aimee asked, much later in the evening, after the dinner dishes had been cleared, the drinks had been refilled several times, and the dancing crowd had grown louder and wilder. Delaney was standing with Grant's sisters near the bar, nursing a watered-down gin and tonic while the music, fast and pulsing, sent her heart thumping along with the rhythm.

The strawberry-blonde sister seemed a little unsteady on those four-inch heels, no thanks to several glasses of wine, but Wendy, the other sister, was next to Delaney, sipping from a bottle of water. Her brown-eyed gaze was speculative. Delaney had the sense she was being sized up by that one, like a python measuring its next meal. Hiccup.

"Living with Grant? It's been fine," Delaney answered, adding a deliberately vague tilt to her head. "He's not there much."

"He'll be around a lot more now that the wedding stuff is over," Wendy said. "We're heading back to school, Scotty is going back to base, and Tyler and Evie will be on their honeymoon. You'll have him all to yourself."

Why did that sound like a dare?

"Well, once he gets my rent money back I'll move someplace else. In the meantime, I'm sure we'll both keep ourselves busy. I've been learning to knit." She hadn't meant to add that last part, but this girl's stare was very unnerving.

Wendy arched one dark eyebrow. "Knit? You mean, like . . . with yarn?"

Delaney hiccupped. It's quite possible she should have come up with something a little more substantial. Something a little more . . . anything. Learning to knit was not exactly a life goal, nor was it involved enough to fully occupy her days. She'd only had one drink, but apparently it had been enough to muddle her mind.

"Did you say knit?" The guest-book attendant in the black-and-green taffeta dress shoved her way into the conversation, parking herself right in front of Delaney. The woman was sixty if she was a day, but her curly hair was held back from her face with a sparkly headband that any six-year-old princess-in-training would have loved. "I find knitting simply delightful," she continued. "My dear friend Anita taught me how to make the most elegant toilette covers. I could show you how, if you'd like."

"Hi, Dody," Wendy said, taking a sip of water. "Have you met Elaine?"

"Why, I don't believe I've had the pleasure, but aren't you a pretty thing? I heard all about you from my son, Fontaine, of course. He's the wedding planner, you know. Aren't these decorations simply scrumptious?"

Delaney nodded. "Um, yes. Scrumptious."

"I know, aren't they?" Dody said excitedly, as if it had been Delaney who brought it up first. "Now, about knitting. Did I hear you say you knit?"

Delaney glanced at Wendy, wondering if either of Grant's sisters found this woman a little kooky, but neither of them seemed alarmed.

"Um, yes. In fact, I'm making baby hats to donate to charity, and I'm thinking about working on an afghan, next." Yes. An afghan. That beefed up her alibi.

Wendy stared. Drunk Aimee tilted. Dody squinted. And Delaney heard her own voice adding, "Well, I mean, when I'm not working, of course." She said that about five seconds too late to be convincing.

"Uh-huh." Wendy took another sip from the water bottle. "And what kind of work do you do?"

She couldn't very well tell them she made soap, because if they'd ever seen an episode of *Pop Rocks*, they very well might make the connection. "I'm a . . . travel . . . agent."

Shit. That was a terrible choice. Why hadn't she just said she was a bank teller? Damn mind-muddling gin and tonic. Damn vulture-eyed staring sister.

"Oh, that's so exotic," Dody exclaimed. "You must go to the most amazing places. Tell me, where is the most fabulous place in the entire world to travel to?"

"Um, Disney World?" Hiccup.

Oh, God. Another terrible choice! Plus she'd sounded like she was asking instead of telling. The evil-eyed sister was getting her all confused.

"Disney World?" said Wendy. "Of all the places in the world, that's the most amazing?"

"Well, I mean, for a family vacation. If you want exotic locations, your brother could probably answer that better than I could. I mean, I've seen brochures for all sorts of fabulous places but he's actually been to some of them." She needed an escape hatch right about now. Just one big chute in the center of the floor for her to jump into.

"You remind me of someone," Wendy said, her brows pinching together like crab claws.

"I was just thinking that very same thing," Dody exclaimed.

Oh, shit. Escape hatch! Escape hatch!

"Me? Oh, I have a very common face." Delaney pulled her bangs down on her forehead.

"I disagree. I think you have a very distinct face." Wendy crossed her arms and studied her more overtly.

Yes. It was official. Delaney liked the wobbly drunk sister better.

Dody stepped forward and practically looked up Delaney's nose. "She looks like a young Elizabeth Taylor, don't you think?"

Delaney leaned back.

Aimee cocked her head to the side and puckered her lips in intoxicated contemplation. "Hey, yeah. You remind me of somebody too. She looks like that one girl in that movie with the guy. Which movie was that, Wendy? The one with the guy and the . . . aliens?"

"No, not that girl," Wendy answered as if she knew just which movie. It was like that with sisters, that verbal shorthand. Under any other circumstances, this would make Delaney laugh because it reminded her of her own siblings, but this wasn't the time for that. This was the time for a distraction. Maybe she could spill her drink, or subtly knock the wobbly sister down.

"I'm telling you, she looks like a young Elizabeth Taylor," Dody insisted. "Or maybe I'm thinking of that model with the long legs. Oh, or that girl who works at the post office. You know, that snippy one who wouldn't let me send a fifth of tequila to my pen pal in prison?"

Delaney's laughter sounded fake even to her own ears. "Well, I'm not a model, I've never been in a movie, and I've never worked at a post office either. So I can't be any of those women."

"But you *are* the woman living with Grant Connelly, aren't you?" Another woman stepped forward, this one a tall, slender blonde, and Delaney couldn't decide if she was glad for the interruption or not. But all at once there were six or seven more women surrounding her, and she decided she was decidedly *not* happy about their interruption. They were all very attractive and dressed in far nicer clothes. She should have worn the Dior. Or better yet, she should have stayed home in that igloo of a house she'd rented because they were all glaring at her as if she were the weakest hyena standing around the fresh carcass of a dead zebra.

She wished her gin and tonic was full. "I'm not *living with him*, living with him. I'm just living at the same place. Grant and I . . . we're just roommates."

Escape hatch! Escape hatch! She glanced around the room to see if she could find him, although adding him to this mix would likely be no help at all.

"I lost my virginity to Grant Connelly," a slender brunette declared wistfully, twirling a lock of hair.

Nope. Having Grant here would be no help at all.

They all turned to gaze at the speaker. She tugged at the neckline of her snug blue dress. "What? Am I the only one?"

"Nope." A different brunette, this one in a push-up bra, raised her hand. "Not the virginity part, but, well, you know."

Two others raised their hands slowly, looking at each other.

"Spring break?" one asked.

"New Year's Eve," the other answered, and then they collapsed into coed-caliber giggles and hugged each other like pageant queens. No shit. Delaney had stumbled into a Grant Connelly sexual conquest recovery group.

"Doesn't she remind you of someone?" Wendy asked, tapping a finger against her lips, not seeming to care in the least that all these women had apparently banged her brother.

"I lost my virginity at a wedding reception," said Dody. They all turned to look at her and she casually fluffed her hair. "Well, not this one, of course. It was my own. And of course, it wasn't Grant because he wasn't born yet."

"I'm telling you, she looks like the girl from that movie," Aimee said, listing to the left and then the right.

All eyes darted back to Delaney, like spectators at Wimbledon.

She'd taken her fake glasses off at dinner because she couldn't see her damn knife and fork, and now she felt completely exposed. Not that those silly glasses had probably done much good, but they were something. Then again, why should *she* feel vulnerable right now? Other than his own sisters and the taffeta-wearing granny, she might be the only woman within ten feet who *hadn't* slept with Grant Connelly.

"She looks like Jeanine Baxter from Channel Six news," Lost Virginity Girl said abruptly, and suddenly they were all nodding emphatically, even Wendy and Aimee.

"Yes! That's who she looks like," Wendy exclaimed, wiping her hands together as if that was a mission accomplished. "Thank you. It's been driving me crazy since dinnertime. OK, who needs a drink?"

That was it? The inquisition was over? Everyone turned toward the bar except Delaney and the busty brunette. The woman stepped closer and leaned in, as if to whisper, but her voice was seagull sharp and loud enough to hear over the music.

"So how is it, really? He's been in the jungle so long he must be like a man just getting out of prison. Is it primal?"

"I have a pen pal in prison," Dody said, turning back around.

Delaney bit back a chuckle and was just about to make her second denial of conjugal relations with her housemate when the man himself appeared. Grant had taken off his coat and loosened his tie. His shirtsleeves were cuffed up to his elbows, and he appeared flushed and flustered.

"Hey, Lindsey," he said to the brunette with much the same falsely jovial trepidation one might display when welcoming a tax auditor into their home.

"Hey, yourself, stranger. Long time no see. Are you in town for long?" She held her wineglass against her cleavage suggestively.

He smiled without showing any teeth. "Oh, you know, all my plans are really up in the air right now."

"Hmm. You know what else is fun to have up in the air?" Her whisper was every bit as shrill as before. "My ankles. Call me."

Delaney let out a shocked bark of laughter as the woman sauntered away and Grant pressed a hand to his face.

"That girl used to be in my Sunday school class," Dody said. "Wicked as a jaybird, even back then. You should stay away from that one, Grant Connelly."

"Thank you, Mrs. Baker. I think that's good advice."

"Of course it's good advice. I'm incredibly wise." She ambled off, taffeta crinkling.

"That is good advice," Delaney added. "In fact, there might be a whole coven of wicked women for you to keep away from." She pointed toward the bar. "All those lovelies were just explaining to me how well they knew you. Biblically. I thought you Catholic boys behaved better than that."

Grant turned to see the cluster of his old conquests and had the decency to blush.

"That's . . . wow . . . sorry."

She should probably be appalled at his sexual history, but if he was a black kettle, she was the pot, and she had the video to prove it. "You don't have to apologize to me. I'm just the human shield between you and your family, remember? And I think I've done my job admirably."

He smiled at her, with teeth. And dimples. That was a real smile. One he hadn't shared with the ankle-waving brunette. "Yes, you have, and thanks. I appreciate it. You've been awesome. I think

I have to do the rest of the fence-mending with my relatives on my own, though. That's what I came over here to tell you."

Delaney felt a sudden shift in her mood, like a balloon wilting from lost oxygen, or one of those toys where you push the bottom and the legs collapse.

Grant loosened his tie a little more. "You're welcome to stick around as long as you like," he said, "but I'm going to spend the night at my mother's house tonight. Scotty and my sisters will both be there, and Aunt Tina too, so I just feel like I should be a part of that. I can drive you home if you want, since the roads are bad, but the power should be back. A couple of our neighbors are here and said it went on about an hour ago."

The balloon went completely flat, and shriveled. He was telling her she could leave. Not that she *should* leave, of course, just that she could. Her value to him had depreciated as his value with the family increased. It made her feel a little used, but that was silly. She hadn't really wanted to come to this thing in the first place, so why feel glum that he didn't need her anymore? It didn't make sense, except that being surrounded by so much love made her realize she missed human beings—when they weren't snapping photos or trying to twist her words for a magazine article. She certainly missed her own family.

That was hardly Grant's problem, though.

"Oh, I can get myself back to the house. It's not very far." She wanted him to insist she stay, but he pulled a folded napkin from his pocket.

"OK, in that case, I wrote my cell number down so you can call if you have any trouble with the power or anything. You sure you're good to drive? How many drinks have you had?"

"Just one." She wasn't drunk. Now that his sisters' interrogation was over, she felt entirely sober. But she wasn't good to drive.

She didn't like that damn snow. It was freezing cold and slippery out there and she was wearing high-heeled Christian Louboutin boots. Obviously Grant had never tried to navigate a snowy sidewalk in fifteen-hundred-dollar boots. But then again, that wasn't his problem either.

"I'm fine to drive. You have a good time with your family."

"Thanks. And thanks for coming. Drive safely." He squeezed her shoulder, like a roommate, then turned and walked away, nudging the cuff farther up his tanned forearms.

But damn, if she didn't feel dumped.

She shouldn't feel dumped. That was stupid. This wasn't a date. He wasn't even *telling* her to leave. He just wasn't *insisting* she stay. Maybe asking her to dance would have been a nice thing, though. Or getting her a drink? She looked around, suddenly feeling entirely awkward. The women from the bar had moved to the dance floor and were wiggling their asses like girls gone wild. Any moment now one of them was bound to have a wardrobe malfunction. A couple of the groomsmen had taken off their shirts and were wearing their tuxedo vests over bare chests. Neckties were long gone, or tied around heads like ninjas. This party was in full swing, and now being the invisible girl wasn't nearly as fun.

"You don't look like Jeanine Baxter from the news," the wedding planner said, popping up over her shoulder like a prairie dog. She hadn't even realized he was near her.

"I don't?" Her voice was pensive as she watched Grant's retreating form disappearing into the crowd.

"No, Delaney Masterson," Fontaine whispered into her ear.

She whipped her head around and watched as an expression of victory spread across his face.

"Hah! I knew it!" He grabbed her wrist and pulled her over to a secluded corner. "You are her, aren't you?"

"No."

"Yes you are. I am a master of subterfuge. I sniff out scandal the way a pig snuffles truffles, and those hideous glasses on such a pretty face were a dead giveaway." He kept his voice low, glancing around furtively. Delaney looked around too, for an exit. Her heartbeat was so fast and shallow it vibrated in her chest. Leave it to the gay man to out her.

"Your secret is safe with me, cupcake," he whispered. "But I must have all the yummy details."

"There really aren't many details," she said.

He shook his head. "Oh, there must be. I live for that sort of thing. Let me guess. You've been having a torrid affair with Grant Connelly for months and came here to meet the family, but you're keeping your identity a secret so they won't realize you're the wildly infamous *Pop Rocks* girl? Right? Am I right? Oh my God, that is so fucking adorable."

"No, God, no. It's nothing like that. Please, Fontaine, I know you have no reason to cover for me, but I'm asking you to anyway." Oh, this was awful. Of all the people to figure her out, there was no way this man would keep her secrets a secret.

His excitement turned to crestfallen despair, like an impersonator changing identities. He drew in a sharp breath and covered his mouth with a slender hand. "That's not it? Then is Grant the father of your secret baby and you came here to tell him? Oh! Trust me, girlfriend, we will all support you—you and your little Connelly bastard."

She wasn't sure whether to feel insulted, shocked, or beholden. "I'm not pregnant."

Fontaine grabbed at her wrists again. "Holy bejebus, is he blackmailing you? Oh my gosh, that's it, isn't it? There's another video and he's threatening to release it. Grant Connelly is a cold-hearted scumbag."

"No!" she said, her voice far too loud, but with the music blasting, no one seemed to be paying the least bit of attention to them over in the corner. Thank goodness for that. "Listen to me, Fontaine. Can you do that?"

Seriously, could he do that? Because this little wedding planner had a crazy gleam in his eye and there was just no telling what he might do next.

"Yes, I'm listening." He nodded and took a deep breath.

Given the complicated and convoluted stories he'd come up with on his own, it seemed going with the truth might be her best option now.

"Grant has no idea who I am. He thinks I'm Elaine Masters, a soap maker from Miami. It was just dumb bad luck that I ended up at his house. I'm in Bell Harbor hiding from the paparazzi until all the fuss dies down about that stupid video, and I'm desperate to keep my identity a secret." At least for a few more hours, until she'd had time to get back to the crooked little house and pack her bags. Now that one person knew who she was, it wouldn't take long before everyone knew. So it was time to leave town.

His narrow shoulders slumped. "That's it. You're hiding from the paparazzi?"

He seemed quite deflated. Maybe she should have said she was a time traveler, or an alien. "Yes, I'm afraid that's it."

He sighed with disappointment. "No blackmail? No secret baby?"

"No. Sorry. Just a sex tape. But will you keep my identity a secret anyway? It would mean the world to me." This time it was her squeezing his hands, pleading, even while knowing he'd never be able to keep this to himself. He was already bursting at the seams for want of someone to tell, but after a moment's silent deliberation, he smiled, showing off unnaturally bright teeth. "Of course I'll keep your secret. I am the soul of discretion." He held up his right hand. "May I never again see a shirtless picture of Channing Tatum if ever I reveal your true identity."

She felt the briefest hint of relief, but shirtless Channing Tatum notwithstanding, she was fairly certain that half the wedding reception would know her real name before she could even get to the door.

"There is a price for my silence, of course," Fontaine added.

Of course there would be a price. There was always a price. "What do you want?"

"Two things. First, you must dance with me because I should very much like to shake my groove thing, and second, promise me you will never, ever wear that ugly sweater ever again."

Chapter 9

"ELAINE?" GRANT STEPPED THROUGH THE door into the kitchen. The sun was shining for the first time since he'd been back to Michigan and it buoyed his spirits as much as spending time with his family had. He'd clearly been forgiven for his extended neglect, and his brother and sisters had stayed up with him until almost dawn, joking around and sharing stories, as if they were all trying to make up for lost time. Even Carl was there, and other than his insistence on making everyone try a sloe gin fizz, Grant realized he was a damn likable guy. Life was looking better. Coming home had been a good decision.

"Hey, hello?" he called out again.

Elaine appeared around the corner wearing dark jeans and a clingy pink top that made his hands go sweaty and his pants get tight. He'd been sorry after she'd left the reception last night. She'd danced with the flamboyant wedding planner a few times and then vanished before he'd had a chance to cut in. Of course, she'd done him a huge favor by going at all, so he could hardly expect her to stick around listening to his relatives talk about crazy old Anita Parker and the cat that had eaten her parakeet.

Elaine set her brown backpack on the floor next to the kitchen table. "Oh, hey. I'm glad you made it home before I left."

He looked past her into the living room and saw a suitcase. He quickly rewound last night in his head to think if he'd said or done something offensive but came up empty.

"Left? Where are you going?"

She dropped her phone into the bag. "Um, I'm not sure. Just somewhere else. It's too cold here."

"Somewhere else?"

That must be relief in his gut, right? Relief he'd finally have the house to himself? Because it kind of felt like he'd gobbled down a big bowl of dog food. Kibble = not good. "I don't understand. What about the money we owe you?"

Her expression was enigmatic, her shoulders barely moving with the world's lamest shrug. "We said this was a short-term solution and it's been a couple of days, so I figured I should move on. I guess I'll be in touch and tell you where to send the money, if you ever get it back."

"Of course I'll get it back. I'm not just going to keep your money. Elaine, what's wrong?"

Oh, Lord. Why was he asking her that? He knew better than to ask a woman what was wrong—because somehow it would end up being his fault. Even if every aspect of her mood was beyond his knowledge or control, it would still end up being his fault—because he had testicles. Whenever a woman was annoyed, somehow it always came around to the Y chromosome.

"Nothing's wrong. Everything is fine."

Sure, she said fine, but he also knew that when a chick said *fine*, what she meant was *Here, hold this hand grenade while I poke you with a sharp stick*. He rewound last night again, but still . . . nothing.

Something here didn't add up. "Let me get this straight," he said. "Everything is fine, and you're not sure where you're going, but you're going to just . . . what? Get into the car and drive? Seems like you might want a destination before you hit the road."

Why was he arguing with her? He wanted her gone. Didn't he? Yet his frustration was as palpable as it was inexplicable. She wanted to go, he should just let her go, but that felt like losing and he didn't like losing.

She reached up and adjusted her earring, a look of uncertainty passing over her features. She wasn't wearing her glasses today. Her eyes were bright in the sunlight, but overall, she looked . . . sad?

"Listen," he said, "go out to lunch with Scotty and me. He has to leave for the airport in a couple of hours, but we were going to go hang out at Jasper's until then. If you're not even sure where you're going, there's not much point in hurrying, is there?"

The corners of her mouth tilted. "I am sort of hungry."

"Good. Put your coat on. The least I can do is buy you lunch after dragging you to a family wedding." He pulled her coat off the hook and handed it to her. "Come on. Scotty's impatient." And so was he. Impatient to understand, and impatient to make her stay.

She looked at him for a minute, and he thought she was about to tell him no. Then she chuckled and slid her arms into her coat.

———◆———

Scotty dropped them back off at the little lavender house with the crooked roof a couple of hours later. Delaney said her good-bye and then went inside so the brothers might have some privacy. It was snowing again, the sky back to gray and splotched with dark, heavy clouds. It was too late to leave today. Maybe she'd go in the morning. Or maybe she'd give the whole situation a little more thought.

Lunch had been fun, and although everyone in the restaurant seemed to know the Connelly brothers, no one seemed to know her as anyone other than Elaine Masters. Maybe Fontaine had kept his promise. Who knew shirtless Channing Tatum wielded such power? Well, realistically, who *didn't* know that? So, all things considered, maybe she'd be safe here for at least a few more days.

A plastic-wrapped plate of wedding cake sat on the kitchen table with a square yellow note on the top. Delaney leaned over to read it.

Enjoy the leftovers—

Mom

Delaney chuckled to herself. If there was cake, she should definitely stick around another day or so. She picked up the plate and put it in the refrigerator because the only thing better than wedding cake was cold wedding cake. Then she hung up her coat, reaching into the pocket for her phone before remembering she'd dropped it in the backpack before leaving for lunch.

Grant came in behind her and a gust of icy air surrounded them. And then another chill nearly knocked her to her knees . . .

"Where's my backpack?"

Grant hung up his coat. "What?"

"My backpack. I left it right here on the kitchen floor before we left for lunch."

He looked around, unfazed, then started to take off his boots. "You must have put it someplace else."

No, she hadn't put it someplace else. She'd left it there on the floor next to the table. She rushed around the kitchen, nerves churning. She went into the living room, propelled by her agitated pulse. Her suitcase was there, right where she'd left it, but no sign of the backpack—or her money, or her phone, wallet, or laptop. Everything was in that bag because she'd packed it up to leave. She raced up the stairs, heart pumping faster than her legs moved, like she was jogging underwater. The bag wasn't in her room or her closet. It wasn't in the bathroom.

"Did you find it?" Grant called up the stairs just as she came racing back down.

"No, I didn't find it. I told you, I left it right here in the kitchen. I remember because I dropped my phone into it before we went to lunch. Grant, all my money was in there. *All of it.*"

A frown started to form on his face. "Well, it has to be here somewhere."

They looked in every nook and cranny, every closet and cabinet, leaving behind a little piece of Delaney's spirit in each one because that backpack was nowhere to be found.

"Somebody must have taken it," she said. "You know that back door never locks properly. Call your mom. Maybe she saw something suspicious when she dropped off the cake."

"What cake?"

"Your mom dropped off leftover wedding cake while we were gone. I put it in the fridge. Grant, I just don't understand this. Who could have taken it?"

Delaney looked around the living room, hands fisted by her sides as Grant opened the refrigerator door and looked inside. She leaned over an easy chair to peek behind it. "Do you think they took anything else?"

He came into the room and sank down on the sofa. Lines formed on his forehead and she noticed he looked more exhausted now than he had the night they'd met. Even his voice sounded tired.

"Elaine, there's a slight possibility I might know who took it, but I'm not sure if that's good news or bad," Grant said.

"Tell me."

He clasped his hands and steepled his fingers. "My mother sometimes has a tendency to . . . help herself to things that aren't hers."

"Your mother?"

"Maybe. If she dropped off the cake and saw that bag, well, it's possible she took it."

"Then you need to call her. Right now, and tell her to bring it back. I'd do it myself but she has my phone." She couldn't keep the sharp edge from her voice, and why should she try?

He pulled his from his pocket and dialed, staring at Delaney the whole time.

This was crazy. How could Donna think she could just take that money without getting caught? That was the first, and most important, question. Delaney's next question was whether or not Donna had looked inside and had found the wallet full of identification. It was stuffed down deep, underneath all the money, but that would make two people in Bell Harbor who knew who she was. Delaney sat down and squeezed her hands together between her knees. No matter what, this was bad.

"Voice mail," he said, then left a message. "Mom. It's Grant. I need to talk to you right now. Elaine's backpack is missing and I have to wonder if you know something about that. Call me immediately."

He dialed again as Delaney waited, her stomach doing the cha-cha-cha.

"Carl, it's Grant. If you've seen Mom, call me. Actually, call me if you haven't seen her either. Just . . . call me. It's very important." He slipped the phone back into his pocket. "God, Elaine, I'm sorry. Maybe I'm wrong and it wasn't her. You're right about that back door. We should probably call the police."

"No!" The word was half shout, half squawk, followed by a hiccup. "No, let's not call them until we've talked to your mom. I mean, if it was her, you don't want the police involved, do you?"

"No, of course not, but mostly I don't want your money to be stolen either. How much was in there?"

She tried to swallow down the next hiccup. "Around forty thousand."

"Dollars?" Now *his* voice was a half shout, half squawk. "You were driving around with forty thousand dollars? My God, I knew it was a lot, but I had no idea it was that much. Why would you travel around with that kind of cash? That's crazy. Why not just use a debit card?"

Delaney pressed her thumbnail against her lip. No easy answer there. She'd wanted to use cash so no reporters could track her down by credit card use, but she couldn't very well explain that to him. Or the fact that she'd had no idea how long she'd be away from Beverly Hills. People lived modestly in this town, but where she was from, forty thousand dollars would last about three months. "I told you, I took all my money out of the bank when I left Be— um, Miami. Cash just seemed . . . easiest."

She needed to pull herself together before she accidentally told him all of it, but she was frantic to get that money back. First, because she needed it, and second, because of all the things that could go wrong if Donna discovered who she really was. The media would have a feeding frenzy and this whole clusterfuck would end up as another episode of *Pop Rocks*. It wouldn't just be her life that would be impacted, but Grant's too. His whole family could be dragged in, just like hers had been dragged into the video scandal.

Grant leaned forward with his elbows on his knees. He sounded as if he might be hyperventilating just a little. She certainly was.

"All right," he said breathlessly. "Let's head over to my mom's house. Maybe she's there, or the bag is, or both. Unless you want to call the police, I don't know what else to do."

Carl met them at the door wearing his blue fuzzy bathrobe. "Why, hello. May I interest you in a sloe—"

"No, Carl. Thanks," Grant said, shouldering his way past. "Where's Mom?"

Carl opened the door wider and Delaney stepped in too, her legs quaking in distress. Her backpack was not going to be here. She could already feel it.

"Your mother?" Carl glanced at his watch. "Right about now she could be flat on her back with cucumber slices over her eyes."

"What?" Grant's frown was fierce.

"She's on her way to a—a whataya call it—a beauty spa with your aunt Tina. You know, one of those places where you take a bath in mud and come out looking ten years younger. Hope she soaks in there for a while." He snickered and pulled a can of Bud Light from his pocket, cracking it open with one hand.

"I think she swiped Elaine's backpack," Grant said, giving Carl a long, hard stare. "It had *money* in it, Carl. Do you know anything about that?"

Carl rubbed a hand over his whiskered cheek. "Money, huh?"

"Yes, it was a brown leather backpack. Have you seen anything like that around here?"

"It was Louis Vuitton," Delaney added. "It was brown with gold initials all over it, and it's about this big." She gestured with her hands. Trembling hands. She looked around the room as she spoke, and winced at the view. This shack was full of so much clutter, that backpack could be hiding in plain sight and still blend in.

"No, can't say as I have, but you're welcome to look around for it," Carl said, motioning to the room in general.

"Which spa? Do you remember the name?" Grant pressed him but Carl seemed unfazed. Then again, Carl always seemed unfazed.

"The name? Nah, not even a little bit. Not sure she told me the name, but it's definitely someplace south of here because they're on their way to Memphis."

"Memphis?" Delaney and Grant burst out in unison, and her chest felt as if she'd been kicked. Hard. With a steel-toed boot.

"Yeah, Memphis. Your mother is going to stay with Tina for a while now that the wedding is over with. I think she needed to get away from this winter weather for a bit. I don't know anything about a backpack, though."

Grant turned toward Delaney. "Now do you want to call the police?" he asked quietly. "We could just say she's a missing person."

"Police? Whoa, whoa there. You don't know for sure she has it, do you?" Carl held out a hand. "That's your own mother you're talking about."

Grant's face was grim when he turned back to his stepfather. "I know it, but there's *forty grand* in the bag, Carl. How fast do you think she'll burn through that if nobody stops her?"

Carl took a big glug of the beer. Then another, and another until the can was empty and he crushed it with his hand. Then he walked into the kitchen and pulled a torn slip of paper from under a toucan magnet on the avocado-green refrigerator door before walking back to them. "Forty grand, huh? In that case, there's probably something you should know. I'm not entirely certain, but it's possible that your mother might have left me."

"Left you? What would make you think that?" Grant said.

"Because she left me this note."

"What's it say?"

Carl glanced at the paper, as if to refresh his memory. He cleared his throat. "It says, 'Sorry, Carl. I'm leaving you.'"

"Jesus," Grant muttered, and Delaney plunked down on the coffee table with a thud because her legs had gone noodleroni under her.

"She's left me before, you know. Couple of times, but she never gets very far and always comes back as soon as her paycheck's gone. Usually it's just a couple of days when she needs a little break, but with that much dough, well, she could be gone a while. All I know is she told me she was dropping some cake off at your place, and then heading to Memphis with her sister, but when I came back from walking the dogs this afternoon, she was gone and this note was on the fridge. Shoot, come to think of it, maybe she's *not* going to Memphis."

"Jesus," Grant said, louder this time.

Delaney dropped her head between her knees, wondering if fainting might make her feel better. Probably not, but she was wishing she could give it a go. A little void of nothingness right now would most certainly feel better than the twirling, swirling anxiety clutching at her insides with nasty claws.

Carl shook his head, finally showing some distress. "I'm sorry about this, Elaine. If Donna does come back, I swear I'm going to have a LoJack installed on that woman."

"If she comes back," Grant muttered.

"If she comes back," Delaney whispered, then her brain shifted into gear. She lifted her head slowly as a thought formed. "Wait a minute. A LoJack? That's it! She's got my phone."

"And?" Grant asked.

She stood and grabbed his arm. "And my phone has a locator app on it. All I have to do is call my sister and she can tell me where it is. If we find my phone, we find the bag." God, she was brilliant. She was practically Jason Bourne brilliant. She reached out her other hand. "Give me your phone and I'll call my sister right now. Your mom can't have gotten very far. It's only been a couple of hours."

He pulled his phone from his pocket and handed it over.

"In the meantime," she said, "maybe you guys could look around here."

She walked toward the kitchen so she might have a sliver of privacy, but the call went to her sister's voice mail. "Mel, it's Lane. Call me back at this number just as soon as you get this message. It's hugely important. Huge. Life-or-death time."

She turned around and there was Grant, like a shadow on her heels. "Lane? Is that what your family calls you?"

She nodded, and watched for any dawning realization, but none came.

"It's cute. It suits you."

"Thanks." She'd take a little time later to appreciate that compliment, and be grateful he didn't know who she was, but right now her main concern was finding Donna the sticky-fingered landlord, and her forty thousand dollars. Technically it was thirty-nine thousand eight hundred and fifteen dollars. And eleven cents. She'd counted it this morning when she packed.

"Listen," Grant said, "I don't think that bag is here. I think our best bet is to get in the car and head south. If your sister calls and says we should be going someplace different, we will."

"You want to just get in the car and drive? Didn't you just tell me a few hours ago that was a bad idea?"

"This situation is a little different, and unless you have any other suggestions, I think it's worth a shot. The sooner we catch up to her, the better chance we have of getting your money before she can spend it, and like you said, she can't have gotten far. With any luck we'll track her down right away. Worst case scenario, she and my aunt will probably stop at a hotel somewhere and we can catch up with them then." He reached up one hand and rubbed the muscles corded along one side of his neck. "Let's just pray to God it's not a hotel with a casino."

Chapter 10

THE LAST THING GRANT CONNELLY wanted to be doing right now was putt-putting down Interstate 196 along the Michigan coast during the worst fucking winter in fifty years. In a Volkswagen. This soup can on wheels couldn't go much faster than seventy miles per hour, and even if it could, the snow had kicked up again, making it nearly impossible to see. The wind buffeted them around like a bull tossing a rodeo clown, and the heater was virtually useless.

This was going to be one miserable trip, and they didn't even know if they were headed in the right direction.

Elaine was grim over in the passenger seat. She'd brought her knitting but the needles were silent and still in her lap. The more dejected she looked, the worse he felt. They'd stopped back at his house to grab a few overnight things in case they were gone more than a day, which was looking more and more likely. They still hadn't heard back from her sister, and every mile on the road could actually be taking them away from the money. Maybe they should have stayed put in Bell Harbor, but he needed to be doing *something*.

"I don't know how to tell you how sorry I am," he said for about the fifth time in an hour.

"It's not your fault," she answered, tucking her pale blue scarf into the neckline of her brown coat. "How could you know she'd take it? Maybe it wasn't even her."

He gripped the steering wheel so tightly his fingers were numb, or maybe they were numb from the cold. All he knew was that he could barely feel them. What he did feel was frustration. Deep down, he knew his mother had taken that backpack. It was the only logical explanation. She'd been in the house, and the odds of some other random burglar just happening by on a Sunday afternoon were about zero.

Fast on the heels of his frustration was guilt because this was just the type of situation he would have left to Tyler to deal with in the past. Now it was up to him to fix. Tyler was on his honeymoon. Scotty, Aimee, and Wendy had all left town too. Elaine was Grant's responsibility, so finding Donna and getting that money back was his job, whether he'd asked for it or not.

"It never occurred to me she'd take it," he said, "but I told you that first night my mother likes to gamble, so maybe I should have seen this coming. It just makes me so mad. I have zero tolerance for people who lie or steal and she's done both." He glanced her way. "My brother says it's psychological. Like, a compulsion brought on by stress, but I don't think it matters why she does it. She has to realize she can't just take stuff."

Elaine shifted in her seat.

He kept on talking, nervous and wanting to fill up that space. "Regardless, you're being an incredibly good sport about this, Elaine. If I were you, I'd have called the police. Shit, I think we should call the police anyway and she's my own mother."

She looked out the window. "We can't call the police." Her voice was quiet, almost as if she wasn't talking to him so much as just lamenting that fact, and it nearly made him slam on the brakes as his brain sorted through the facts.

He was an idiot.

The only reason somebody losing forty large would refuse to call the police was if the money wasn't theirs to begin with. Jesus. He was on this highway to hell to get back *stolen* money that had already been *stolen*, and Elaine was no better than his mother. He'd been suspicious that first night, but he'd tucked the concern away because Elaine was cute and quirky. And because she did yoga and had a mouth made for kissing.

A full minute passed before he could make himself ask.

"Is that what it is for you, Elaine? A compulsion?"

It took her a few seconds to look back over at him. "What? For me? What are you talking about?"

"Stealing things. I'm a little slow to put the pieces together but I just figured out why you don't want to call the police. Where'd the money come from?"

She rolled her eyes in an Oscar-worthy performance, as if his accusation was the most ridiculous suggestion imaginable. She was a better performer than Blake Rockstone.

"Are we back to that again? It's my money. God, I told you that. You still don't trust me?" She huffed in frustration, real or otherwise.

"Why would I trust you? I can't even trust my own mother, and you haven't been very forthcoming with information in the few days we've known each other."

Her cheeks went pink. "Fine. What do you want to know?"

His phone vibrated on the dashboard, and Elaine jumped in her seat before grabbing it and tapping at the screen. "It's my sister."

She put the phone to her ear. "Mel? Thank goodness. What took you so long to call back?"

There was a murmur from the other end so all he could hear was Elaine's side of the conversation.

"Well, just because you don't recognize the number, don't you think you should listen to your messages? I left you, like, five of them."

Murmur. Murmur.

"Fine. Whatever, but here's the deal. I need you to use the location finder on your phone to find mine. Somebody stole it and we're trying to track them down."

Murmur, murmur, murmur. Grant saw Elaine's cheeks go pinker still.

"Just me and a friend. We think my phone may be on its way to Memphis."

Murmur, murmur.

"A friend, I said."

Murmur, murmur, murmur, murmur. Pause. Murmur.

Elaine sighed and glanced his way. "His name is Grant and we live in the same apartment . . . building. *Now* will you tell me where my phone is?"

Murmur, pause, murmur.

"Kankakee, Illinois?" She looked at Grant. "Does that sound right?"

"I've never heard of it but Illinois is the direction we're headed," he said. "Now at least we know they're going south."

Elaine nodded. "That's really helpful, Mel. Thanks, but I need you to do me another favor. This is important. I need you to keep an eye on that phone's location. If it stops or changes directions or something, we need to know, like, immediately, but don't tell Mom or Dad, OK? I don't want them to worry."

Murmur, murmur.

Grant watched her from the corner of his eye, talking earnestly to her sister, her face animated. What kind of thief would be so concerned about worrying her parents? After a few more minutes, and a bit more vague but very nonfelonious-like discussion, she hung up and put the phone back on the dashboard.

"She's going to check in every half an hour. So as long as my battery doesn't die, we're in good shape."

They drove on for another mile or so, the scrape of the windshield wipers and the soft ka-thunk, ka-thunk of the tires rolling over snowy highway the only sounds.

"I told you my family had a soap business, right?" Her voice was soft, her words hesitant, but relief pulsed through him. Finally, she was going to give him some solid answers.

———

"Yes," Grant answered. He looked straight ahead but she could tell she had his full attention. His curiosity was obvious, and logical, and she didn't want to lie. It just wasn't in her nature, but if she told him her *real* story, he'd think she was nothing more than a poor little rich girl who'd run away from home. Which, technically, she was. And try as she might, she knew she couldn't bring herself to tell him about Boyd. It was just too mortifying. She liked Grant. She liked the way he looked at her as if she were sweet and innocent, but all of that would change the minute he knew about her sex video. So for her sake, and his own, she had to keep the falsehoods to a minimum.

"Well, we do have a little soap business, but it doesn't bring in much money. My dad used to work, but then he had a long dry spell where he didn't do much of anything at all. Bills piled up."

All of that was true. Not even an exaggeration. Once the record label dropped her dad, her parents kept on spending, trying to keep up with the illusion of success as if money was still coming in, and they fell further and further into debt. Delaney and her sisters worked as celebrity stylists, but it wasn't until *Pop Rocks* came along that things began to improve.

"Now he's working again, so that's good," she went on. "The family is all pitching in and we're finally getting back on our feet, but with everyone living in the same house, it's a little too much, you know, family time. Actually, my oldest sister moved out years ago but my middle sister and I stayed. Apartments are pretty pricey in . . . Miami so living at home works OK."

She took a breath. Teetering on the edge between fact and fiction was exhausting work. "Anyway, I felt like they could manage without me at the moment so it seemed like a good time to, well, make a break for it, I guess. You left your family once. That should make sense to you."

So close, so very close to the truth. She *was* trying to make a break for it. She'd become a stylist by default, because her mother and sisters were absorbed in that world, but she'd never planned it that way for herself. She'd just . . . followed. Like she'd followed along with doing the reality show. She was doing it for her parents, not because she wanted the fame or the attention. She couldn't tell him all of that, though. Not right now. Not knowing how he felt about the soulless masses of Los Angeles—because he'd think she was one of them.

Once Grant had helped her get that stupid bag back and she had her money and identification, she'd tell him everything. All of it. Even the awful stuff about Boyd, but until then, she needed his help. It was a weak justification, but she wasn't prepared at the moment to deal with the emotional fallout of piling on the grittier details. They were stuck in this car together until they found Donna, after all, and telling him more about her situation would only serve to make this trip more awkward.

"So, you took all your money and moved to a new town." He said it as a statement, as if to make sure he understood her.

"Yes."

"Why the hell did you pick Bell Harbor? Especially now?"

She felt her cheeks heating up. "If I tell you, you'll think it's a frivolous reason."

The look he cast her way said *try me*.

"I read an article in a travel magazine that said the dunes and beaches were really pretty. It showed a picture, a charming little picture of Bell Harbor, and I stared at that for days and days, and finally I thought, if I could imagine a perfect little town on a perfect little beach, it would look just like that. So . . . that's how I picked Bell Harbor. How was I supposed to know this whole side of the country was going to have the worst weather event in modern history?"

Her aspersions must have offended the weather gods—because one second she was talking about beaches, and in the next second, their car was spinning wildly out of control, careening across the highway at sixty miles per hour. The phone went flying in one direction, the knitting from her lap went flying in another. Round and round they spun, like that awful teacup ride at Disneyland. Faster and faster.

"Hang on," Grant shouted.

Still they spun, until Delaney couldn't tell which direction they faced or if they were even on the road. A blur of lights flashed past as another car spun around and barely missed them. Grant's hands were white-knuckled on the steering wheel as he fought against the momentum of the spiral. On they flew, until the thunder of hard-packed snow crunched against the metal of the car as they plowed into the ditch. Scraping, metal crushing, followed by a bang, and at last, the car came to an abrupt and total stop. Her body flew forward, the seatbelt jerking her back and kicking the breath from her lungs.

How many seconds had passed? Ten? Ten thousand? Dazed, she looked over at Grant. His face was as white as the winter sky outside.

He looked back and reached over to clasp her arm. "Are you OK?"

She nodded. "I think so. Are you OK?"

"I think so."

Their rapid breathing hung like fog in the car. Delaney looked past him, out his window, to see that they had stopped ten or twelve feet away from the side of the freeway, but it felt as if they could have spun around for miles. Her own window was nearly covered in snow because they'd plowed into a drift. The engine had cut when they collided. Taking a breath, Grant turned the key with an unsteady hand. The engine sputtered, but unbelievably, turned over and revved up.

"Do you seriously think you can drive us out of here?" She pointed at the snow out her window.

"No, but I'd like to know if we can keep the car warm until somebody rescues us."

He felt around on the floor until he found his phone. She watched him dial 9-1-1 and press the speaker button.

"Nine-one-one. What is your emergency?"

"We just spun off the road on Interstate 94, just past the Portage exit. We're on the side of the road, not the median, and we're in a yellow Volkswagen."

"Is anyone in the car injured?"

"No, we're both fine, but there's structural damage to the car and no way we're driving out of this. We're definitely stuck. We have about half a tank of gas."

"All right. What's your name, sir?"

"Grant Connelly. My passenger is Elaine Masters."

She flinched as he lied to the dispatcher. If they were rescued by the police, she was going to have to give them her real name. This alias thing was tricky. It was most certainly a crime to give a false name to law enforcement, but in the scheme of crimes committed, swiping a backpack full of money was worse. Hopefully the police graded on a bell curve.

"All right, Grant," said the dispatcher, "I'll notify the sheriff's office. We've had lots of accidents this evening and they'll get to you just as soon as they can. In the meantime—" Her voice disappeared.

Grant looked at his phone. "Shit. We lost the signal." He looked around as if trying to get his bearings. "Do you have anything in the trunk? Like flares or blankets or anything."

She shook her head. "No, nothing like that. Sorry."

"No, I should have thought of that myself. It was stupid to head out in this weather with no supplies. You'd think a survival guy would know that, huh?"

He turned off the engine, then pressed the silver handle, pushing his shoulder against the door.

"Now what are you doing?"

"I need to make sure there isn't snow plugging up the tailpipe. I've already tried to kill us once today. I'd rather not poison us with car exhaust."

Cold wind and snow rushed in as he climbed out and shut the door. He was back in minutes, but was already covered in white as he settled back in behind the steering wheel.

"It's really coming down out there. We'll be damn lucky if they see us. I can't get the trunk open to get our overnight bags. What color bra are you wearing?"

"Excuse me?" This hardly seemed the time.

"I want to tie something bright to the car antenna to help the police spot us. Something dark might work too, but I thought you might be wearing one of those neon-colored bras you like to hang all over my bathroom."

"I don't hang . . ." Yes, she did, but they weren't neon. Neon would be tacky. "They're not neon. They're just . . . whimsical."

"Yeah, that's what I'm always thinking when they fall all over the floor. What a whimsical C cup that is."

She was a B cup, but no woman in her right mind ever told a man her breasts were smaller than he thought they were.

"I don't remember which bra I'm wearing," she said, but she unzipped her coat and tried to reach inside the neck of her sweater to see the strap. The seatbelt hampered her actions and she reached down impatiently to unlatch it, her chest aching in the process. That had been a hard hit. Finally she'd wriggled around enough to hook her thumb in the strap and pull it up so he could see.

"What color is it?" she asked.

"Oh, it's the red one. I like that one. Take it off."

"Are you kidding me? You think I'm going to take my bra off?"

"I'm not kidding. It's getting darker by the minute and the sooner we get something bright on the antenna, the better chance we have of somebody figuring out we need help. I have no idea when the police are going to show up and it's cold as hell."

Take your bra off. Was he joking? But Grant's face was serious, even as he said, "It's either your bra or my plaid boxers. What's it going to be?"

"I'd like to see you try to take your boxers off inside this clown car," she said as she unzipped her coat the rest of the way.

"Under any other circumstances, I would be most happy to oblige you." His eyes darkened as she reached up inside her sweater.

"Could you turn around, please?" she asked.

"We could die in this car. Are you going to begrudge a dying man the chance to see your breasts?"

She stopped moving. "Could we really?"

He shook his head. "No, of course not. I'd never let that happen. But if I say, 'yes, we could,' would you show me your breasts?"

"Do you really think this is the time for this?"

"I'm just trying to keep warm."

"Turn around." Her voice was stern, but his teasing had warmed her up a little too. He finally complied and within seconds she had shimmied out of her bra and back into her coat. She reached over and tickled his ear with the strap and was rewarded by his sharp intake of breath as he caught it with his fingertips.

"Yes, I definitely like this one. Be back in a minute." With a quick smile in her direction, he was out of the car again. It was already several degrees colder, and the light was just beginning to fade. What if they did die out here? Did that really happen to people? They were on Interstate 94. Surely the police or some motorist would spot them soon.

It seemed like forever before he was back in the car. It might have been one minute, it might have been ten. Her brain was as frozen as her breath in the air, but at last he tugged open the door and climbed back in. He was twice as snowy as before. His pant legs were coated with it.

"Are you all right?" she asked.

"Awesome. It's colder than the fucking South Pole out there. And I've been to the South Pole." He rubbed his hands rapidly up and down his arms, then tried to brush off the snow. Delaney reached over and helped him, bumping her head against his in the process.

"It's OK. I've got it," he said. He turned the key. The car moaned and choked before the engine finally turned over. "We've got about ten minutes to heat up the car and then we have to turn it back off. Enjoy it while it lasts."

Chapter 11

TEN MINUTES TURNED INTO THIRTY, and the temperature inside the car plummeted. It was beyond frigid. It was whatever temperature came right after ice age and just before the end of days. Delaney couldn't stop shivering. She was like one of those creepy little wind-up monkeys that clashed brass cymbals together and clicked their teeth.

"I don't suppose you could knit us a blanket, could you?" Grant tried to tease, but mostly he sounded frozen.

"I don't think so. My fingers are numb." She'd retrieved the yarn and needles from where they'd flown to the floor and stuffed everything into a bag that now sat uselessly in the backseat.

"OK, in that case, I'm totally not making a pass at you, but we need to share some heat. Tilt your seat back as far as it will go."

She didn't care if he was making a pass. Whatever it took to get warm. She pulled the metal bar under her seat and it creaked backward until it hit the backseat cushion. She looked at him for further instructions. Her brain was too frozen to formulate a question.

"Good. Now unzip your coat."

What? That her brain needed clarification on. "Unzip? Why would I unzip it?"

"Because we're going to combine body heat and that will work better if we're . . . sweater to sweater instead of coat to coat. Just trust me." He unzipped his own coat.

She didn't have much choice but to trust him. She unzipped her coat and leaned back. Grant moved his right leg around the stick shift and pushed off from his seat. He got stuck for a minute, his hip caught up against the steering wheel. Then it popped free, and he landed on Delaney with a thud. The air burst from her lungs and the seat belt bruise ached again. She gasped loudly.

"Oh! Sorry," he said. "That could've gone better. Are you OK?"

She nodded and drew in a deep breath as he lifted his chest up off of hers. Their legs were tangled, and he moved so that one of his was between hers and the door, as if he was trying to completely cocoon her in the shell of his making, which would be nice if it wasn't so completely and utterly awkward.

"Put your arms around me, inside my coat. I know this is a little . . . personal, but trust me, we're going to be a lot warmer this way."

She believed him. She felt every inch of her skin heating up, some spots more than others, as he settled himself on top of her like a big blanket of Grant. She slid her arms up under his coat and around his waist, lacing her fingers together.

"I'm sorry if I'm heavy, but you'll be warmer underneath me."

He adjusted his legs again, settling in against her. He was heavy, but it felt good. Not just because he was warm but because she felt safe, for the moment, and if she could feel safe under these circumstances, well, that was saying something.

Grant's face was inches from hers. There was no avoiding eye contact.

It was as if he was about to kiss her. And she wanted him to kiss her. It wasn't just because he was all pressed up against her business. She'd wanted to kiss him for days. It was partly why she'd been so ready to leave Bell Harbor. Her attraction to him was a problem she didn't have the emotional strength to overcome.

His smile turned sheepish and at last he rested his head against the crook of her neck and sighed. His breath was wonderfully warm against her skin. It was all so unavoidably intimate.

"So . . ." he said about fifteen seconds later. "What do you want to talk about?"

She giggled at that, but the sound held a hint of hysteria. She could feel the edges of it tapping at her mind. She'd just wanted a little peace and quiet, a little privacy. She hadn't meant to end up here, but oh, what irony would it be if her ultimate fate was death by cameraman?

"How about if we don't talk at all?" she said.

"Oh, I need to talk. I need us to talk about something completely unsexy. Like the most unsexy thing imaginable." He lifted his head and his hazel-green eyes met hers. His voice was terse and stretched thin.

"Why do you need—? Ohh . . ." Delaney caught his meaning. Poor man. Poor testosterone-driven man with no control over the blood flow inside his own body. Now her laughter was prompted from genuine humor.

He let out a puff of icy breath. "God, don't do that. Don't laugh. When you laugh your whole body wiggles and that'll make it even worse."

Delaney laughed harder, making Grant harder too.

"Seriously. Have some mercy here, woman." He pressed his face into her shoulder.

"I'm sorry. I'm not doing this on purpose."

"Yeah, OK, well, just try to remember that my dick isn't doing this on purpose either. I don't want you to think I'm some defiler of damsels in distress. I'm not trying to take advantage here."

She could feel his arousal, deliberate or otherwise, pressed against her thigh. Maybe she should feel worried or offended, but mostly she just felt amused. And maybe a little turned on. OK, probably a lot turned on. It all felt quite delicious, really. What a way to die.

"I don't think you're trying to take advantage."

"Good, but for what it's worth, I may as well admit that even if we were not in this life-or-death predicament, I'd still want to kiss you. I've wanted to kiss you since the first moment you walked into my shower."

A rush of warmth burst through her. "Then why haven't you?"

"Quite frankly, you haven't been very approachable, and because I can't shake the feeling you have a jealous husband or possessive boyfriend out there who might like to show me the business end of his shotgun."

"I don't. There is no jealous gunslinger from anywhere in my past."

He stared down at her for a moment, his eyes intense. This body heat swap was delightful.

"So you're telling me you really are just traveling around with a bag full of money and it's got nothing to do with a man?"

Technically it had everything to do with a man. Boyd Hampton. But he wasn't a jealous ex in any sense of the word, and that's what Grant was asking. Add that to the list of half-truths she'd told.

"There's no man."

Grant's smirk was relieved and mischievous. "A woman, then?"

Delaney chuckled. "Nope. Sorry, no girl-on-girl action for you to fantasize about either."

"Oh, God. Now why would you go and say something like that?" He pressed his hips against her to emphasize his body's reaction. "It's thirty-five degrees below zero in here but somehow I'm sweating."

He wasn't sweating but he certainly was hot, and his hard-on was demanding some attention. "You really have no control over that thing, do you?" she asked.

"I have control over what I do with it, but I can't, you know, make it go back to sleep once it's wide awake. So I suggest we start that unsexy talk now. Tell me about making soap. Or better yet, let's talk about grandmas or food-borne illnesses. Let's talk dysentery."

Delaney burst out laughing again, her body trembling in good humor. He groaned into her ear, nuzzling his head against the curve of her shoulder. "You're killing me."

God, he felt good, and so warm. She splayed her hands over his back and moved one of her legs. She was trying to get more comfortable but heard his breath hitch in his throat.

She gasped at the even more intimate contact. "Sorry."

"No, it's OK. It's just . . ." He lifted his face from her shoulder. It was nearly dark outside, with everything cast in shadows of muted gray, but his eyes were still green. His breath was shallow and warm, soft against her cheek.

"Kiss me," he whispered.

It wasn't a question, or even a demand. Simply a declaration that now was the time. She'd known for days that things were leading to this, and so had he. It was as unavoidable as this accident had been, and now it was her taking the wheel. Or maybe it was her letting go of it.

Her left hand slid from his back to reach up between them and touch his jaw, tracing a line over his cheek before cupping the back of his neck. Just the slightest tilt of her head, the softest pressure from her fingers, and then he was kissing her. The full weight of his body pressed down and she welcomed it, pulling him closer and twining one leg around his. His lips moved over hers, their tongues teased and tangled, and their breaths grew fast. His mouth was warm and tasted like mint and heaven. She hadn't been kissed in a while, a long while, but nowhere in her memory had she ever been kissed like this. She was lost in it. In him.

He kissed down the column of her neck, nudging her scarf down with his chin.

"God, Elaine," he murmured against her skin.

"Lane," she whispered. "Just Lane." It was a small thing, but it felt important to her in that moment, that little bit of honesty in the puddle of lies. She wanted him to know her, the real her. Not the brand of Delaney Masterson, or the ruse of Elaine Masters, but just . . . her. The essence of her that was true.

He raised his head and gazed down at her. "OK. Lane. You are a beautiful woman, you know that?"

She smiled back, and believed it for a moment.

"And you're a very handsome man. I didn't realize that when I first saw you."

"Really? Because it seemed like you got a pretty good look at me while I was in the shower."

Delaney felt the heat stealing over her cheeks. She had gotten a pretty good look, but judging from the bulk pressing against her thigh right now, she'd actually underestimated him. "You ruined my book."

"That book is fine. It just needed to dry."

"It's still ruined. I can't read it now. Every time I open it I keep wondering which pages were pressed up against your . . . you know."

Grant's laughter was full of teasing. "Can't you even say it? Pressed up against my what?"

The blush turned scorching. "Oh, you know. Your . . . *penis.*" She whispered the last word and glanced away, sending him into a fit of laughter.

"Wow, you really are a Girl Scout. How did you get to be twenty-five years old and still be so innocent?"

Her smile faded. She wasn't twenty-five, and she sure as hell wasn't innocent either. But it felt so nice having him think that. It made her feel shiny and new, untarnished by Boyd and her own bad judgment. She should tell him the truth now, but everything inside of her was glowing at his appraisal—even if it was misguided and inaccurate. If she told him the truth, he'd stop kissing her, and right now all she wanted in the world was for him to do it again. So she told him to.

"Shut up and kiss me."

Chapter 12

SHE WAS SO INTENT ON Grant's kiss, she didn't know why he stopped, but he lifted his chest from hers and reached toward the door.

Then she heard it, a rapping at the window. A bare hand swiped at the snowy glass and bare knuckles knocked again as Grant tugged on the manual window lever. Snow whipped inside and swirled around, a miniblizzard leaving the driver's seat speckled with crystals.

"Hey, in there!" a pleasant, masculine voice called in over the wind. "You folks need some help or are you too busy to care you're in a ditch?" He stuck his head inside when the gap was large enough and grinned at the two of them.

Relief at being rescued mingled with disappointment at ending this interlude.

The man looked to be about her age, and he was wearing a brown hoodie with no overcoat. His eyes were espresso dark, and she could see enough of his face to know he sported elaborate, sharp-edged sideburns. He was cute, if a little devilish in appearance, but honestly, she was so cold that a trip to hell didn't sound half bad.

"Yeah, we could use some help! We've been waiting on the police for more than an hour," Grant answered.

"There's a huge mash-up about two miles back that way," the

man said. "They're probably stuck in that. We took a different exit but barely made it through ourselves. The roads are for shit right now and we've got the tour bus."

Delaney almost burst out laughing. Tour bus? Of course it was a tour bus. With her luck, this guy was probably part of a Jesse Masterson cover band.

"Well, we're sure glad to see you. Do you think you could give us a ride to the next town?"

"Of course, no problem. Come on." He pulled open the door and a blast of arctic air carried along pellets of ice to slap at Delaney's face. She instantly missed Grant's body heat as he moved, but it was past time to be out of this car. He untangled his legs from hers and clumsily climbed toward the driver's seat and out into the elements. The man popped his head back in to reach for Delaney.

"Watch your step there, honeybun," he said, gently grabbing her arm and tugging. "You all right?"

"I'm good, thanks. I think you saved our lives."

"My pleasure."

She managed to grab her knitting bag, then clambered from the car. Her legs sank into two feet of snow. Grant turned back and caught her other hand. The wind was howling all around, biting at her face. A monster-sized tour bus loomed before them, just feet from where they'd skidded off the road. It was sleek and black and a welcome sight. Even if it was full of musicians.

"Is there any way to get our clothes and stuff?" she called to Grant. She had to shout to be heard over the storm.

He looked back at the car and shook his head. "I don't think so. The trunk is jammed up in the snowdrift."

"Let's boogie," their rescuer hollered from behind. "We can't stay here long or somebody is going to crash into the bus and then we're all screwed."

Delaney stared for a second longer at the blocked-up trunk where her overnight bag was trapped. She hadn't brought much for this journey. Just a few pairs of jeans, a few sweaters, and some toiletries and styling products. Damn, she really wanted her styling products. And her underwear. She wanted that too. She was now utterly and completely at the mercy of strangers. She would have cried then, but the tears would just turn to cubes on her face so what would be the point?

Grant put an arm around her waist. "Sorry about your car. We can let the police know we'll be back for it, but it's stuck there for now."

She hadn't even thought about the car. Her crappy little Volkswagen that had gotten her out of one mess but right into another. She wasn't sure she'd miss it all that much.

They made their way up the short but steep incline, trudging through the snow and getting soaking wet in the process. Brown Hoodie Devil Man pounded on the door, and when it opened, he climbed aboard first. Delaney followed with Grant right behind her. The bus was blissfully warm, and for that alone, she had to be thankful, yet the feeling of déjà vu was overwhelming.

As a kid, she'd spent hours on her father's bus, along with Melody and Roxanne. They'd played with Barbie dolls on the bunks and had tea parties at the little folding dinette table. Her mom would let them have Kool-Aid and Swiss Cake Rolls and Delaney had always unrolled hers before eating it. Some of her favorite childhood memories were from days on that bus. It had sat in the driveway for a while after the last Jesse Masterson CD came out, but eventually her parents had sold it to pay other bills. No need for a tour bus when there were no tour dates to play.

"Welcome aboard," said a chubby, balding man behind the mammoth steering wheel. He had a shiny head and a friendly expression. That missing tooth was hardly noticeable at all.

Their rescuer pushed the hood from his head, revealing dark brown hair that was either wildly styled or had gotten severely messed up in the gale-force winds they'd just hiked through. "Yes, welcome aboard the Paradise Brothers' home away from home," he said. "I'm Reggie. This is Sam, our driver." He pointed to the chubby, bald guy. "This here is my brother, Finch."

Another man, just slightly taller than Reggie with auburn hair and rust-colored freckles, came forward and extended his hand. "Howdy. Glad to see you folks are OK. That car of yours is damn near buried in the drift. Good thing our Sammy here has got a sharp eye."

Sammy grinned. "Is that there a brassiere on the antenna?"

Delaney blushed. That brassiere had cost her ninety dollars, but all things considered, it was money well spent.

"Sure is," Grant answered, smiling at her.

"Hey, folks. How y'all doin'? I'm Humphrey." A fourth man appeared behind Finch and his velvet voice accompanied his dark brown arm as he reached around the redhead. Humphrey had the sweet-natured face of a third-grade spelling bee champion, but his suggestive wink told Delaney he was every bit a grown-up man. They all looked to be in their midtwenties. Handsome, fit, cocky too. She could tell just by their bright smiles. She'd spent her life surrounded by musicians. She could read these guys like sheet music.

Grant and Delaney shook hands with everyone while he introduced them. "I'm Grant. This is Elaine. Thanks so much for picking us up. It was starting to get damn cold in that car."

Reggie chuckled. "Oh, I don't know. It looked downright steamy in there when I peeked in the window, yeah?" He patted the driver on the shoulder. "Sammy, let's get this rig moving before somebody plows into the back of us, yeah?"

Sammy nodded, and Reggie motioned for them to sit down. There were two rows of pine-green suede sofas, one along each side the bus, and a small kitchenette just past that. Delaney knew with a quick glance that curtained sleeping bunks were toward the back, along with a bathroom. Standard-issue tour bus, and although this one was nice, it didn't have the flashy rock 'n' roll style of her dad's old bus.

These guys were honky-tonk. Up-and-comers, most likely. If the *y'all*s and the *howdy*s hadn't tipped her off, they oozed a certain Southern comfort kind of charm.

"Where you two headed?" Reggie asked, sitting down next to Humphrey. Humphrey picked up a guitar pick and began toggling it over his fingers.

Delaney sat down near Grant while Finch leaned against the counter, his arms crossed loosely over a green-and-black plaid shirt.

Grant looked her way. "That's a good question. Memphis, maybe."

"Maybe?" Finch said. "Kind of shitty weather for a random road trip, ain't it? Pardon my French."

Delaney beamed up at him. She needed to spin this her way before Grant went and said too much.

"That's kind of a funny story, actually," she chimed in. "You see, Grant's mother accidently took my phone when she left to visit her sister in Memphis and we're hoping to catch up with her to get it back. So I take it you guys are musicians, huh?"

Of course she already knew that, but she also knew getting them talking about themselves would distract them from asking questions about her. The old bait-and-switch technique. She tried to look starstruck, as if musicians were the coolest thing ever. As if Eric Clapton didn't play golf with her dad.

"Yes, ma'am," Finch answered proudly. "We're the Paradise Brothers. Based out of Nashville but we just played a couple of gigs up in Michigan and Indiana." He leaned over and playfully cuffed Reggie on the back of his head. "Remember next winter, only shows down south, Reg. This weather is a crazy bitch. Oh, sorry for that French again, ma'am." He looked apologetically at Delaney, but there was more sparkle in his eye than genuine remorse.

Delaney smiled back and batted her lashes in pseudo-awe. There were platinum records hanging on the wall back at her parents' house, but these guys did not need to know that.

"Well, fortune smiles, yeah?" said Reggie. "We just happen to be headed to Memphis ourselves. We're booked on Beale Street in a couple of days, so you're welcome to ride along with us."

"Are you sure it's not too much trouble? We don't want to put you guys out," Delaney said. An hour or so in their company was one thing, but it was a ten-hour drive to Memphis from where they were, and in this weather, it could take twice that long. Even though these guys were country, they would have heard of her dad. He'd been out of the scene for a long time, but his reputation lingered. And it was a small step from knowing Jesse Masterson to recognizing her. She pulled her bangs down over her forehead.

Reggie's dark brows pinched together. "What kind of gents would we be if we just dropped you off at the next rest stop with no car? It's no problem. We've got plenty of room, yeah? But if you want us to leave you someplace, of course we can. We're probably stopping off near Champaign tonight."

Delaney turned to Grant. "I need to call my sister. Is your phone working?"

He pulled it from his pocket and handed it to her. "I don't know if you'll get a signal but you can try."

"Um, do you mind if I use your bathroom?" She glanced up at Reggie.

"Of course not, but if you just want privacy, feel free to go in the boogie-woogie room."

Grant started laughing and she couldn't hold back her smile. "The what?"

The rest of them snickered like sassy frat boys. Finch leaned forward and pointed down the hall to the room at the end. "The boogie-woogie room. It's the only real bedroom on the bus, so whoever brings a lady on board gets to sleep there. Guess you're in luck, sweetness." He nodded at Grant and Delaney felt the entire women's movement take a giant step backward.

"Meanwhile," Reggie added, peeling off his hoodie, "this thing is soaking wet. I'm going to change and throw this stuff in the dryer. Say, are you two as wet as me? You want to toss your stuff in to dry?"

She was wet. That trek through the snowdrifts had left her jeans soaked, and wet denim was not comfortable, but neither was the idea of taking off her clothes on a bus full of men.

Humphrey jumped up from his seat and pulled a duffel bag from one of the bunks. "I got some stuff you can wear." He rifled around in it for a minute before pulling out a pair of black athletic pants with a white stripe down the leg, and a T-shirt. He handed them to Delaney. "Here, you can wear these while your stuff dries."

Finch pulled another bag from a second bunk and pointed at Grant. "Yeah, I got some stuff you can wear."

Grant held up a hand. "No, that's OK. I'll—"

Finch shook his head and interrupted. "Do unto others, man. You can change in there." He pointed to the infamous boogie-woogie room.

Delaney looked at the offered garments. A white T-shirt? It couldn't have been a coincidence.

"I don't suppose you have a bra inside that duffel bag, do you?" she asked.

Humphrey's grin split wide, making him look even younger, yet even naughtier.

"Oh, hells yeah. We got bras. We got lots of bras." He stepped to the side and opened a drawer. Full of bras. Then he pulled open the drawer beneath it. "We gots panties too."

His eyebrows did a little hula dance and Delaney laughed.

"Now, that might seem a little strange, sweetness," Finch offered, "but the ladies, you see, they like to toss us things when we're onstage, and we don't want to hurt anyone's feelings. So we scoop up whatever they send our way, and when we have a bagful, we drop them off at Goodwill. Everybody wins."

"And some of these have just been left behind. You know, *souvenirs*," Humphrey added, as if there were any question. "But don't worry. All these feminine undies have been freshly laundered." He lowered his voice. "Reggie loves to wash the panties."

She looked over at Reggie, who was still sitting on the sofa. He just flipped his palms up, like *yeah, I love to wash the panties*.

Delaney had been in some interesting situations before, some of her own making and some created by fate, but this might be a new low. Reduced to wearing a groupie's discarded underpants. But she was low on options right now. Her own bra was still flapping in the wind on Interstate 94, and heaven only knew when or how she'd get to a store. She had no car, no money, no phone, no anything. All she had was Grant and the clothes on her back. The very wet clothes on her back.

"Thanks," she said to Humphrey. "I might just have a look."

She reached into the drawer as if it was a snake pit.

"Anything in there for me?" Grant asked, peering over her shoulder.

"Only if you're into women's panties," Humphrey answered.

"Only when I'm invited," Grant answered.

"Nice," Delaney murmured. "That's very nice. Very gentlemanly of you."

"You guys hungry?" Reggie called out. "We got Hot Pockets, yeah?"

———•———

Delaney stared into the mirror in the boogie-woogie room and tried to wrestle her damp hair into a ponytail. Her new skanky-ho bra fit pretty well, and the T-shirt and pants from Humphrey were soft and warm. Certainly better than wet jeans, and she was finally starting to thaw. Now she just needed to call Melody and figure out where the heck to have the Paradise Brothers drop them off.

Grant came in and shut the door just as she was about to dial, and he started to undo his pants.

"What are you doing?" she whispered.

He glanced around the room as if wondering who she was talking to. "I'm changing my clothes," he said when he realized he was it.

"You can't wait until I'm out of here?"

His smile was classic big bad wolfy. "You've seen pretty much all of me, remember?"

She did remember. Very clearly. She remembered what he looked like naked and sudsy, and she damn well remembered what he felt like pressed up against her in that Volkswagen. Her cheeks flamed, and he chuckled.

"Such a Girl Scout," he whispered and continued to get undressed.

She turned her back to him and dialed Melody's number. Her sister answered on the fourth ring. "Mel, it's Lane. I need an update."

"It's not a good time right now," her sister murmured into the phone. "The producers are here and Mom—"

"Delaney, is that you? Hello, darling," her mother's voice cut in, bright and chipper, the fake kind of bright and chipper. It was the voice she used when things were terrible but she wanted to pretend they weren't. "I was just telling Harvey the producer, you remember Harvey our producer, right? Well, I was just telling him how you are out scouting locations for another Master-soaps boutique. Have you had any luck?"

Oh, God. She couldn't do this fake song and dance right now. Not with Grant in the room. "Hi, Mom." Delaney used the same fake bright and chipper tone. With any luck, her mother would get the hint and give the phone back to Melody. "Um, yes, I have been doing that little thing. I don't have much to tell you right now, though."

Delaney gave a fast glance over her shoulder and saw Grant's muscular back as he peeled off his shirt. "Let's talk in a few days. Meanwhile, can I talk to Melody, please?"

Her mother's voice came through again, but more muffled and low, as if she'd covered her mouth with her hand. "Lane, where are you? Melody said your phone had been stolen. Is everything all right?"

There was legitimate concern in her tone, and Delaney felt her eyes well up with tears. She wanted to tell her mother everything and have a good, long cry, and then her mother would make her cookies and tell her everything would be fine. But it wouldn't be fine. Her mother couldn't get that awful sex tape back. She couldn't make people stop saying mean things on Delaney's Facebook page, and she couldn't stop magazines from printing pictures of her. Her mom also couldn't tell her what to do about incredibly sexy Grant, who was taking his clothes off right behind her in the boogie-woogie room of a tour bus.

He'd stripped down to his boxers. She could see him in the mirror's reflection, and damn if they weren't really plaid, just like he'd said.

None of that mattered right now, though. All that mattered at this precise moment was getting her phone, her wallet, and her forty thousand dollars back.

"Yes, I'm fine, Mom, but I really need to talk to Mel. She's helping me with something important."

"Oh, well that sounds fabulous, darling." Fake-voiced mother was back. "Keep in touch, then. I'll have you just chat with Melody about those details while I fill Harvey in."

She heard the sounds of a phone being passed and a door shutting, and the clunking of bracelets as her sister came back on the line. "OK, so I just checked your phone's location about ten minutes ago and it says it's in Bentley, Illinois, just north of Champaign."

Delaney watched in the mirror as Grant pulled a white T-shirt over his head and threaded his arms through. He was bigger than Finch, and the shirt filled out.

"Lane? Are you there?"

"What? Oh, yes. I'm here." She'd been distracted by the plain white tee. "So, Bentley, you said? Does the phone signal seem to be moving?"

"I think so. Still heading south."

"OK. Thanks. Can you keep an eye on it, and text me at this number if it stops moving or looks like it's heading someplace other than Memphis?"

"Of course. So where are you guys now? Anywhere close to Bentley?"

"Not exactly. We had—" she was just about to say they'd had an accident, but that would just worry everyone even more. This was Delaney's mess to clean up as best she could. No sense dragging Melody further into it than necessary. "We had a little car trouble but we're rolling again. Tell Mom everything is fine."

"We? As in you and this Grant person? Who is this guy?"

Delaney glanced in the mirror to see him pulling up a pair of dark gray sweatpants. "I told you, he's a friend from my apartment building. Gotta go, now, OK?"

By the time she'd said her good-byes to her sister, Grant was fully dressed in dry, borrowed clothes and he had their damp things draped over one arm.

"Everything good?" he asked.

"As good as can be expected. Looks like your mom is just north of Champaign and still on the move. Do you think you could try to call her again?"

He nodded. "I've left half a dozen messages with her, and I left a message at my aunt's house because she doesn't have a cell phone. And you tried to call your own phone, right?"

Delaney nodded. "It went to voice mail."

"Well, that's the best we can do, I guess. I told Carl to let me know if he heard anything too. Should I mention again now how sorry I am about all this?"

She knew he was, but of all the people involved in this fiasco, Grant was the only one *not* to be blamed. This was Donna's fault for taking the money, Boyd's for releasing that video, and Delaney's for running away. Oh, to rewind. But if she did, she never would've met Grant, and the idea of that caused a little trip and stumble to her heartbeat.

"Stop apologizing. Let's just hope we get lucky and can still catch up with your mother tonight."

His laugh was low and suggestive. "I am all about getting lucky."

But luck was nowhere on their radar.

Chapter 13

"HEY, GUYS," SAMMY CALLED OUT from the driver's seat as Delaney and Grant came out of the back bedroom and headed up the narrow aisle. "This storm is getting worse. I think we should pull over at the next rest stop and call it a night. We're still on track to make it to Memphis in plenty of time if we get an early start in the morning."

Delaney's optimism vanished. So much for catching Grant's mom sooner rather than later. Her disappointment must have showed. Grant looped an arm around her waist, whispering low, "Lane, I'll get your money back to you. I promise."

She blinked fast and nodded. "It's OK." It wasn't, though. Not even a little bit, but what could he do about it?

"I'll take those wet duds," Reggie said.

Grant handed them over with a nod. "Thanks."

"Your lady all right?" she heard Reggie ask.

"She's just anxious to get her phone back," Grant answered.

Reggie didn't respond. He just took the damp clothes and walked back to the rear of the bus.

Minutes later, they pulled into a truck stop parking lot, and before the wheels were done turning, Finch was standing up at the kitchenette, rubbing his hands together.

"Well, looks like it's time to party. Who wants a drink?" He pulled a fifth of Honey Jack from the cabinet, along with a couple of glasses.

"I'll take one," Delaney said immediately. She'd have just one. Facing a day-long bus ride tomorrow was going to be bad enough. Facing it with a hangover would be unbearable, but she needed something to fend off her distress. Hopefully this drink would cheer her up and not send her into the boogie-woogie room crying like a little girl. Delaney Masterson was not a crier.

Drinks were poured, and soon they were all sitting on the couches along either side of the bus and getting acquainted. She took a sip of the whiskey, and the heat was instantaneous and welcome.

Sammy, Finch, and Humphrey were on one side, and Delaney sat between Grant and Reggie on the other. Judging from appearances, Finch and Reggie were truly brothers, but the other two were clearly no relation.

"So, besides looking for a lost cell phone, what's your story? Where are you guys from?" Finch asked.

Grant stretched, and rested his arm along the back of the sofa, letting one hand dangle over her shoulder. She leaned into him, liking it.

"I'm originally from Bell Harbor, Michigan," he said. "I was born there, but more recently I was based out of Los Angeles."

"Ah, Los Angeles," Reggie said in a poor rendition of a Latino accent. "City of Angels, yeah?"

"Hardly," Grant answered. "No angels around there that I could find. Just a lot of false perfection. Everything there is so glossy. Everybody is a voyeur, but nothing you see is real. Just a bunch of D-list celebrities saying *look at me*."

Delaney felt a little dizzy, and it wasn't from the whiskey. Her whole job revolved around LA glitz and gloss and voyeurism. But she wasn't on the D-list. Worse than that. She was a *stylist* for the D-list.

"I didn't spend much time in the city," Grant added. "I travel mostly."

"In a Volkswagen?" Humphrey asked, the guitar pick still flicking over his fingers.

Grant chuckled. "No, that's Elaine's car. You ever heard of *One Man, One Planet*?"

"Hells, yeah!" Humphrey exclaimed. "I love that show."

"I'm a coproducer and the director of photography. Well, I was. I just quit." He cocked his head. "And it *still* feels good saying that."

"That's the show with Rock Blakestone, yeah?" Reggie asked.

"Blake Rockstone," Humphrey corrected him before Grant had the chance.

"Whatever. That guy is badass." Reggie lifted his glass. "Here is to the badassery of Blake Rockstone."

Grant shook his head. "Can't drink to that. Blake would like you to think he's a badass, but trust me, the only thing bad is his attitude. And his real name is Ned Beidelman. He's an asshole. It feels good saying *that* too." Then he took a drink.

Humphrey fell back against the cushion, both hands pressed against his chest in a display of mock agony. "Blake Rockstone is an asshole? No, say it ain't so. I love that guy. Y'all remember that episode where he wrestles the alligator? Man, I thought for sure he was a goner."

Grant shook his head. "That poor alligator. The thing was half dead, shot up with so many sedatives we thought we wouldn't be able to revive it."

"I remember that episode," Reggie said. "Looked like the gator was fighting him pretty hard, yeah?"

Grant took another drink. "The assistant director put bungee cords on the poor thing's back legs so they could make it twist and turn. Couple of poor sap production assistants were in charge of jerking it around to make it look ferocious. Add a few close-up shots and a little editing, and poof." He spread his fingers wide. "Cinema magic. To the untrained eye, Blake Rockstone dry humping a sleeping animal looks pretty intense. That's why I quit."

"Because of the bestiality?" Finch asked.

Grant chuckled. "Yes, that, and the way it's edited to manipulate the audience. When we first started the show, we had just one or two cameras. We were right in on the action. We had to be or we'd miss the shot, but now it's too slick. There's nothing authentic about it. Just like LA, I guess."

Delaney took a big swallow of her drink. It burned, but not as much as Grant's obvious disdain for television fakery, which she was very familiar with. *Pop Rocks* was full of it, thanks to sound bites and clever editing. In one episode, they'd made it seem like Melody had broken her foot, when in reality all she'd done was stub her toe. And in another episode, a well-articulated discussion about gun control was made to look like a *heated argument* between her and Roxanne about where to go to lunch. Every conversation she'd had on camera had been somehow twisted into something different. The trivial became significant, while the substance was boiled down to nuggets.

Delaney gave a little hiccup after swallowing the whiskey, and Grant squeezed her shoulder. She didn't look his way. She didn't dare. She just pulled her bangs down over her forehead.

"So you quit. What now?" Finch asked. "What does an ex-director of photography do when he's out of work?"

"Well, if I can get the money Blake owes me, I've been kicking around this idea for a new show."

Now she looked at him. "New show? What kind of show?"

He ran a hand over his jaw, as if he wasn't fully on board with sharing, but then he started talking and his enthusiasm became evident. "Kind of an extreme makeover show, only with charities. Traveling all over, I've seen some truly devastated areas. The kind of places most people don't want to think about. We're pretty desensitized to seeing human suffering on a TV screen. You know, you hear about a village of a hundred hungry kids, and you think, 'Oh, that's so sad, but it's too big a problem for me to solve.' So, my idea is to personalize it. Take a different charity each week and do a feature about just one person or one family who that organization has helped. I think if people can see how even a little participation can impact the life of a real person, they'd be more apt to get involved. I mean, if you saw one hungry kid crying on the street in your neighborhood, you'd never forget it, right?"

They all nodded, including Delaney.

"So, that's my idea. Follow a different charity each week, show what kind of conditions some people are forced to live in, and provide the average urban dweller with a tangible method of helping. I don't want to manipulate things in any way, just give an authentic view of people's individual circumstances and hope it's motivational."

"That's a cool idea," Finch said. "I'd watch that."

Grant looked over at him. "Would you? Some of the outreach workers I met in the Philippines triggered this idea. I was there right after a hurricane and I was so impressed with the way they pulled together to get things done. I wanted to do a documentary about it but my producers thought it would be depressing. I guess watching Blake try to shake a scorpion out of his sleeping bag is better television than saving a kid's life."

He took a swig from his glass and added, "All you see on American television is the same kind of beautiful people doing the same kind of irrelevant shit, over and over. It's boring. I think people are ready for something with a little more substance."

Beautiful people? Irrelevant shit. He was describing *Pop Rocks* again. He just didn't know it. But his idea for a show was brilliant. And full of heart. When it came right down to it, Grant Connelly was sentimental.

"I love that idea," she said, locking him in her gaze. She wanted to kiss him right then and there. And she would have too, except Reggie cleared his throat loudly and stood up, breaking the spell.

"I could use another drink, yeah? Finch, get me more whiskey."

"So, who wants to play strip poker?" Reggie asked after two or three more drinks had gone down the hatch and the night's conversation had covered everything from trends in music to the best place to get fried calamari, from favorite pagan holidays to where one might find the most radical wave for surfing. It was close to midnight and Grant was feeling the one-two punch of fatigue and booze. He'd stopped drinking after the second glass of whiskey, but since he'd stayed up late last night with his family after Tyler's wedding and spent much of today chasing down his mother, he was tired. Elaine was leaning against him, still nursing that first drink. Smart woman.

"Anyone, strip poker?" Reggie asked again, grinning at the only woman on the bus.

Elaine shook her head but smiled. "No, thanks. I'd hate to lose the clothes that Humphrey so generously offered me."

"No one wants to see your hairy ass, Reg," said Finch, standing up. "And I'm ready for some shut-eye."

Sammy stood at the same time. "That's it for me too, folks. I got a long day of driving ahead of me tomorrow." He moseyed on past the rest of them and went into the spatially challenged bathroom.

Reggie tossed back the rest of his drink. "All right, but, Elaine, consider this an opportunity missed. I play cards lousy and you could've had me naked in just a couple of rounds."

Grant slid his arm around her shoulders again. He knew the kind of guy this Reggie was, casting a wide net with his over-the-top flirtation. Blake was the same sort, just looking for a vulnerable woman to come along and take that bait. The kind of woman swayed by celebrity propaganda and a clever line. Elaine seemed too smart to fall for Reggie's good ole country boy persona, but then again, chicks always seemed to dig musicians.

Grant stood and pulled her up with him. "Thanks again for housing us tonight, guys. We really appreciate it."

Reggie slapped him on the back good-naturedly. "No sweat, man. *Mi casa es su casa.* Or . . . I guess, *mi bus-o es su bus-o*, yeah? Anyway, you need anything, let me know. We got extra toothbrushes and stuff in the bathroom. Help yourself."

"Thank you," Elaine said. "You've all been so great."

"My pleasure, honeybun."

She turned to walk down the aisle and Reggie caught Grant by the sleeve. "Seriously, anything you need, we got. Ibuprofen, water bottles." He lowered his voice. "Rubbers, lubricant. It's all in the drawers in the boogie-woogie room."

Grant let out a chuff of laughter, even if Reggie was as obnoxious as hell. This bus sure was a one-stop party shop, but he'd had a little too much whiskey and his head was foggy, not that he thought for a minute that Elaine would go for it anyway.

And he was right. He walked into the bedroom after his turn in the bathroom and closed the plastic accordion door behind him. The space was just big enough for a double-sized mattress, one nightstand—not to be confused with a one-night stand—and a closet barely deep enough to hold two shirts. One, if it was fleece. The room was surrounded by long, horizontal windows covered in short, green curtains, and a modest amount of light came from a single-bulb lamp. A couple of faded quilts sat in a pile on top of dingy beige sheets, but Elaine was standing off to one side, staring at the bed like it was littered with roadkill.

"What's the matter?" He kept his voice low.

She whispered back, frowning, not taking her eyes from the center of the mattress. "Do you have any idea how much DNA is in this bed right now?"

Grant smiled at her unease. He'd slept in virtually every possible condition, in dirt, on rocks, and in between stinky motel sheets that were far more infested than these were. This was nothing for him, but for her, it was obviously different. "It beats sleeping in the car. I didn't want to tell you this, but I was getting a little nervous about being found."

"Oh, I'm grateful. Don't get me wrong. It's just, things in here are a little . . . crusty." She nudged one quilt with her index finger and then wiped it on her borrowed sweatpants.

God she was cute. "It's the boogie-woogie room, Lane. In fact, I've heard rumors there are party favors in the drawers."

Her eyebrow arched and she finally looked at him.

"Party favors?"

"In the drawer." He nodded at the nightstand and her gaze snapped to it as if the thing might come to life and get its freak on all over her. He couldn't resist. He stepped over and tugged open the drawer. An abundance of brightly colored foil wrappers glinted in the dim light, and an industrial-sized tube of KY jelly rolled forward.

"I'll be damned," Grant murmured. "I thought he was kidding."

Elaine let out a slightly breathy chuckle, and he realized she was not nearly as traumatized as she'd first appeared. She reached into the drawer and plucked a white square packet from the pile. It looked like a wet wipe from a restaurant. She flipped it over. Then burst out laughing and handed it to Grant.

He squinted a little to read the label. "Sweet Sack Ball Swipes. Get fresh before you *get fresh*." He smiled at Elaine. "That is marketing genius right here."

"That is the tackiest thing ever."

"I think it's thoughtful, and it says right here it's cinnamon scented. I wonder if it's *flavored* too?" He smiled optimistically.

"It doesn't matter. I'm not tasting it. I'm not even smelling it. Put it away." She clasped her hands to prevent touching anything else.

There was no doubt in his mind she was serious, but she was smiling and he felt himself going rigid again—for about the tenth time since they'd climbed aboard that bus. She was adorable, and funny and sexy, and the way she'd gazed up at him and whispered, "I love that idea," had nearly made him push her down on that sofa and kiss her senseless. He tossed the packet into the drawer and nudged it closed with his knee. "OK, but just so you know, I really want to kiss you again."

She moved around, evading his arms. "No, you don't. You're drunk. You're just imagining things."

"Oh, trust me. I'm imagining all sorts of things." Oh, God, he really was.

"Well, stop it, because it won't do you any good. And check your phone, will you? I want to see if Melody has sent any updates."

He pulled the phone from the pocket of his jacket, which had been hung to dry on a hook on the wall. He checked the screen.

"Two messages," he said. "First one says PHONE IS STILL IN BENTLEY." He moved his thumb over the screen. "And the second message says, PHONE IS STILL IN BENTLEY. WHERE THE FUCK ARE YOU AND WHO THE FUCK IS GRANT? LOVE, MELODY. XOXO."

He smiled at her, and she smiled back. "It's too late to answer her now. I'll call her tomorrow."

He set the phone on the little shelf above the bed as she stared at the mattress once more.

"Which of these pillows do you suppose is the least nasty?" she asked, reaching down and spreading the quilts over the bed using just her thumbs and index fingers.

"No telling. But here." He pulled off his shirt. "Put this around one. It's not much, but it's clean and smells like fabric softener. Apparently Reggie likes to wash shirts too."

Elaine chuckled. "Won't you be cold?"

He'd be lying next to her. No chance he'd be cold. In fact, he'd be lucky if he got any sleep at all. "I'll be all right." He slid under the blankets and sheet and patted the spot next to him.

She stared for a minute, and he sat back up. "Do you want me to go sleep on a bunk or the couch? Because I will if you ask me to." Every speck of testosterone in his body was calling him a dumbass right now. What kind of moron offered to go sleep someplace else?

Elaine paused for the briefest hesitation, then sighed and flipped off the light. "No, it's fine."

She climbed in next to him, covered a pillow with his shirt, and lay down, her back to his front. His chest whumped in relief and he wasted no time in snuggling up behind her and wrapping an arm around her waist. He left a little room between them—as Father Lawrence would say, *leave room for the Holy Spirit*—but there was nothing holy about his thoughts right now. Even so, he didn't need her to know the extent of his desire, or of his suffering. As she relaxed into him, he knew this was going to be the longest night of his life. Her hair spread over the pillow and smelled like flowers. He didn't know what kind of flowers because he was, after all, a dude, but the scent was flowers for sure, and her skin smelled like that fancy bar of soap back at home in their shower. He wanted to savor it. He breathed in deep, slow, and apparently loud.

"Grant? Are you . . . smelling me?"

His pause was infinitesimal. "Get over yourself. Of course I'm not smelling you."

He was totally smelling her. He nudged a little closer, pressing his chest against her back and slipping his hand up under her shirt to rest it on her warm abdomen.

"Hey, now what are you doing?" she whispered and caught his arm at the wrist.

"Touching you," he whispered back.

"I know you're touching me, but you should stop. These walls are wafer thin." She didn't push his arm away but her grip tightened.

Still, the whiskey made him bold and silly. He nuzzled the back of her neck and took another obvious breath. "So . . . no boogie-woogie, then?"

He felt her body move with silent laughter. "Absolutely no boogie-woogie. You said you'd never take advantage of a damsel in distress."

"I never said that. If I did, I was just trying to get laid."

He felt her laughing again, though no sound came out. "Go to sleep."

"Won't you at least kiss me good night?" He sounded more desperate than sexy. Damn whiskey. Damn dick that felt no sense of shame or pride.

Elaine rolled slightly so that she was looking up at him. Lights from the parking lot lampposts shone in through the seams of the curtains, making her look dark and mysterious.

She lifted her mouth and gave him a fast, tight kiss on the lips, but he followed as her head fell back to the pillow. That tiny taste had only made him want more. His hand slid farther around her, turning her onto her back. She didn't resist, and the kiss deepened briefly, until one of the goddamn Paradise Brothers slammed the bathroom door and the moment was over.

Elaine kissed him once more, a soft brush of the lips at the corner of his mouth, then she rolled to her side once more. "Go to sleep, Grant."

Yep, this was going to be one long, uncomfortable night.

Chapter 14

"WHAT DO YOU MEAN THERE'S no signal?" Three hundred and fifty pounds of virtual linebacker plowed into Delaney's chest, and Grant's phone shook in her hand. She pulled the quilt back up to her waist as she sat in the bed. It was barely daybreak, and with the time difference between Illinois and California, she'd woken her sister up.

"I'm sorry, Lane," Melody said, her voice drowsy. "I don't know what to tell you. I checked when I went to bed last night and it showed that your phone was still in Bentley, Illinois, but when I check it now, it says it's offline. So either your burglar turned it off, or your phone died."

"Crap! Crap, crap, crap." Elaine punched at the mattress with her fist.

Grant rolled over and scrubbed a hand across his face. "What's the matter?" His voice was as scratchy with sleep as Melody's.

"Who's that?" her sister asked. "Your mysterious Grant person? Let me talk to him."

"Oh, hell no." That's all she needed. Melody and Grant exchanging information. "Just let me think." But her brain wasn't booting. After a few seconds of blank nothingness where her cognitive reasoning should be, she spoke up. "OK, listen, Mel, I guess we'll head to Memphis. I'll call you when we get there, but don't tell anyone about any of this. Not about the phone or the car trouble or anything. I want to take care of things myself, without having to worry about what the people worrying about me are actually worrying about. Got it?"

Her sister's voice rose. "But what if *I'm* worried? You're acting nuts, you know. I don't want the next picture I see on *People* magazine to be a mug shot of you, or one of you shaving your head or something. What do you even know about this guy? Is he trustworthy?"

Elaine looked down at Grant. His short hair was a little bedheady and he had a pillow line on his cheek. Very threatening.

"Are you trustworthy?" she asked him. "My sister wants to know."

She was making a joke, scrambling to find some humor in this latest twist, but his sleepy gaze turned serious. "I am trustworthy. Tell your sister I'm going to get your phone, and your money, back and get you home safely."

"Money?" Melody said. "What money?"

Ah, shit.

Delaney tore her gaze from his. "It's nothing. Just a little cash I had with my phone. It's all good."

If she told Melody that forty thousand dollars had been stolen along with her wallet and laptop, there was no way her sister could keep that quiet. She'd tell her parents, and then her parents would call the police, and then Donna would get arrested, and then Delaney would be all over the news again in yet another ridiculous scandal, and Grant would be dragged in right along with her. No police, no media. No way. "It's all under control," she lied to her sister. "Go back to sleep. I'll call you later."

She disconnected the call before her sister could ask anything else, and set the phone on the nightstand. She slid back down so

she was lying on her back next to Grant. Her heart thumped errati-
cally. Pure stress. Probably. She pulled in a deep breath through her
nose and blew it out slowly. That did nothing to calm her mind.
It only made her feel light-headed.

Grant was on his side, facing her, with his arm drawn up
under his head, and since his shirt was wrapped around her pillow,
protecting her from all manner of boogie-woogie ickiness, he was
bare chested. That wasn't helping to calm her state of mind either.

"My sister doesn't have a signal for my phone anymore. We
are flying blind."

He reached over and rested his hand on her belly. The move
wasn't so much sensual as it was comfortable and comforting. Her
heart took an extra whump and began to slow. She covered his
hand with her own but stared up at the dingy ceiling.

"So, we'll do like you said," Grant said quietly. "We'll head to
Memphis. We can go to my aunt's house, and if they're not there,
we wait. She's got pets and a job. It's not as if she can disappear
the same way my mom can. And she's not batshit crazy like my
mom either, so I have to believe as soon as she hears the message
I left at her house, she'll call us. I'd bet your forty grand that Tina
doesn't even know my mom has that bag."

Delaney turned her head toward him. "What if they've separated? What if your aunt comes home but your mom has gone
off someplace else?"

His lips pressed into a line and his eyes clouded. "If that hap-
pens, Lane, then we call the police. Yes, she's my mother, and God
knows I don't want to do that, but she broke the law and stole
your money. You don't deserve this. This isn't about some twenty-
dollar watch from a jewelry store. This is serious cash we're talking
about. Money you've worked for and saved. Right?"

The question was tossed out as an afterthought. A reminder that he wasn't wholly convinced she hadn't just stolen it herself. She could hardly blame him for doubting her. No sane, logical person would be in this predicament. Still, she couldn't keep a little edge from her voice.

"Yes, Grant. It's my money that I worked for and saved. I got my first job when I was fifteen and I always put part of every paycheck into the bank. My grandmother taught me to do that. God knows, I didn't learn it from either of my parents."

He looked convinced, finally, and began tracing a design over her abdomen with his index finger. "So, what was your first job?"

"Piano tutor." The answer slipped out before she'd had a chance to think it through. That finger on her stomach was like a magic wand dissolving her ability to lie, and although he was touching her stomach, she felt it farther south.

"A piano tutor? Really?"

She nodded. "Yes. There was this little place by my house, kind of a pay-as-you-can sort of music studio, so most of the people who went there didn't have very much money. I only made a few bucks a lesson but it was probably my most favorite job. The little kids were adorable and sweet, and so excited about using real instruments. The place was noisy and hot but I loved it."

She hadn't thought about that studio in a long time. It was founded by a handful of musicians and her father had talked her into taking the job. Then he'd come in every Wednesday just to volunteer his time. It wasn't much of a secret he'd hoped one of his girls would catch the fever and follow in his footsteps, but only Melody had any real talent. Delaney was a marginally decent singer, but she'd never felt the drive, the hunger to go professional. Maybe because she'd seen what it did to him when the bright lights faded and the fans went home. Still, she was pretty good on piano, and loved to play. She mentally added that to the growing list of things she missed about home. Her piano.

"You must be pretty good if you can teach other people," Grant said, still tracing, still sending ripples.

"I'm OK. I started playing when I was about three, so I've had lots of practice."

"What was your next job?" That index finger trailed downward, circling her belly button through the cotton of Humphrey's T-shirt. Shivers danced along her nerve endings, down to her toes and back up again.

"My next job? I don't even remember. I think I worked at The Gap." Back to the lies. Her job after the music studio had been at a swanky boutique in Beverly Hills. She'd worked there while she dabbled with college. It wasn't a bad job, just sort of mindless. She went from dressing emotionless mannequins to dressing overly emotional starlets. Conversations with the mannequins were more riveting. "What was your first job?" she asked.

His hand stilled, his palm flattened on her stomach. "Um, I mostly worked with my dad. He had a charter fishing boat based out of Bell Harbor Marina."

He wasn't looking into her eyes now, but staring at her shoulder instead. There was more. She could see it.

"And?" she prompted softly.

"And he died in Iraq. So no more charter company."

"Oh, that's sad. I'm sorry." Her parents were a pain in the ass, but she loved them and couldn't imagine life without them.

His head gave a single shake, shooing away a memory. It was subtle, but she noticed. Or maybe she was learning to read him. His eyes came back to her.

"My brother and I used to talk about starting the company back up," Grant continued, "but things went crazy pretty fast after my mom married Hank. Ty says the boat is still sitting in her barn, though. He told me he'd nearly sold it to pay off some debts last fall but Evie talked him out of it."

"He still has it?"

"Apparently, although he's got a job and a wife, and they're about to adopt some kids so I'm not sure when he thinks he's going to fish."

"You're out of a job. Maybe you could do it now, although I really like the idea you have for a TV show."

Grant shook his head, finally smiling again, showing off his subtle dimples. "I'm not cut out to be a fisherman. I like my feet on dry land, or at least dangling over dry land." The finger tracing began again. "And I also like that you like my idea for a TV show." Mildly melancholy faded away, turning to sweet and sexy. "Maybe you could be the host of my show? That would be fun, right? Any interest in being on TV?"

Delaney's laughter came forth so fast and loud she had to clap a hand over her mouth. The S.S. *Irony* had just set sail. "No," she said, shaking her head. "I have no interest in being on TV."

━━━◆━━━

"What'cha making there, honeybun?" Reggie asked, sitting down next to her on the green sofa. They'd been on the road for a while, but another arctic blast had paralyzed the entire east side of the country, making travel slow and treacherous. They were still hours away from Memphis and Delaney was about ready to get out and push this bus just to make it go faster.

She paused at Reggie's question and held up a wad of soft blue yarn. "A baby hat."

His expression registered surprise, followed by tenderness as he glanced at her stomach, then back at her face. "Aww. Congratulations, darlin'."

Grant looked up quickly from the magazine he was reading, eyes rounding like a startled cartoon character. Finch and Humphrey stared at her too. This must have been how Snow White felt when the seven dwarves came home from the mines—assuming Snow White had just announced her unexpected pregnancy.

Delaney let out a short burst of laughter. "Not a baby hat for me. I'm not . . . well, I'm just . . . not. These hats are to donate to charity, although I'm not very good at knitting. I'm not sure any charity will want them."

"If they take used bras and undies, I think they'll take your hats."

"Let me see that," Humphrey said, moving to sit down on the other side of her. "You're doing that wrong. Wrap the yarn around this way."

She let him take the needles from her hand. "You're a knitter?"

His smile was confident. "My grandma taught me. I can crochet and sew too."

"Humphrey is going to make someone a wonderful wife one day," Finch said.

"Hey!" Reggie reached over and cuffed his brother on the kneecap. "That is pure chauvinism talking. If he wants to explore his feminine side, we should encourage that."

"Yeah?"

"Hells, yeah. Somebody on this bus should learn to cook." The brothers snickered but Humphrey seemed unfazed.

"I didn't realize those were baby hats you were making," Grant said. "What made you decide to make baby hats?"

Delaney shrugged. "I don't know. It just seemed like something I could do to make the world a sweeter place."

His gaze held hers, and she didn't know why he was looking at her that way, as if he was working through something in his mind. Almost smiling, but mostly not. It sparked a fire down low, and she wondered how much longer she'd be able to resist him. Had they been in any other setting last night, things would have gotten much hotter, so maybe getting snowed in with this bus full of chaperones was for the best.

"What?" she finally said. "They're just baby hats."

"Here, like this," Humphrey said, directing her attention back to the needles. She let him show her, but all the while she could feel Grant's eyes on her.

"That doesn't look that hard," said Reggie, leaning in over her arm.

"It's not hard," Humphrey said. "You just have to have some patience, and be skillful with your fingers."

"I got loads of patience, yeah? And everyone knows I am skillful with my fingers. You got any extra needles?"

Delaney chuckled. "Um, sorry, no. I have lots of yarn but only these needles."

"I can fix that." Humphrey grinned. He stood and went to one of the bags lying on a spare bunk and rifled around in it for a minute. "How about these?" He stepped toward them again, whipping out drumsticks from behind his back.

Snickering circled the bus. "Nice going, MacGyver," Reggie said, then he tilted his chin at Finch. "Grab another pair of those. I challenge you, bro."

"To what?" Finch arched a ginger brow.

"A knitting contest, yeah? This blizzard ain't going anywhere and we got hours to kill before we get to the hotel. I challenge you. Honeybun here gets to be the final judge, and she'll decide which one of us makes the best fucking baby hat north of Tennessee. You man enough to take me on?"

"You want me to knit. On drumsticks. Baby hats."

"I'm in," Humphrey said, going back and grabbing four more sticks. "How about you, Mr. Cameraman. You want to knit?"

Grant shook his head. "I'm more of an observer. Maybe I could just film the rest of you with my phone."

A tremor went through Delaney at the suggestion. No filming. Not her. She pulled her bangs down.

"Shit, yeah. Film us," Reggie said, bouncing a little on his seat. "A roadie documentary. We can post it to the band's Facebook page. Like, *look at us doing good*. Think the chicks will dig that? Think these baby hats will score us some honeys?"

"The chicks will totally dig it," Humphrey said.

"I'm in," declared Finch.

And thus began the Paradise Brothers Best Fucking Baby Hat Competition.

Chapter 15

GOD ALMIGHTY, GRANT WAS GLAD to be climbing off of that Paradise Brothers tour bus. He was grateful for their hospitality, but the only thing more boring than knitting was filming someone knitting. And one more hour of listening to Reggie's inane stories, followed by another night of lying next to Elaine without closing the deal, was going to give him a stroke—and not the kind of stroke he was looking for. It was close to eight o'clock in the evening when they pulled into Memphis, but at last, they'd arrived.

The lobby of the Heartbreak Hotel was like a 1960s movie set on psychedelic drugs. The walls were a purply blue. Red velvet curtains trimmed with gold fringe hung from fifteen-foot windows, and asymmetrical sofas of gold and silver filled up the area along with zebra-fur chairs. And perhaps not surprisingly, the lobby was chock-full of Elvis. Impersonators, that is, maybe thirty in all, wandering around, chatting in groups, or talking on cell phones. There was something inherently odd about seeing Elvis on a cell phone, but Grant's brain was too tired to process the incongruity. All he wanted right now was a room with a view—a view of Elaine on the bed. He was making assumptions, of course. She might not share a room with him, but last night's bout of restless dick syndrome made him hope against hope she'd be amenable to the idea.

Reggie walked in through the double lobby doors with a big duffel bag over his shoulder and did a slow 360 turn, pointing with his index finger. His lips moved as he counted. Then he looked back at Finch.

"Am I stoned right now? Did we get high on the bus and I just don't remember, or does everybody else see a room full of Elvises?"

"I don't see any," said Humphrey.

"Me neither," said Finch.

But Sammy pointed to the poster near the door. "That might have something to do with it."

A bright red-and-pink sign with rhinestone letters sat on an easel by the front door.

This week in the Jungle Room Lounge—
Happy Birthday, Elvis Celebration!

"May I help you?" called out a woman from behind the tall purple counter. She was petite, with a tubular bun on the top of her head that looked like a stem. Not a good look.

Finch stepped around Reggie. "Yes, thanks. We're the Paradise Brothers, here to check in."

"Welcome to the Heartbreak Hotel. We're glad you made it. My apologies for the weather. We've never had it so cold here in Memphis. By the way, the other two guests in your party have already checked in."

"Other two guests?" Elaine asked, glancing at Humphrey.

"Our manager and his wife," he answered. "Sissy won't travel on the bus with us no more, not ever since Reggie proved you really can light ass gas on fire."

Grant chuckled at Elaine's expression, which was much like the one she'd had when staring at the DNA-encrusted boogie-woogie bed.

"I'm not sure what my manager has reserved," Finch said to

the desk clerk, "but do you happen to have another room available? We picked up a few strays on the road."

Grant stepped up to the counter as the desk clerk shook her head.

"Mm, I'm sorry. I don't think so. It's Elvis's birthday weekend and we've been sold out for months, but we may have some cancellations due to the weather. Let me check." Her fingers flew over the keyboard, clickity-clack. "No, I'm sorry. There's nothing right now."

"Well, in that case, how many people can our rooms handle?"

Her fingers clacked some more.

"It looks like you have a couple of our themed rooms. Let me see. The Graceland Suite has a king bed in a private bedroom and there's two sofas. The Burning Love Suite has a private king room, a sofa, and a chaise lounge. I'm afraid we're out of roll-away beds, though. Several of our departing guests have added on another night's stay because of the storm."

Finch frowned and looked at Grant.

"Don't worry about it," Grant said. "We'll figure something out." Although he didn't know what.

"No, no, we're good," Finch said. "I'm not sure why Clark got us two suites, but you and Elaine take the Burning Love room and the rest of us will crash in the Graceland. A little whiskey down the hatch and that floor will feel like a feather bed."

"I'm afraid I can't let you do that, sir," interrupted the desk clerk. "Fire safety regulations stipulate we can only allow a certain number of guests in each room. You'll have to divide up four and four if you want to add guests to your party." She glanced at Grant. "I'm sorry, sir."

"No worries," Finch assured her. He turned to Grant. "Sorry, bro. Looks like you're stuck with me and Reg tonight, but you can have the bedroom and we'll take the sofas. Humphrey and Sam can bunk with Clark and Sissy in the other suite."

This wasn't the night Grant had planned, but then again, nothing had gone as he'd planned since the first moment Elaine had shown up in his bathroom back in Bell Harbor. "I guess that'll have to work, but let me pay for the room."

"Don't sweat it. It's a business expense. A tax write-off."

"I just don't feel right about that, Finch. You guys have been so generous already. Let me pay for something."

"I know how you can pay us back, Cameraman," Reggie said enthusiastically from over Grant's shoulder. "How about you let me sleep with your woman in the big king bed?"

Elaine chuckled, but it was all Grant could do not to pop him in the jaw. This guy was getting on his last fucking nerve. It must've showed in his glare, because Reggie chortled and held his hands up in self-defense. "No? OK, then. Just a suggestion."

Grant turned back to Finch. "Look, my aunt doesn't live too far from here, and if I can get ahold of her, we can probably stay there tomorrow, but it's too late to go over there tonight."

"Honestly, no worries, man. As long as I can get a hot shower and a cold brewski, I'm good to go."

They finished checking in, grabbed some luggage and guitars from the bus, and walked to the elevator. A vintage poster commemorating Elvis's comeback tour hung on the wall. It was a red-and-blue image of the King with a banner across the top. *Elvis '69.*

Reggie pressed his cheek against it and pointed. "You see that, gents? Sixty-nine? I'm going to love it here."

———◆———

Five minutes later Delaney stood with Finch, Reggie, and Grant outside their room. The door was painted a rich, deep red, and two overfed cherubs floated above a gold banner. Fancy gold letters declared this to be *The Burning Love Suite*. It even had little hearts dotting some of the letters.

"Burning Love, yeah?" Reggie murmured, elbowing his brother. "Sounds like an STD to me. Let's see what's behind door number one."

Delaney couldn't help but marvel at the decor as she stepped inside. It matched the tacky charm of the door, with bold, rich colors and shiny gold accents. Grant flipped a switch and a crystal chandelier dangling over a glass-topped dining table scattered glimmers of light around the room. A purple velvet chaise and a red, heart-shaped velvet stool filled one corner. On the other side of that was a dining area, painted white with gold trim, and a pink-and-gold seating area came next, complete with a sky mural painted on the ceiling.

The men walked in and looked around, heads tilting this way and that as they soaked it all in.

"Wow. Very understated," said Reggie, nodding. "Even the cabinet handles are fat angels."

"Those are cherubs, you ignoramus," Finch said.

"What are cherubs?"

"Fat angels."

Delaney stepped forward through a short hallway into what was a fairly tame-looking bedroom, considering the rest of the decor. Emerald-green velvet curtains and gold satin bedding. She'd be sleeping there next to Grant. With Reggie and Finch right outside the door. She couldn't decide how she felt about that, or about any of this.

All day she'd waited to hear something from Grant's aunt, or his mother. She'd checked in with Melody once more but the phone finder app still showed hers as offline, and Melody asked so many questions, she didn't dare call her again. Carl didn't have any news either. But he did suggest a sloe gin fizz might be tasty.

Grant walked in behind her. "You OK?"

She nodded. "I'm OK. You?"

He let out a big sigh and scratched a chin in desperate need of a shave. "I'm good, but if that Reggie doesn't stop coming on to you, I'm going to punch his lights out and he'll have to try singing with his jaw wired shut."

Grant didn't have any jurisdiction over her. It wasn't his right to make such a jealous declaration, and yet it warmed her through. They were on this adventure together, a team whether they'd intended it to be that way or not. Delaney smiled and stepped nearer, wrapping her arms around his waist. She rested her head against his chest and he pulled her in tight.

"Reggie's not my type."

"Good. What's your type?"

"I don't know. Whatever you are. Maybe that's my type." It was a foolish thing to say. Far too sentimental. She should be stepping back instead of encouraging him. She had enough things to worry about without adding this man to the picture. But he was already in the picture. In fact, he was the only constant she'd had in days. At the moment, he was all she had.

And at this moment, he was enough. She lifted her face up to his and he kissed her lightly.

"Pay no attention to me, kids," Finch said, coming through the door and stepping around them. "There's just one slight problem with this room."

Delaney looked over at him as he walked around to a doorway on the other side of the bed. "Problem?" she asked.

He opened that door and peeked inside. "Yup. Little problem. This here is the only shower in the joint. Looks like Reg and I will have to tiptoe past you lovebirds. No worries, though. We've seen a little bit of everything on that bus so nothing you two do could shock us."

Reggie strolled in next. "We could shower in pairs to speed things up. Elaine, you're with me."

She felt Grant start to move in Reggie's direction but she squeezed him around the middle and he stayed put.

Finch pulled a phone from his pocket. "Hey, Sam just texted me. He says he and Humphrey are heading to the Jungle Room Lounge with Sissy and Clark to get some dinner. They want us to meet them. You guys in?" He glanced at Delaney and Grant. "Sissy is about your size, Elaine. She might have some clothes you could borrow."

The thought of food and fresh clothes was probably the only thing more appealing than a shower right about now. She and Grant were back in their own original clothes, but she had nothing to sleep in and nothing clean to put on after bathing. Still, food was the first order of business. She looked up at Grant. "Hungry?" she asked.

She could see what he was thinking. He wanted her alone in that room more than he wanted food, but she wasn't ready for that. As much as she was drawn to him, as much as the idea of a long, hot shower followed by long, hot sex with Grant appealed to her, she had to focus on basic survival first. She needed food and clothes. She needed her phone, her wallet, and her money. And she needed to tell him who she was. She needed to tell him about the sex tape. Then, if he even still wanted her, she could give in to the temptation of Grant.

"I'm hungry," she added, before he'd had a chance to come up with a reason to say no. "Will you buy me dinner? I seem to have lost my wallet."

Chapter 16

THE JUNGLE ROOM LOUNGE WAS really just a hotel dining room with a ten-foot bar off to one side and a fifteen-foot-square dance floor in the center. There was a stage of sorts, a raised platform, maybe two feet off the ground, covered with royal-blue carpet. A piano sat to one side, and of course, there were the ubiquitous Elvis spottings. They were everywhere, bellied up to the salad bar, eating chicken wings, or posing for pictures with other hotel guests. Strains of "Blue Hawaii" could be heard over lulls in the conversations.

"So, I got a speck of bad news and I got two heaps of good news, fellas," said the Paradise Brothers' band manager when they were all seated around a table with drinks in their hands. Clark was a barrel-chested cowboy from the pointed toes of his black snake-skin boots to the top of the brown ten-gallon hat perched on the back of his head. Sissy, his wife, was a giggly little thing with long cleavage and a short attention span. Her enormous white-blonde hair was sprayed so stiff it looked like a plaster cast, but Delaney liked her instantly. It was impossible not to with all her *oh-sugar-this* and *God-bless-that*. Something about her Southern accent made everything she said sound entirely gracious. Even when she said, "My ex-sister-in-law is a gap-toothed, hump-backed, mercenary whore, God bless her little heart."

"How about the bad news first," Finch said to his manager, twin frown lines meeting up between his eyebrows.

Clark adjusted that enormous hat. There must be a lot of head room in whatever car he and his wife drove. "Well, it seems the Blues City Café where I had you boys booked just had a frozen water pipe burst. Place is shut down while they make repairs."

Disappointment spread around the table.

"Oh, but don't you boys worry, ya hear?" Sissy chimed in, waggling her red-lacquered fingernails at the group. "Sugar bear here has everything all worked out. You tell 'em, honey. Go on."

"I do. I do indeed. That's where the good news comes in. Seems that the band hired by this here hotel has been waylaid up north by the same storm that's freezing pipes down here. I tell you, this weather is about as welcome as a two-dollar whore in church. Anyway, I figured, them being in need of a band, and y'all being in need of a venue, whah-lah! Goes together like country music and a pickup truck."

"You want us to play here?" Humphrey asked.

"Right here in this very room." Clark nodded and took a big chug of beer.

Finch looked around, squinting, and Delaney understood his concern. The acoustics would be lousy in a room like this, and they'd have to play unplugged or all that framed Elvis artwork would rattle right off the walls.

Clark tipped his hat back a little farther with the lip of his bottle. "It's better than nothing at all. Just a couple of nights, anyway. Plus they pay almost as much as the other place, and they're gonna comp us the rooms, and all our food's included. So eat up, boys. You got a show to do tomorrow."

Finch looked around at his brother and bandmates.

"We don't have to dress like Elvis, do we?" Humphrey asked.

"Do they cover booze?" Reggie asked at the same time.

Clark shook his head. "No to dressing like the King, and no to the booze. If you want free drinks you'll have to flirt with the waitresses. Knowing you horny devils, you'd have done that anyway. So, we all good here?"

The Paradise Brothers exchanged another round of glances before Finch finally nodded. "We're in. Let's eat."

They ordered ribs, catfish, cornbread, and several more drinks, and passed the time swapping stories with Delaney managing to avoid giving anything but the vaguest of answers. Sissy here was exactly the type to watch a show like *Pop Rocks*. One word about making soap or even the names of her sisters and this woman could be on to her.

"So where did you say y'all are from?" Sissy asked, licking barbecue sauce off her thumb as she ate a french fry.

"Grant and I have a house up in Michigan," Delaney answered. That was true. They did. Sort of.

"Really? 'Cause you look sort of familiar to me. You ever done any modeling?"

Delaney's dismissive chuckle ended in a hiccup. "Me? Oh, gosh no. I was a bank teller." Shit. Maybe she should have said travel agent? She glanced at Grant from the corner of her eye, but fortunately he seemed to be engrossed in something Humphrey was telling him. Just to be safe, she added, "Um, a bank teller in college, I mean."

Sissy's penciled-on eyebrows rose. "A bank teller? With a body like yours? What a waste."

"Hey, speaking of bodies," Finch interrupted, "Elaine here could use some clothes. Did you bring anything extra she might borrow? Not that Humphrey doesn't enjoy having her in his pants."

Clark chortled loudly and tapped his hand against the table. "Anything extra? What do you think, Fincher? My little missus here brought enough clothes to change her outfits six times a day."

Sissy tilted her shellacked head from side to side and smiled like Miss America. "Y'all didn't marry me because I was so smart, Clark Doolittle. You married me because of how I fill out a sweater, so don't you go giving me grief now about wanting to look pretty for you."

He leaned over and kissed her cheek with a big, juicy smack. "Damn straight, doll. First time I set my eyes on this lady I knew she was the one for me. Pretty as the day is long. And I knew she was smart too, on account of when I asked for a dance, she said yes."

All the band members smiled blandly and nodded at the insipid cuteness of a story they'd obviously heard before. Meanwhile, Delaney felt Grant's hand slide down her thigh. The touch was light on her leg, but deliberate enough to set off firecrackers in the sensitive spot right between them. She bit her lip and moved a little in her chair to ease that unexpected tremor. A sharp inhale of breath came from his direction, then that naughty dog dared to move his fingertips closer to the source, moving his hand back up. Delaney let out a gasp of shocked laughter.

Everyone looked at her and she felt the heat blossom on her cheeks. "That's . . . why, that's just such a romantic story."

Sissy squinted her eyes and took a sip of her champagne cocktail. "How did you two meet?"

How did we meet? Delaney looked at Grant. Her mouth wouldn't quite work just then, which was probably a good thing, because her brain had shut off the minute his hand hit her lap. A slow, lazy smile tilted up the corners of his lips as he stared at her instead of Sissy.

"Oh, I'd say our first meeting was similar to that," Grant said. "Elaine walked in the room and took me completely by surprise. In fact, she took one good look at me, I looked back at her, and damn, she nearly blew me away."

Blew him away? Oh, that's right. With a blow-dryer. Clever bastard. His smile heated up, and she felt it from her toes to her scalp and every delicious detour in between. Damn it. How was she supposed to *not* have sex with him when he looked at her like that?

"Is that how you remember it, Lane?" he asked.

"Pretty much," she said softly.

No one said a word for the space of a heartbeat, and Delaney didn't even realize she and Grant were gazing at each other like moony-eyed teens until Reggie raised his arm and called out, "Check please!"

"Well, ain't that cute," Sissy said, wiping her hands on a napkin. "Let's you and I head on up to my room now, Elaine, and I'll see if I have any outfits that fit you. We could stop in the gift shop too, for a few things. You boys stay here and finish your drinks and let us have some girl time."

A ringtone sounded as Sissy stood up, and everyone shifted around, going for their phones.

"I think that's mine," Grant said, pulling his hand from Delaney's lap and taking the phone from his pocket. He glanced at the screen, then handed it to her, his gaze intense.

"It's your sister."

———————————◆———————————

"Where the hell are you?" Melody said as soon as Delaney answered. "Are you in Memphis yet?"

Delaney had jumped up from the table as fast as she could and practically sprinted into the hallway outside the lounge. "We just got here about an hour ago. Sorry, I didn't have a chance to call you yet."

"Well, don't scare me like that! God! I had no idea where you were, and then the police called. Lane, it's all over the entertainment news."

"What? What is?" Dizzy time struck, and she tipped against the wall for support, then realized she was pressed against Elvis '69 and had to move. She sat down on an oversized planter instead.

"The police found some old abandoned car on the side of the road that was supposedly registered to you, but of course we told them it couldn't possibly be yours because you wouldn't be caught dead in a piece of shit Volkswagen. Then a while later, I started to freak out a little bit, thinking maybe this Grant guy *had* killed you and maybe you *were* caught dead in a piece of shit Volkswagen! I couldn't help it, Lane. I had to tell Mom and Dad. I know you didn't want me to, but honest to God, if you don't tell me what the fuck is going on I'm going to find you just so I can kill you myself."

Grant came around the corner and touched her shoulder. "Everything all right?"

Delaney nodded and tried to smile as if everything was hunky-dory, although what she really needed to do was put her head between her knees and hyperventilate. She held up a hand. "Just a little . . . family drama. I'll be back in a sec." Hiccup.

She stood up and wobbled farther down the hall, past a super-fat Elvis, a super-hairy Elvis, and an Asian Elvis in six-inch platform shoes.

"OK, explain this to me again," Delaney said to her sister. "What exactly is being reported on the news?" Hiccup.

"They're saying that you're missing, and that your family has no idea where you are. You need to come home now, Lane. The longer this goes on, the bigger the story gets. Mom and Dad want to know if you're OK. They've already called our lawyer, and they hired a publicist."

Delaney nearly laughed at that. Or she would have if she could breathe. They'd tried to hire a spin doctor as soon as Boyd's video surfaced but Delaney had thought she could work this out on her own. She'd thought a little break from the spotlight would be all it took for this story to go away. Obviously that wasn't the case. And now that the police and lawyers were involved? Fuck.

"Which lawyer did they call?" she asked, pressing a thumb to her lip.

"Tony, I think."

"All right. First, tell Mom and Dad I'm fine, because I am. Then tell Tony to call the police and tell *them* I'm fine. He can play the lawyer confidentiality card or whatever, but I want to make sure the police understand I'm not missing. I'm hiding, but that's not a crime. And as far as the publicist goes? God, I don't know. Maybe she should make a statement that the car belonged to a different Delaney Masterson or something. There must be more than one of us around."

"You are freaking me out right now."

"I'm not trying to, but you guys are all overreacting. The truth is I can't do anything about this right now. If I call the police, they're going to want to ask me a bunch of questions, and I'm not in a position to talk to them at the moment. If I do, Grant and his family will get dragged into this too, and there will be no way to keep the whole mess from the paparazzi. They'll end up in the news right alongside me, and I will look like an even bigger fool than I did with just the *sex tape*."

She'd meant to lower her voice when she said *sex tape* but apparently she'd only made it slightly more strident.

Asian Elvis lowered his gold sunglasses and stared at her above the rim. Note to self: never say *sex tape* in a crowded hotel lobby.

"Why can't you just get on a frickin' airplane and come home?"

"Because I don't have any money! Or my wallet, or my ID, Melody. All that stuff got stolen with my phone, so I couldn't book a flight and get on a plane even if I wanted to."

"Everything got stolen?" Alarm bells were sounding but Delaney was determined to curtail the drama.

"Yes. I'm sorry I didn't tell you that sooner, but I didn't want you to worry." That was partly true, but the other part was she knew Melody couldn't keep a secret, and the last thing Delaney wanted was for this to become another episode of *Pop Rocks*. "Please help me out here, Mel, and tell everyone I'm totally fine."

Melody scoffed into the phone. "I think *fine* is a pretty strong word. I am legitimately concerned about you."

"Don't be. I'm actually . . . I'm kind of having fun."

"Fun?"

Delaney hadn't realized it until just then but . . . yes. This was fun. It was fun because Grant was here, and everyone was being nice, and no one expected anything from her. She wasn't performing in front of a camera for a nameless, faceless audience. She wasn't trying to cater to her family's needs. She wasn't trying to impress her Beverly Hills clients. She was just . . . being herself. And she liked it.

"Yes. I'm having fun."

"God damn it, Delaney. It's time to come home. This shit is getting serious."

Deep down, she knew it was. Her problems weren't going to disappear just because she had. They were multiplying. She was Dorothy with the flying monkeys circling her head, but no simple heel-clicking would fix all this. She had to fix it herself. She took a great big breath.

"I know I do. And I will, soon. I should have my wallet back in a couple of days, and as soon as I do, I'll come home, talk to the police, I'll do whatever the damn publicist wants me to. OK? I just need a couple more days."

"You have no money at all? And no ID? How are you managing?"

"I'm managing just fine."

"There is that word again. I'm not sure you know what the word even means. Just put yourself in my shoes, Lane. I don't know exactly where you are, and you've obviously put your trust in some total stranger. I don't even know his last name. All I know is his cell phone number."

Delaney had put her trust in him. It had been easy. Trusting men hadn't typically worked out in her favor, but Grant wasn't like most men. She didn't really know how she knew that, but she just did. Down deep in her heart, where it mattered the most.

"His name is Grant Connelly and we're at the Heartbreak Hotel."

"The Heartbreak Hotel?"

"Yes. In the Burning Love Suite."

"The Burning Love Suite?" Melody's voice went from surprised to dubious.

"Yes."

"With some guy named Grant Connelly." Now she sounded downright suspicious, and maybe she had a right to all of that. The situation *was* a little unusual.

"Yes. I'm in the Burning Love Suite of the Heartbreak Hotel with a man named Grant Connelly, and I'm asking you to trust me because it's not quite like it sounds." No, it wasn't quite like it sounded, because she hadn't mentioned the bus full of musicians or the steady stream of Elvis impersonators trying to eavesdrop on her conversation, but given that her sister was poised to commit her to a psychiatric facility, Delaney decided to keep those details to herself. Instead, she simply added, "And I'm having fun."

Chapter 17

REGGIE STRUTTED FROM THE BATHROOM of the Burning Love Suite with a white hotel towel barely wrapped around his hips and his clothes tucked into the crook of his elbow. Arrogant jackass. It was close to midnight and he was the last one to shower. Took his sweet time about it too, just to make Grant wait for some alone time with Elaine.

She was sitting on the gold satin coverlet of the bed wearing new pink pajama pants and an *I love Elvis* T-shirt that Grant had bought for her in the hotel gift shop. He'd gotten a shirt for himself too, the same one as hers because there wasn't much selection. He needed to get to a real store soon, though, because while she might look adorable, he looked like a tool. Real men don't wear *I love Elvis* T-shirts.

Reggie chuckled when he saw it and patted Grant's shoulder as he walked by to go into the other half of the suite.

"Nice shirt, Cameraman," he murmured.

"Nice towel, dickhead," Grant murmured back.

Reggie didn't miss a beat. He just smiled bigger and spoke louder. "All righty then. Good night, Mary Ellen. Good night, John-Boy."

The bedroom door had nearly shut when Reggie turned around and stuck his face back inside. "FYI, you crazy kids, Fincher and I sleep like the dead. Nothing that goes on in here will wake us up. Unless you invite me back in to pinch hit. Then I'll totally wake up."

Grant stepped forward and pushed on the door so hard he nearly caught Reggie's head. "Seriously, get the fuck out."

He could hear Reggie chuckling on the other side but that was all good, because he was out there, and Grant was in here—with Elaine. He turned the lock on the door, the click loud and decisive, and Reggie laughed again, but the sound faded as he walked away. Grant turned to see Elaine pull her legs up in front of her and wrap her arms around her knees as she leaned her back against the velvet headboard.

He rubbed his hands together and lightened his tone. "That guy's annoying."

She just smiled and tucked a curling lock of damp brown hair behind her ear. All of a sudden he was nervous, which made no sense at all. They'd been together nonstop for days, and now he was nervous? Now, when it was time to be suave and seductive? It was the shirt. It was making him impotent. Elvis was only sexy on Elvis.

"I feel like a doofus in this shirt," he blurted out. "This is the kind of shirt Carl would wear."

She burst out laughing and his impotence faded. What a delicious sound, that laugh. It was one of those loud, unladylike bursts that told him he'd hit his mark.

She patted the spot next to her, telling him he just might hit another mark if he played his cards right. Not that this was a game to him. Elaine wasn't a sporting sort of girl. He'd figured that out within the first five minutes of meeting her. Any woman who covered her eyes at the sight of a penis, and in fact could not even *say* the word *penis* without blushing, was not the type looking for a meaningless fling, even if you were spending the night in the Burning Love Suite.

He sat down next to her but turned so he was facing her and the headboard. The lighting in here was dim, making her long-lashed blue eyes dark. "So, how did the conversation go with your sister?" he asked. "You seemed kind of off after that. Or was it something with Sissy?" Elaine had spent time with the band manager's flighty-headed wife after taking that phone call, and had been quiet ever since.

Still, a smile played across her lips, a hint of her humor remaining. "Sissy was fine. Nosy, but fine. She gave me a few things to wear. They're not quite my style but it was still very sweet of her. And at home, things are . . . well, there's some drama."

"Drama at the soap factory? Like a soap . . . opera?"

She laughed again and it made him feel victorious, but her smile faded too quickly.

"I may have to go home soon. Sooner than I had planned."

Gut punch. Bad feeling. "Why?"

"Well, for starters, we forgot to tell anyone about the car, so when the police found it, they called my family and my family thought something awful had happened."

Shit. That was basic survival skills 101. Leave a note when someone is looking for you. "I'm sorry. I meant to call the police but I forgot," he said.

"It's not your fault. I should have told my sister about the accident but I was trying to manage this on my own. Now they're all worried I'm somehow at risk, which is exactly what I was trying to avoid."

"You're not at risk. I'll take care of you." The words were out there before his brain had even wrapped around them, and he didn't know where they'd come from. Where any of this was coming from—this urgent need to stake a claim—this drive to protect her. Maybe it was guilt over his mother's involvement. Maybe it was simple red-blooded lust. But whatever it was, all he knew for certain was that he felt it, and he wanted to follow it.

Her smile was sweet but unconvincing. "Thanks, but I have some stuff back home I have to handle in person. I can't do it from here, and I can't do it from Bell Harbor either."

This was entirely unacceptable. They were just getting started. She couldn't go back home already. He wanted more time. He hadn't had enough of her yet. He wanted all of her.

Her damp hair had created wet marks on the shoulders of her shirt. He picked up a tendril and twined it around one finger, staring at it, because looking into her eyes was just too dangerous. He'd scaled mountains and traversed ravines, but nothing had ever made his heart jackhammer inside his chest like this. "I don't want you to go back to Miami already."

"You don't? You could have your house all to yourself." Her voice was whisper soft.

"I don't want my house all to myself. I like you in it. I like watching the yoga."

"You could get cable. They have lots of yoga shows on cable."

He moved a little closer, and she stretched her legs out in front of her. "It wouldn't be quite the same as watching it live," he said.

She moved to readjust the pillow behind her and the tendril fell from his fingertips. She leaned back, resting one hand on his leg. It wasn't the same maneuver he'd tried at dinner but he was glad she was touching him. Really glad. He wanted her to touch him all over. The thought sent blood rushing to his groin, and in another ten seconds his dick would be tapping at her hand. That might be awkward. Or awesome.

"I think these walls are pretty solid," he said, looking around. "Pretty . . . soundproof. We could probably make a lot of noise in here without being heard."

He looked back at her and was only partially teasing.

No, actually, he wasn't teasing at all.

That door was locked, the walls were real, and this bed was as inviting as the sweet scent emanating from Elaine's warm skin. He wanted her, badly. And he wanted her bad. In ways too wicked and loud to be contained inside this room. But for tonight, he could keep things on the quieter side. If that was the only option.

The color rose in her cheeks. "You've been really good to me, Grant. And I appreciate all you've done," she said.

The rushing of the blood slowed. Those weren't the words he expected. Gratitude wasn't what he wanted from her. Gratitude came from people feeling indebted, and he wanted her to know they were on equal footing. She didn't owe him.

"You've been really good to me too, Lane. You could've called the cops on my mother, or demanded I leave my own house. And you went to a family wedding as my human shield. That takes real generosity."

The sound she made was half giggle, half sigh. "OK, I guess we're even, but maybe what I'm trying to say here is that, just because we're stuck together in this hotel room, with this incredibly comfortable bed surrounded by everything Elvis, I don't want you to *love me tender* just because you think I'm . . . convenient."

Her words made sense, in theory, but in reality, nothing could be further from the truth, and he chuckled at the irony.

"Nothing about you is convenient for me, Lane. Driving hundreds of miles through a snowstorm to track down your money sure isn't. Having you live in my house isn't convenient. Knowing my family has screwed you over six ways to Sunday isn't convenient either. But honestly, what's most inconvenient is the way I feel."

Her eyes lifted to his. "Why? How do you feel?"

His breath caught, and his gut took a big, bold leap. He slid his hands up to cup her face and ran a thumb over her lip, that full, lush bottom lip that left him weak in the knees but courageous in his pursuit.

"How do I feel? Like I need to make you mine. Soon."

———————●———————

Grant's eyes were dark on hers and held no hesitation, no doubt. Just passion. Fierce passion, with none of the teasing from the last few days, or even from the last few minutes. She'd asked, and he was giving her his answer.

He was making it easy for her—so very easy to give in—to all of this, to the moment, and the emotions, and the madness. She wanted him in the most brazen way. Even while knowing Reggie and Finch were just outside that door. Even while knowing this was more about biology than destiny. Even while knowing she should stop this and tell him the truth about who she was and why she was on the run. But she didn't because she craved his touch. His gaze had been on her all day and she'd felt it, like a whisper passing over her skin. A constant reminder that he was near.

His thumb was teasing over her lips, making her hungry for him. Her breath went shallow and her mind went blank of everything except this man and this moment. She pushed aside the past and gave no thought to the future. There was only here and now.

She moved forward, closing the last of the distance between them, and kissed him hard, with all the pent-up desire she'd held inside. Grant groaned low in his throat and wrapped his arms around her, deepening the kiss. He pushed her back into the pillow, bumping their heads against the headboard, but the contact only added to the moment. His lips were insistent, demanding, the textures of his mouth divine, and Delaney knew she was right where she wanted to be. She was—

Knock, knock, knock.

"Hey! Really sorry, kids. I need my contact lens case," Finch said, his voice as loud and as casual as if he were just interrupting them from watching cartoons.

Grant looked back at her like the Hulk trying to collect his emotions, and Delaney pressed fingers to her mouth to hide her humor. "You've got to be kidding me," he muttered under his breath.

She sat up straight on the bed as Grant stood. He opened the door without a word while Delaney avoided eye contact. Finch walked through fast and was back out in five seconds.

"Really sorry. Carry on."

Grant shut the door—pretty hard—and turned the lock—again.

He looked over at Delaney, and she bit her lip. This was her chance to change direction, to stop them from doing something she might regret. But it was too late for that. "Maybe we should turn on the television?" she said. "You know, for a little . . . noise canceling?"

He smiled, relieved. "I like the way you think." He picked up the remote from the bedside table and turned it on, flipping the channel to some old Elvis movie—since that's what was on every channel.

Delaney pushed the covers down on the bed, exposing crisp white sheets under the coverlet, and rose up on her knees. Burning Love was about to meet boogie-woogie. This probably wasn't her wisest decision but she was past the point of caring. Heat whooshed through her as Grant pulled his shirt up and over his head and came forward, kneeling on the mattress in front of her, breast to chest. Delicious.

"This is the first part of you I noticed," she said, running the backs of her knuckles up his taut stomach before trailing her hands over his shoulders. She swayed against him and pressed a light kiss on his collarbone. His skin was warm and tasted slightly sweet.

"Yeah? What was the next thing you noticed?" His voice was low and raspy as his hands clutched her hips.

She ran her lips along to the other side, kissing that collarbone too and feeling his pulse quicken under his skin.

"Mm, probably your nice personality," she teased, murmuring against the side of his neck. She felt as much as heard his elongated exhale.

"I don't have a nice personality."

"Don't you?" She was coy, like a woman about to shed her inhibitions along with her clothes. She ran her fingers up and through his hair. It was soft, the only thing about him that was, and she pulled his face a little closer, her lips hovering near his. "I think you do. Either way, I like you."

She did. She liked him a lot, and her simple declaration seemed to be all the encouragement he needed. His pulled her close, almost roughly, and kissed her soundly, catching her bottom lip in his teeth for the tiniest nip. It made her gasp, and it made her melt. Then his hands were everywhere, sliding up her back, tracing her spine and then back to her hips to pull her against him. She marveled at the sensations as their bodies swayed on the soft mattress. He kissed her throat, then leaned backward to slowly, slowly, ease the hem of her shirt up and off. She lifted her arms, letting the fabric tease her skin.

No chance for shyness or hesitation now. She was topless, and not at all sorry about it. The air in the room was cool, but his admiration was hot, his gaze paying tribute to her body as his hands followed. He cupped her breasts, running his thumbs against the peaks. She pressed into his palms, getting a squeeze and a growl from him for her efforts. Then his arms wrapped around her once more, and she was pinned breathless beneath him as they tumbled to the mattress. The smattering of hair on his chest added to the delicious friction, sending tendrils of heat outward through her limbs, turning all her muscles to liquid as he kissed her, his tongue a miraculous thing.

Everything inside her was functioning on instinct and need. His mouth lit up her senses, setting her on fire, bringing her alive. She heard the mumbled dialogue of the movie, faint in the background, but concentrated on the throaty sounds and hushed breaths exchanged between them. He grazed his teeth along her shoulder, threaded his fingers into her hair, tugging it. This wasn't tender, it was urgent.

"God," he murmured into the curve of her neck.

She nodded at his sentiment and arched upward. "I know. Me too," she whispered.

Her hands explored, feeling the smooth muscles of his back bunch up and release at her touch. She moved one leg up and around and pressed her heel into the back of his thigh.

"Lane, I hope you're in a hurry." His voice tumbled out from deep within his chest, and was laced with both humor and desperation.

"I am, but do you have any . . . party favors?" She felt as desperate as he sounded.

He lifted his head and smiled down at her.

"I do. Compliments of our hosts."

She reached around his waist and grabbed his ass, giving it a squeeze. "Then how about a little less conversation, a little more action, baby?"

He kissed her fast and hard. "You are my kind of girl, Elaine Masters." Her heart wobbled at his words, like a flat tire on sticky pavement, but she pushed the thought away. Her name was a technicality at the moment. He wanted her, *her*, not some reality TV rendition of her. Not some old sex tape version either. She'd tell him the truth tomorrow for sure.

He rolled off the bed and found his coat, unzipping one of the interior pockets. She sat up and smiled.

"That's where you put them? In your coat?"

He pulled out a foil packet, then smiled at her and took out a second one, and a third, tossing them onto the nightstand.

"I was in a hurry. We were getting off the bus. Where would you suggest I put them?"

She laughed and fell back to the bed, crossing her arms over her breasts. "I don't know. I'm just glad you brought some."

He came back to her then, eyes gleaming. "Me too. And I grabbed at least ten, so I hope you weren't planning on sleeping." He leaned over her, kissing her belly and working his way up, tantalizing her. She sighed from deep within. She needed this, this loving attention, this release, and the freedom to just *feel*. To just *be*. Everyone she'd ever been with before had come to her with expectations because of who she was, because of who her parents were, but he knew none of that. He wanted her for *her*, and she meant to make the most of it.

He lavished patient attention on her most sensitive spots until she was breathless. She wrapped her legs around his hips, drawing him closer. The fabric between them was a frustrating barrier. He must've thought so too because he rolled away slightly and tugged at the waistband of her pajama pants.

"These need to go," he said, his voice decisive.

She hesitated, knowing this was truly the point of no return. Those pajama pants were the only thing between her and being full-on naked. And once she was naked, well, then she'd be *naked*.

Grant looked up at her face, his eyes drunk with desire, but he sensed her reservation and kissed her, soft and slow. She felt it from her lips to her toes, and everywhere in between.

"Please?" he whispered, and she was lost. She would give him anything. Everything. She'd known that, deep down, since the first moment she'd seen him. All he'd ever had to do was ask nicely, and in this moment, he was asking, very, very nicely.

She covered his hand with her own and pushed at the waistband, lifting her hips to help him slide the pants over her bottom and off her legs. Then she reached for him, and his jeans quickly joined the growing pile of discarded clothes next to the bed, until it was just her and Grant tangling between the sheets. He kissed her and caressed her, teased and rewarded, murmuring sweet encouragement until all her senses coiled tight, and burst. A dizzying spiral that left her breathless and blissful. He joined her soon after, his breath ragged and welcome as he pressed his mouth against the curve of her neck.

"Beautiful, Lane," he whispered moments later. She didn't know if he meant her or the experience, but it didn't matter. She was one and the same. All good. Her surroundings began to take shape once more. The voice of Elvis singing floated into her ear from the television, some song about being all shook up. She could relate. Her body still crackled like a downed wire, with Grant the only thing grounding her. She could feel his heart thumping against her ribs. Or maybe that was her heart. They were so close it was impossible to tell where one started and the other ended.

After another moment, uneven breathing returned to normal, and Grant shifted his weight, rising up on his elbows to gaze down at her. "I've made a mistake," he said, but his smile showed no remorse.

"A mistake?"

He nodded. "I should have grabbed twice as many party favors. We're going to need them."

Chapter 18

THE SUN SHONE BRIGHTLY THROUGH the hotel window, casting pale yellow beams over the gold bedspread. Delaney's body sizzled with aftershocks from the third mind-blowing orgasm she'd had in the past eight hours spent in bed with Grant, and for the first time in her life, she was thinking about having a panic attack. She'd never had one before. Not once in her whole stupid life. Not even when she'd seen that awful video for the first time and realized it was her. But she was giving serious consideration to having one now—a panic attack—because she'd just realized she was totally, madly, deeply in love with Grant Connelly.

If anything could trigger a panic attack, that had to be it.

He didn't even know her name.

She had to tell him.

She had to tell him everything.

She had to tell him. She had to tell him. She had to tell him. *SheHadToTellHimSheHadToTellHimSheHadToTellHim.*

But she didn't want to tell him because it felt so good to be adored. Since the moment they'd first touched, he'd strummed her body like an instrument, and now every cheesy love song Elvis ever sang made sense to her. She was all shook up, she was a fool rushing in, she couldn't help falling, all of those . . . and all because Grant

Connelly was a hunka, hunka burning love. But it wasn't just the sex. It was the way his eyes changed from hazel to green depending on the light, and the way those same eyes crinkled in the corners when he laughed. It was the way he talked about wanting a more meaningful job and a better relationship with his family. It was the way he was trying to protect her and get her money back. It was the way he looked at her, *her*, as if she were gorgeous and fragile and fresh. As if she was valued for simply being herself, and she wanted to hang on to that glorious feeling for as long as she could.

Annnnnd—there was the sex, which had been pretty fucking phenomenal. Really. Truly. The sex alone could have been enough of a reason to fall in love with Grant Connelly. But just as the aftershocks of her climax faded, so did her fantasy that she could keep her identity a secret. Guilt and anxiety swooped in like fake Elvis at a polyester jumpsuit factory. Grant deserved better than this. He didn't deserve to be lied to, but oh, everything would shatter once she told him the truth. Everything would be different. Maybe he would forgive her deceit. Hopefully he could, but even so, once he knew who she was, once he knew about Boyd and the video, everything—everything—would be different.

Even so, it was time to come clean—and she would—just as soon as she was *actually* clean. She needed to shower, and she needed to get dressed because this was not a conversation to be had during this post-coital glow, while the sheets were still twisted around their feet and Grant was breathing raggedly against her shoulder. No, this was not the time.

She'd tell him all about Delaney Masterson just as soon as they were dressed.

Only she didn't because he'd followed her into the bathroom, and then the shower, and by the time they came out, Reggie was pounding on the bedroom door.

"Hey! Honeybun, me and Fincher need our toothbrushes. How long are you two going to be takin' care of business?"

"I hate that guy," Grant muttered as he pulled on brand-new Elvis boxers. They had pictures of little blue suede shoes all over them, and she bit back a smile as she called out toward the closed door, "Hang on a sec. We're almost dressed. Five more minutes."

"Please don't laugh at me in my underwear," Grant added, quietly, but his own smile tilted at the corners of his mouth.

"I promise. You make those look good," she said.

"No one could make these look good."

They quickly finished dressing and unlocked the door. Reggie sprinted through and went straight for the bathroom, his hair wild from a night spent on the couch, and Delaney felt a little bad, now. She'd been so wrapped up in Grant, she hadn't thought much about how the Paradise Brothers had fared during the night.

"Good morning, Reg," she called after him, then she and Grant walked into the other side of the suite.

"Good morning, Finch."

He was lying on the white vinyl sofa still wrapped in a blue hotel blanket.

"Good morning, sweetness. Oh, you too, Elaine," he teased.

"How did you sleep?" she asked.

He offered up a naughty grin. "I'm guessing I slept about as much as you did."

Heat blossomed on her face, but Grant just smiled. He practically thumped his chest. Men.

By the time Reggie and Finch were done in the bathroom, Sam, Humphrey, Clark, and Sissy had all showed up. Humphrey was wearing the sweatpants he'd loaned Delaney the other night, and Sam had on a Paradise Brothers T-shirt. Sissy and Clark, however, were resplendent in matching head-to-toe denim outfits. His, a suit, and hers, a one-piece jumpsuit that would have made Elvis weep with envy.

"Got any coffee?" Humphrey asked, sitting down on one of the cherry-red suede chairs and putting his feet up on the glass-topped coffee table.

"Um, I think so," Delaney said. "I'll make you some." She busied herself at the one-cup pot while the rest of them sat down. With everyone making themselves right at home, it was obvious there would be no privacy, and nowhere to talk to Grant. True confession time would have to wait, and every single part of her was relieved.

"Hey, check out all these Facebook hits," Reggie said a few minutes later. He was sitting on the white vinyl sofa with a laptop computer resting on his long legs. "The honeys are commenting on our Best Fucking Baby Hat contest pictures. They love it. Humper, I think even you might get laid after this one."

Humphrey's laugh was genuine. "My momma didn't raise no fools, Reg. I told you, the honeys love a man in touch with his do-mes-tic-i-tee."

Finch leaned over from his spot next to Reggie, peering at the screen. "Here's a comment about you, Elaine."

"Me?" Her throat clogged up as if she'd just chugged motor oil. She coughed to clear it. "How did I get on there? What's it say?" Hiccup.

"It says WHO IS THE LUCKY CHICA IN THE MIDDLE OF A PARA-DISE BROTHERS SANDWICH? That's you, sweetness." Finch beamed over at her like *aren't you excited?*

She wasn't excited. She'd kept her damn head down every single time somebody on that damn bus had pulled out a damn cell phone. How had they caught her in a picture? She handed a cup of coffee to Humphrey.

"That is an enviable spot to be, yeah?" Reggie nodded. "Why don't you come on over here and do it again. Sit between me and Fincher. Cameraman, take our picture."

Delaney heard Grant's jaw click shut.

"No pictures of me today, boys, but I'd sure like to see that one." She stepped closer and Reggie turned the computer as she bent over to look. Oh, damn it. There she was, right there on Facebook, an image of her sitting on the green sofa of the tour bus, wedged in between Finch and Reggie. Her face in the photo was turned so she was almost entirely in profile, and her normally high-lighted hair, which was now dark brown, covered part of her face. She knew who she was, of course, but how many Paradise Brothers fans would figure it out? Probably not many. Hopefully not any.

"Want me to tag it, honeybun, so your friends back in Bell Harbor can see what fun you're having?"

"No." Her voice was too sharp, her follow-up laughter too insincere. Hiccup. "No, I wouldn't want them to be jealous." And she didn't want herself to be nauseous. She hadn't been on her own Facebook page in days, and that was probably for the best, but she grimaced at the thought of what garbage had been dumped there. She really should have shut that thing down before she'd even left Beverly Hills. It felt like a lifetime ago since she'd been in sunny California, and in many ways it was. She'd become a different person since leaving home behind. Not just because of the alias. She was actually starting to *feel* like a different person.

"You OK?" Grant asked.

She stood up straight. "Yeah, I'm just hungry. Is anyone else hungry?" She needed some air and she needed them to stay off Facebook.

"I'm hungrier than a bear waking up from hibernation," Sissy said, standing up from her spot on her husband's lap. "And I want to try me one of those grilled peanut butter and banana sandwiches that Elvis used to love."

Clark stretched his legs out. "Well, I don't know about hungry, but I sure could use a Bloody Mary. 'Cause you know, just like my daddy always told me, 'Son, you can't spend all day drinking . . . unless you start first thing in the morning.'"

Sissy giggled and swatted at his shoulder. "Your daddy was a teetotaler and never said any such thing."

"Didn't he? Well, somebody's daddy said it. So let's head down to the lounge."

———————

The meal was raucous, the conversation inappropriate, just as Delaney had come to expect from this group. These guys were fun, and funny—flirty for certain, but with such a Southern gentleman flair it made her snicker right along with them. Their overt attention toward her was harmless, but still flattering. Plus she was in a damn fine mood after last night. How could she not be? Grant seemed to be in a similar state of mind, and even now couldn't manage to be next to her without there being some kind of physical contact between them. Yes, she needed to tell him the truth, but she'd worry about that later.

After everyone had finished eating, the Paradise Brothers and Sammy made short work of getting what they needed from the bus and setting up the stage. Besides their group, there were only a handful of people milling around in the Jungle Room Lounge. Even most of the Elvis impersonators had disappeared, probably to go back to their lives as accountants and dentists. Delaney excused herself to use the ladies' room, and when she came back, Reggie was tuning some instruments. She wandered over to the stage and lightly tapped a few notes on the piano.

"You play, honeybun?" Reggie asked, glancing her way.

"A little."

"I'm trying to tune some stuff. Want to give me a hand?" he asked.

She glanced over at Grant. He was sitting at the table with the rest of the group while Sissy told some animated story that involved much waving of her hands. Judging from his expression of consternation, it was either a very involved story, or he was just trying very hard not to stare at her cleavage. Delaney could hardly fault him if he had been staring at it. Sissy's cleavage was spectacular.

"Sure, I can help you," Delaney said to Reggie. She sat down on the piano bench and felt an eager tremble run through her. She hadn't played in weeks. Add that to her list of things she missed about home.

She stroked a few keys, played a few more notes, and Reggie plunked a bass string.

"Can you give me an A?"

They worked together for a few minutes, her plunking, him tuning. "You know any songs?" he asked.

She sat up straighter. "I know lots of songs. Pick one."

"'Ode to Joy'?"

She looked over her shoulder and frowned at him. "Seriously? Everyone knows 'Ode to Joy.' Even people who don't play piano know 'Ode to Joy.' I've got something better for you."

She started playing one of her favorites, a song her dad had written but never recorded. She knew this one by heart, every note, and as soon as she'd struck the first note, she got all caught up in it, forgetting there was anyone else in the room. It was just her and the piano.

When she finished, the smattering of people in the lounge clapped, and she flushed all over with the heat of her stupidity. She'd let her ego get the best of her. So much for keeping a low profile.

Reggie stepped closer and leaned over the piano, his dark eyes gleaming. "You're pretty good on that thing, honeybun."

"Thanks." She pulled her bangs down. Hiccup.

He flashed a Reggie-style grin and his eyebrows twitched. "In fact, watching you tickle those ivories is getting me a little aroused."

She plunked a few sharp notes. "You sure know how to charm the ladies, don't you?"

"I do, actually, but I'm just messing with you." Still, he leaned forward even closer and lowered his voice. "But I gotta say, even though I've charmed a lot of ladies, and I do mean, *a lot*, I'm damn good with faces, and yours has been distracting me since the first moment you climbed on board our tour bus."

All of a sudden, the oxygen felt a little thin in here. She stared down at the keys and started playing "Ode to Joy" just as a distraction. "Um, thank you, I guess?"

He chuckled. "Honestly, I'm not hitting on you. I mean, don't get me wrong. You got that gorgeous face, and a rockin' body. I can think of at least twenty-three things that I'd want to do to you." He looked her up and down so blatantly she could only laugh, and yet, she already knew this was leading to no place she wanted to be.

"So, yeah," he continued, "I'd have remembered you for sure if we'd gone horizontal, which is why I found myself so perplexed when you got on the bus. Now I've finally figured it out."

A sensation of imminent doom made her fingers stumble and hit a wrong note. Dun-dun-dunnnn.

Reggie's voice sank so low it was nearly coming from his chest, and he leaned so close she could smell his honky-tonk cologne.

"I know who you are."

He said it so quietly she might have imagined it, but one look at his expression and she knew she'd heard him correctly. Still, she tried to deflect him. "I'm nobody special. Just Elaine."

His eyes narrowed, that black-coffee stare nearly knocking her from the piano bench, but still he whispered. "You're Delaney Masterson. You're Jesse Masterson's runaway daughter."

At least he'd called her a runaway instead of a video star. She glanced toward Grant and saw him watching, scrutinizing. Her smile back at him was half-assed. She couldn't fake this one. She looked at Reggie again to see where he intended to take this.

"Who else knows?" She began playing an Elvis song, or maybe it was Huey Lewis, or the Stones. Her brain wasn't quite paying attention. Her fingers just moved from stress and habit. And "Ode to Joy" was just too damned ironic at the moment.

"Nobody knows, I don't think. If they do, they haven't said anything to me, but why the cloak-and-dagger? Why the alias?"

"Haven't you seen the headlines? I'm in hiding from the press."

"Well that much is obvious, but why are you hiding from the press? Who does that?"

Reggie was new at this, the whole fame game, and he was a man, so maybe he couldn't understand the downside of notoriety.

"I'm hiding because my name is a punch line right now. I figured if I disappeared for a bit, the frenzy would die down, but I didn't expect to leave my car behind for the police to find."

Reggie nodded but still looked confused. "That's where we came in, right?"

"Yes." Her fingers continued to play but she hardly heard the notes.

Reggie scratched his head, making his wavy hair sway. "So I have to be honest here, sugar. I don't pay much attention to celebrity news, unless it's about me. In that case I'm fascinated, but you have some sort of reality show, right? So why was the press hounding you in the first place?"

She looked up at him. Was it possible—?

"Oh, wait . . ." he interrupted her brief speck of hope. "Was there a naughty bit of video?"

So much for that.

"Yep."

He nodded slowly. "Yeah, I guess maybe I did hear something about that. Weren't you giving—"

"Yep." She glanced over at Grant but Sissy had him distracted again.

Delaney lowered her voice and looked up at Reggie. "But I didn't know about the camera. That's the kind of stand-up guy my old boyfriend was. Not only did he film us without telling me, but then he sold it to the tabloids."

"What a douche bag!" Reggie exclaimed, then scowled and lowered his voice. "Worse than a douche bag. That guy is an ass-sucking douche bag. Can't you go after him? I mean, legally. Or otherwise? I think Sammy might know some guys who could do a little damage to his kneecaps."

Delaney had been giving that some thought. The legal aspect, not the physical injury aspect, although Melody's offer to kick Boyd Hampton in the nuts was still very much on the table. "I may. I'm trying to sort out my options right now, but I got a little waylaid by this storm, and the fact that Grant's mother sto—accidentally took my phone. She has my wallet and some other things too. It's all just been one clusterfuck after the other ever since that video surfaced."

"I'm sorry, honeybun. What does Captain America think of all this? He must want to fillet that SOB. I sure would."

Delaney reached out and clutched Reggie's wrist where it rested on the top of the piano. It was reflex, but she quickly pulled her hand back before Grant noticed. She leaned forward. "Reggie, Grant doesn't know anything about . . . about anything. He doesn't even know who I am."

God, that sounded so awful when she said it out loud. She sounded like a horrible person. Oh, God. Was she a horrible person? How had that happened? Shit. She really should have told him by now.

Reggie's dark eyes went round for a second, then a sassy smile took over his face. "Wait a minute. Are you telling me your boyfriend doesn't know you're Delaney Masterson? He doesn't know your daddy is Jesse Masterson? And isn't your momma somebody famous too? Victoria Secret or somebody like that?"

Breathe, Delaney. Just breathe.

"My mother was a model but now she makes soap. And Grant is not my boyfriend. We're just sort of . . . well, traveling companions."

"Traveling companions?" Reggie's voice was flat disbelief wrapped around a stick of *get-the-fuck-outta-here*.

"Yes, traveling companions. Technically, he's my landlord, but that's another whole story."

Laughter overtook Reggie and he collapsed over the top of the piano. Delaney's misfortune was apparently of little consequence. Maybe she should be offended. Or maybe she should just laugh along with him. Really, it was either one or the other.

Reggie lifted his head. "He's your landlord? Wow, I need to get me some rental properties right quick and find myself a honey like you," he said between his chuffs of laughter.

Delaney shook her head and sighed. "There you go being all charming again."

"Well, I'm a charming kind of guy, but sugar, if you think that dude is *just* your landlord, I will French kiss a baboon's bright red ass because, let me tell you, that is a man in love." He said the word *love* as if it had a dozen syllables, and Delaney flushed with both denial and hope.

She glanced Grant's way. Sissy was still trying to engage him but now he seemed to be paying more attention to what was going on up on the stage. Delaney began playing another song, something from Coldplay, or maybe Maroon 5. Honestly, her brain wasn't registering it. It was just all in her fingers.

She shook her head at Reggie. "He's not in love. He can't be. We hardly know each other. There hasn't been enough time to fall in love."

Reggie set his chin on one fisted hand, elbows on the piano. "Not enough time? How much time you think it takes, sugar? I can fall in love in fifteen minutes. Ten if I'm between sets."

Delaney chuckled. "That's not love, Reggie. That's hardly even lust."

His smile was broad as he tipped his head in agreement. "All right. You might have me on that, but trust me, sometimes a minute is all it takes if it's the right one, and that guy is not kidding around with you. I've seen that look in a man's eye before."

She started playing "Love Me Tender," as if her fingers wanted to help convince her brain that Reggie might be speaking some truth.

"What look?" she asked him.

"The one that says he's about ready to come over here and kick my ass. He doesn't like me. He thinks I've been flirting with you for the past three days."

"Haven't you been?"

"Hells, yeah, but that's just me. I mean, I *could* fall in love with you, if you wanted me to, but it seems like you got enough going on right now. Plus I'd rather your fella didn't go all King Kong on me and start ripping off my appendages, starting with my Little Reggie."

Delaney might have laughed again, but her nerves were frayed. "I think you're exaggerating, and I think you're misreading this whole situation, but either way, please don't tell anyone. I'm going to explain all this to him soon, very soon. Either tonight or tomorrow, but right now I have nothing but the clothes on my back and no way to get home. I have to get my wallet and stuff back. It's complicated, but keep this secret for me and I'll owe you. I promise. I'll even introduce you to my dad if you want."

Reggie scoffed at her. "Hey, I'd love to meet your dad, yeah? But you don't have to worry about me keeping your dirty little secrets. I might not come across as a very reputable guy, but in spite of my voracious appetite for frisky women, I'm actually a pretty decent human being. You can trust me."

Her stomach felt like a cement mixer. "Yeah, well, no offense, but the last guy who said *you can trust me* ended up getting me on film."

"Douche bag," Reggie said shaking his head, then he stood up and leaned away from the piano.

Delaney spotted Grant from the corner of her eye coming their way.

"Well, shucks," Reggie said, chuckling. "Looks like I've exceeded my time limit, yeah? Here comes your landlord to open up a can of whup-ass, but he won't get any details out of me. I promise. Secret to the grave, honeybun." He kissed his fingertips and held them out in a vow.

A few more strides and Grant stepped up on the stage. He sat down on the piano bench next to Delaney. "You two look like you're plotting something." His smile was for her alone, but Reggie spoke up first.

"Just talking about monkey butts and movies we didn't like, yeah?"

Grant's gaze was still on Delaney. "Yeah?" he said.

"Yeah," Delaney answered. "Reggie here is partial to kissing baboons."

Grant smirked. "Well, I don't know what any baboon might have done to deserve that, but if it keeps Reggie busy, I'm all for it."

Reggie's laugh was good-natured and Delaney started to relax once more. He'd keep her secret. There was no advantage in him telling anyone, and the offer of introducing the band to her dad had been genuine. That was a free spin in Reggie's pocket and he was smart enough to keep it.

"Monkey business is just monkey business," Reggie said. "But your lady here isn't interested. Guess she's not the girl I thought she was."

Delaney shot him a look, but he winked at her and jumped off the stage. "Nope. Oh, and by the way, Clark landed us another free room, so you two will just have to make due in the Burning Love Suite without me and Finch."

Now Grant looked over at Reggie. "Really?"

"Finch already moved our duds to the other room. You're welcome." He bowed, then turned and walked away.

"Is he serious?" Grant's gaze was optimistic.

"I guess so. That's the first I've heard of it, though."

"Maybe we should go up there and check." He picked up her hand and kissed the back of it and her heart went all fluttery again. It had been doing that all day. Maybe she should see a cardiologist. This could not be healthy. Neither was keeping secrets. If they went upstairs, she'd really have no choice but to tell him. He deserved the whole truth but the thought of giving up what they currently had was enough to make her cry, so she leaned over and kissed him, just to capture another moment.

She heard Reggie's voice from across the room. "Damn it to hell, I have got to get me some rental property."

Delaney giggled into the kiss, and Grant leaned back.

"Is he serious?" he asked.

"Is he ever?"

Grant looked ready to answer, but before he had the chance, his phone chimed in his pocket. He pulled it out and looked back at her, eyes intense.

"It's my mom."

Chapter 19

"HELLO?" GRANT CLEARED HIS THROAT.

"Grant? Oh, thank heavens. I'm so glad to get ahold of you." The voice was breathless and a little frantic, but it wasn't his mother.

"Aunt Tina?" he said. Stress jolted through all his joints, and he sat up straighter on the piano bench.

"Yes, it's me. I think we need to talk."

"Where are you?" Grant asked. "Is my mom with you?" He could hear noises from the other side of the call, like someone blubbering into a pillow.

"Yes, she is," Tina said, "but something is wrong. She just listened to your phone messages, and now she's hysterical and won't tell me what's going on. She's just crying and crying and told me I should call you and tell you she's sorry."

She was sorry? For all this trouble? Sorry was so not going to cut it. "Put her on the phone, would you please?" His voice was terse, but he added the *please* because there was no sense getting testy with his aunt. It was quite possible she didn't have any idea what was going on. Even if she did, he needed her cooperation.

Elaine looked over at him, concern etched all over her face. And no wonder. She was about to find out if her life savings was gone. The color had all but drained from her complexion.

Tina's voice cut in. "She can't talk to you right now. She's too distraught. She just keeps saying 'tell him I still have it.'"

Breath was a sharp stab in his chest. "She still has it? All of it? Every penny?"

He could hear his mother's muffled voice in the background. It tugged at his heart for about a tenth of a second before he remembered that she'd stolen forty thousand dollars from Elaine, and his mother was not the victim here.

"Donna," Tina said, "he wants to know if you have all of it." There was some more blubbering, then Tina was back. "She said she has nearly all of it. What is going on here, Grant? What does she have?"

"Where are you guys?" he asked instead. "Have you gotten home to Memphis yet?"

"No, we're in Effingham. The roads were bad so we decided to stop at a hotel for a few days. We've been having a lovely time too. Then this morning at breakfast your mother finally decided to turn on her phone and the next thing I knew she was having a nervous breakdown at the Bob Evans. Now we're sitting in the parking lot and she won't tell me what's going on. So you tell me. What's going on?"

Grant put his head down, a fist against his forehead. Naturally his mother would make a scene inside a restaurant instead of falling apart someplace discreet. She'd probably stolen all the mints from next to the cash register on the way out too.

"I really need to talk to her, Tina. Tell her . . ." he took a deep breath. "Tell her I'm not mad, I just need to ask her some questions." That was a big Effingham lie. He was as furious as hell, but if his mother was sincere, if she really did still have *nearly all* of Elaine's money, he didn't want to make the situation worse by adding to her panic. Although, when his mother said *nearly all*, she could mean *next to none*. There was just no hope of getting the honest truth from her until they were physically together and he had that bag in his hand. Right now he was mainly a hostage negotiator.

He waited, clenching his jaw. He wanted to look over at Elaine, to reassure her that everything would be fine, but he didn't dare because he didn't want her seeing the doubt on his face. He stared down at the piano keys instead while she sat next to him, motionless. He could hear his aunt trying to cajole his mother to take the phone—his dear, batshit crazy mother, the catalyst of all this.

Lord knew she never should have taken that money, but then again, if she hadn't, he wouldn't be with Elaine right now. Shit. If Donna had never rented out his house in the first place, he and Elaine might never have met at all. Crazy how the world worked sometimes.

His dad had always said, "Son, things happen for a reason," but then his dad had gone and gotten himself killed in Iraq. There was sure no good reason for that, so Grant had decided his father was wrong. Now here he was left wondering again, about fate and destiny and coincidence while he waited for his batshit crazy mother to come to the goddamn phone.

He had every right to be mad at her, but if there *was* a grander scheme to life, then maybe, just maybe, his mother had done him a favor.

Elaine reached over and squeezed his wrist. "Grant, there's something I need to tell—"

"Grant?" His mother's voice cut in, her voice warbling like her throat was full of marbles.

He sighed. "Hi, Mom."

Donna started crying all over again, and he finally looked over at Elaine. She looked positively stricken. She needed that money.

The fear was plain on her face. He'd get it back to her. If he had to sell his house or call up Blake fucking Rockstone and get his old job back, he'd get Elaine her money.

"What did you do, Mom? How much did you spend?"

His mother snuffled in a big gulp of air. "About four hundred dollars."

The Mack truck that had parked on his chest backed up. "Four hundred dollars?" That was nothing! Sure, it didn't take care of the six grand they owed Elaine for rent, but they could certainly work that out. He held the phone away from his mouth and turned to Elaine. "Four hundred dollars. That's all she spent," he whispered.

Elaine didn't look that relieved. Her smile was of the *I-just-swallowed-bad-medicine-but-I-know-it's-good-for-me* variety. Maybe she thought his mother was lying. That was certainly within the realm of possibility. The sooner they could see Donna in person, the better off he'd feel, and the more he could assure Elaine this would all work out.

He brought the phone back to his ear. "You know you did a terrible thing, right, Mom? Elaine did you a huge favor by not calling the police."

Elaine shook her head at him, frowning.

Donna warbled again. "I know. I just . . . I saw that backpack and I really liked it, and Tina and I were going on a girl's trip and I thought how nice that bag would go with my brown coat. Then I saw the money inside and I just couldn't stop myself. Please tell Elaine that I'm sorry and I will give it all back."

His mother was reckless, and impulsive, and she had more than a splash of kleptomania, but he couldn't fix it over the phone. This was something he'd have to deal with once they were all back in Bell Harbor. "You will give it back, and we're going to get you some help so that you don't do this kind of thing anymore. In the meantime, we need to figure out where we can meet because you've also got Elaine's phone and some other stuff that she needs inside that bag. Tina says you're in Effingham. How far is that from Memphis? That's where we are."

"You're in Memphis?" His mother's voice squeaked. "You and who?"

"Me and Elaine. We're here waiting for you and we need that bag back."

"They're in Memphis," he heard Donna say, undoubtedly talking to his aunt. The phone was clumsily passed once more and Tina's voice came through.

"Grant? We should be in Memphis tonight, but not until late. It's about a five-hour drive but we'll have to stop for gas and to eat again. If the roads are still bad, it may take a bit longer. Can you come to my place in the morning?"

"Yes. Sure. Of course, but meanwhile, Tina, lock that bag in the trunk, OK? Don't let my mother anywhere near it."

Delaney Masterson had received a stay of execution. Or more accurately, Elaine Masters had. She could hear both sides of the conversation from her spot next to Grant on the piano seat. His mother was loud, loud and clearly distraught. Delaney should probably be furious with her for causing a shitload of misery and worry! But mostly, at the moment, all Delaney felt was relieved. She'd be getting her money and phone and wallet back tomorrow morning. But even better than that, Donna had referred to her as Elaine. She hadn't mentioned the name Delaney at all. Was it possible she'd never found the wallet? True, it was stuffed down near the bottom of the bag, underneath the money, but Donna wasn't a very good thief if she hadn't even searched through her loot. But then again, Donna Beckett didn't strike Delaney as very bright.

Then again, *again*, who was *she* to accuse someone of being not bright?

Who was the one hiding in plain sight under an alias?

Who was the one running from a sex-video scandal?

Who was the one falling in love with a man who didn't even know her real name?

That would be Delaney.

If anyone was stupid in this whole mess, it was her. And she needed to fix it. Her euphoria swung back in the other direction, toward anxiety. She just didn't know how to feel. Maybe it was this weather, this bi-polar vortex.

"Tomorrow morning," Grant said, smiling wide. "We'll get all your stuff back tomorrow morning." He put his arm around her waist and pulled her closer. "That's good news, right?"

She nodded. "Right."

"OK, then why don't you seem happy about it?"

She looked at him, feeling very much like the world was crumbling in all around them because there was one more issue neither one of them had really addressed. "Well, for one thing, once I have my stuff back, I have to go home."

He touched her cheek and smiled. "Just for a little while, though, right? This isn't it. We'll figure something out."

Her heart swelled with hope, but Grant had no idea what he was talking about. How could he? He was talking to a girl who didn't exist, so she needed to tell him. Right now.

"Grant—"

"Y'all want to go on over to Graceland with us?" Sissy's voice cut through Delaney's thoughts like a scythe. "The boys don't have to start playing for another couple of hours, so if you two can keep your hands off each other for a spell, we can go see where the King slept, then go get some ribs at Marlowe's before tonight's show. Interested?"

Delaney could not hold back a smile. Another reprieve. She couldn't possibly tell him at Graceland. And she couldn't tell him at a restaurant either. She'd just have to tell him later tonight. Or . . . tomorrow. Tomorrow would work.

Chapter 20

THE PARADISE BROTHERS WERE A hit with the Heartbreak Hotel crowd, and Grant had to hand it to Reggie. The guy might be as obnoxious as hell, but he could sing, and he was a natural entertainer. They all were, Finch and Humphrey too, joking with each other onstage as effortlessly as they had on the bus. Playing guitars and bass, keyboards and drums. They were masters, offering up a mix of Elvis classics, old country western, and some original honky-tonk songs with lyrics so raunchy the audience cheered and Elaine blushed.

Still so innocent, even after last night.

God. Last night. His body went hot at the memory. It was the best night he'd ever had, and the fact that they had the room completely to themselves for this evening? Damn. That had been on his mind since the moment he'd heard. Unfortunately that also left him touring the entire Graceland mansion this afternoon with a semierection, but certainly he wasn't the first one. Everybody loved Elvis.

"Let's slow it down for the lovers in the crowd tonight," Reggie said into the microphone, and Grant wondered if that was just for them or for lovers in general. Either way, Grant pulled Elaine to the center of the dance floor and then into his arms. The song was something sad, an old story of woe about love gone wrong, but nothing about this felt wrong.

Everything about this was just right.

The truth was, he'd never felt this way before. He'd been with plenty of women, some who he'd been fond of, a few he thought he might have even loved, although he never told them so. But this was different. He and Elaine were in sync, every rhythm, every breath. He wasn't naive, of course. He understood she was shiny and bright, and everything about this had that new car smell. Sure there would be bumps in the road, and yes, he still had more to learn about her, but if Elaine could put up with the amount of stress they'd encountered over the last few days with such grace and patience and good humor, well, he couldn't imagine ever growing tired of her. He'd definitely never grow tired of her lips, because they tasted like caramel and set his skin on fire. He wouldn't grow tired of her laugh and the way it burst like a firecracker. He'd certainly never get tired of the way her body moved like water under his palm either. Nope. Never getting tired of that.

Grant pulled her closer, breathing in the sweet, fresh scent of her. That curve where her shoulder glided into her neck. He could spend the rest of his life there, breathing in the scent of that curve. He'd always trusted his instincts. They'd rarely steered him wrong, and if he followed them right now, he'd end up strolling down the aisle right toward a preacher. Who the hell would have thought his idiot brother was right? When you knew, you just *knew*. And right now, he knew Elaine Masters was the one for him.

He was punch-drunk with it, the idea, the surreal quality of all that had gone on since he'd met her. He'd never been one of those fanciful dolts who believed in fate, or love at first sight, but whatever elements of destiny had brought this woman into his life, be it coincidence or the actions of his batshit-crazy mother, well, he was thankful because Elaine was beauty and heartbreak and everything in between. Learning all about her would be like having an endless gift to unwrap.

His hand slid up her back and threaded into her hair. He had to kiss her. Right now. In the center of a crowded dance floor in the middle of the Jungle Room Lounge, he had to kiss her. So he did. She kissed him back, and he knew this night would be even better than the one before. It needed to start right now.

As soon as the last strains of the song floated out over the crowd, Grant pulled her from the dance floor and around the corner. He pressed her up against the wall next to the elevator and the big Elvis '69 poster and kissed her again.

She chuckled, low and sultry, as he reached around blindly for the elevator button. When the door opened, they practically fell inside.

"Want to go upstairs?" he asked, as the elevator started to rise.

She laughed again. "I think we're halfway there."

"God, I'm halfway there."

The door opened with a soft glide and then they were almost sprinting down the hall. His hands shook as he stuffed the key into the slot at the suite door. Maybe that hand tremble wasn't manly, but he didn't care because they were still in the hallway and Elaine was already pushing the edge of his shirt up from behind.

He slammed down the handle and shoved open the door, pulling her inside. He wondered, briefly, if there was a security deposit on this room, because there was a good chance they were going to break something.

They rushed past the burgundy walls and into the bedroom, falling to the bed with a bounce and a bit of laughter. His shirt came off first, then he caught the hem of hers, pulling it up, fast, urgent. What he lacked in style he'd make up for in pure enthusiasm.

This wasn't the time for finesse, it was the time for raw need. He didn't want to slow down, he just wanted to be buried deep inside her. He kissed her neck, and bit. She arched up against him and he caught her around the waist, turning them on the bed so that their heads were near the pillows. Her soft gasp of encouragement would have buckled his knees if he hadn't already been lying down.

She knocked the pillows aside so she was lying flat on the mattress. He gazed down at her, marveling once more at his good fortune that this woman had stumbled her way into his life. Maybe some things really did happen for a reason.

"God, you're beautiful," he whispered and dipped his head for another kiss. She reached down between them and tugged at the waistband of his jeans, popping the button. She may as well have been pulling the pin from a grenade because there was no stopping him now. He growled down deep, the sound scraping in his throat. She pulled at the zipper but his pants were uncooperative, given that they were stretched to capacity by his extremely optimistic cock. He reached down and moved the zipper on his own. She reached inside his boxers and set him free, running her hand along the length of him. Everything inside him turned to chaos and want.

"God," he ground out again, and pressed another kiss along the slim expanse of her neck. "I need to lose these pants before I lose my mind."

She offered up a sweet huff of annoyance when he rolled away to take off his jeans, but he was back before the sound ended. He moved lower, his face nuzzling her belly. Her laughter was breathy and she tried to turn but he held her steady.

"That tickles," she gasped, and pulled at his hair.

He might have kept at it, just to hear her laugh again, but he had more serious matters on his mind. He reached down and unzipped her jeans. She sighed with relief as he caught the waistband with his hands and inched them slowly off. They got caught up at her ankles and he had to stand up to get them all the way off, but that was OK. He dropped them on the floor as a wickedly delicious idea took hold. Yes, he was in a hurry, but he still had time for one small and luscious detour.

———•———

Delaney was so happy to be naked. Grant's hands and lips and tongue seemed to be everywhere, leaving her mindless and blissful. Everything else faded away. It was just them, and this bed. An oasis of pleasure. She heard her jeans land on the floor and then Grant was kissing her ankle, and then her calf. His tongue traced a path upward, sending tendrils of desire right to the center of her. Delicious. Hot and delicious.

He kissed the inside of her knee, his fingers gripping her hips tightly. A confusion of sensations competed for her attention, some rough, some gentle. The sweeping glide of his fingers, then the scrape of his whiskered cheek brushing against her skin before he dipped his head and kissed her. There. Right there.

She bit her lip, but the moan escaped her anyway and she pulled at his hair again. This tickled in a completely different way. He was good at this. Really, really good at this, and she let herself be swept away on that tide, the roll and the swell, until her body crashed and broke apart and all her muscles turned to water. It felt like the only thing holding her together was his embrace.

Then he was beside her, inside her, riding his own wave, and she wondered if he had any idea that she was falling in love with him.

They lay together under the blankets a little while later, facing one another as he curled and uncurled a strand of her hair around his finger.

"Do you want to hear something kind of funny?" he asked, staring at that strand.

"Sure." She was feeling sleepy, and thoroughly satisfied, and would've said *sure* to just about anything he'd asked her at that point.

"When I came home for my brother's wedding, I was going to tell him he was an idiot for getting married."

Some of her blissful euphoria waned. That wasn't funny. It was mildly distressing.

"Why is that funny?"

He twined the hair back in the other direction. "It's funny ironic . . . because I thought he was crazy for marrying someone he'd only known for six months. But I think I'm starting to see the appeal. Now that I've met you, I think I finally understand."

Her heart tumbled clumsily over itself at his words. "You do?" she asked.

He looked at her, and all her euphoria swelled back into place. He was talking about her. He was talking about them.

"Yes." He chuckled then, kind of dazedly and self-consciously, and turned his face into the pillow for a few seconds before looking back at her. "Yes, I do. I'm guess what I'm trying to say here, Lane, is that I'm falling for you. I'm falling . . . all the way."

His smile fell away too, and he was gazing at her with such honesty that it nearly stopped her breath altogether.

"Falling . . . all the way . . . in love?"

"Somewhere very near there. I know it's fast, and illogical, but I'm kind of hoping I'm not out here on this ledge all by myself."

It was a ledge, and once they jumped, there was no going back. But she was out there too. If he was going to jump, she would jump right next to him. He was looking at her expectantly, optimistically. Her heart felt the plunge, the sense of weightlessness before gravity took over and began its inevitable pull.

"I'm with you, Grant. I'm falling too."

"You are?"

She nodded, and nearly felt like crying because she had so much to tell him, so much to say that was important. She needed to tell him her story, but it would keep for a few more hours. Right now, she would exist in this beautiful, timeless bubble of perfection, awash in this glow.

"Yes, I am. I'm crazy about you," she said. She kissed him then, sealing a promise. No matter what tomorrow brought, she'd always love him.

Chapter 21

GRANT WALKED INTO THE HOTEL lobby with a spring in his step and a slightly sore back. The sexual gymnastics from the last two nights were taking their toll, but hot damn, it was worth it. He was in love, Elaine was in love. The world was a beautiful place. Today, they'd get her bag back from his mother, and whatever came next, they'd face it. Obviously there was shit in Miami to deal with, but it couldn't be that bad. She was obviously close to her family, and no matter what it was, he'd help her work through it. That's what a man did for the woman he loved. He took care of her.

Grant had never taken care of anyone before. At least, no one except himself, but since the moment Elaine had shown up at his door, his bathroom door, he'd been striving to look after her. And he liked it. It was rewarding in a way different from any other accomplishment, and now he understood what had driven Tyler to make that commitment with Evie. It just made sense in a way that nothing else did. When you knew, you just knew.

Grant chuckled to himself as he crossed the lobby, his feet in Memphis but his head somewhere else entirely. He could see life stretching out before him, a life with Elaine. The two of them would live in that little house in Bell Harbor for part of the time and travel the world the rest of the time. She'd left home to find adventure, so damn it, he'd show her adventure. He'd give her a lifetime of adventures. They'd make love on every continent. Now there was a goal to look forward to.

It was sunny outside and the Memphis cold snap seemed to be over. Good news because they had to figure out how to get back to Bell Harbor, and driving through another blizzard did not appeal to him. It already felt like they'd been away for weeks, but it had only been a couple of days. Amazing how a couple of days could change a man's life forever.

He walked into the gift shop for coffee. He'd already showered and dressed, and since Elaine needed a little extra time, he'd been sent on a java run. A rotund woman in a pink shirt behind the counter greeted him with a big, toothy smile.

"Good morning, sir. Can I help you find anything?"

"I just need a couple of coffees, please."

"We got Krispy Kreme doughnuts too, and you know Elvis loved to have himself a Krispy Kreme doughnut now and then."

Grant was unaware that Elvis had an affinity for Krispy Kreme doughnuts, but it appeared this young lady had enjoyed a dozen or so. In fact, there were little pieces of glaze on the front of her shirt.

He smiled and shook his head. "No, thanks. Just the coffee today."

"Sure thing. Here are the cups. You can fill them up over there." She set two disposable cups next to the cash register and pointed to a coffee station on the other side of the store. "That'll be two dollars, please."

He tugged his wallet from his pocket and pulled out some money, then watched with teenage-boy horror as a foil-wrapped condom flipped out from between two bills and landed with a slap on top of a stack of magazines next to the counter.

The girl's eyes widened, then she burst out with a big hearty guffaw that shook her whole body, which was no small amount of mass. Those little pieces of doughnut glaze hopped around on her breasts like hot popcorn. He guessed it was lucky she had a sense of humor but heat still suffused his face. He hadn't carried a condom in his wallet in years but had tucked one in there as a joke for Elaine.

He chuckled a little at his own expense. At least he and the shop girl were the only two in here. Thank God Reggie was nowhere in sight. He'd never hear the end of it if that guy was around. Grant bent over to retrieve the brightly wrapped party favor—and stopped short. The air kicked from his lungs and he reached over to grip the counter for support. Because there—right there next to the Paradise Brothers condom—was Elaine's face on the cover of a tabloid magazine.

WHERE IN THE WORLD IS DELANEY MASTERSON?

That's what the headline said in big, bold letters across the top. Delaney Masterson? Who the fuck was Delaney Masterson? The glossy image of the woman on the cover of the magazine had much lighter hair than Elaine, and gobs of makeup, but the eyes and the smile and the curve of her chin were pure Elaine. He couldn't breathe. The air inside the little gift shop pushed down and all the muscles in his love-sore back clenched.

"Aw, shucks, honey," said the clerk, "you don't need to go getting all embarrassed. I've seen all sorts of stuff at this hotel. One little rubber ain't nothin' to fret about. In fact, we sell them right here from behind this counter. You need some more?"

"No. No, thanks." He managed to stand upright but the room was spinning. "I'll take this magazine though." He slapped it down on the counter next to the cups and took more money from his wallet. He grabbed the condom and put that in his pocket.

The woman looked at the magazine and tsk, tsk, tsked. "Now ain't that a shame? That pretty young girl with so much going for her and then she went and did something so naughty. And now she's missing. Her sister says she's hiding out with some other man, not even the man from the video."

Jesus Christ. "What video?"

"Oh, honey, where you been at? It's all over the news. That girl has a sexy-sex video. I read all about it though I ain't seen it. Apparently," she leaned forward to whisper conspiratorially, "and I heard this from my cousin Bernice when we went to get our nails done, she said that this Delaney Masterson released the video just to boost the ratings for her TV show. Now isn't that sad?"

Wind from some unknown source roared in his ears so loudly he could hardly hear this girl. He had to concentrate very hard. "What TV show?"

"*Pop Rocks.* That's the show she's from. Her daddy is Jesse Masterson. You've heard of him, right? Everybody has heard of him." The girl jabbed a neon-orange fingernail against the cover of the magazine. "But anyway, nobody knows exactly why she took off, but they found her abandoned car up in Illinois and nobody has seen or heard from her since."

He looked down at the cover of the magazine. It was Elaine Masters. He was as certain of that as he was of his own name, but snippets of their past conversations started jumping around in his head like an old record skipping. Questions from the night they'd met screeched to the forefront. Questions he'd let her explain away without much effort. What had he missed? How was this possible? He picked up the magazine and turned to leave.

"Hey, mister. Here's your change," the girl called after him but he didn't turn around. "What about your coffee?"

He just kept going. He left the shop and went into the Jungle Room Lounge. It wasn't open yet because it was only nine in the morning, so there were no overhead lights on. He walked over to a seat by the window and sat down with a thud. He was numb, except for his stomach, which was roiling like water about to boil over. He looked at the cover and tried to breathe.

She'd lied. Clearly she had lied. But why? And to what extent? His hands nearly tore the paper as he opened the cover and flipped pages until he found the article.

Police have canceled their search for the missing Delaney Masterson, 27, youngest daughter of '80s rocker Jesse Masterson and supermodel Nicole Westgate after learning from relatives that she is hiding out in a super-secret love nest with a new beau. Even her closest friends and family don't know exactly where she's holed up, but one thing is for sure, absence only makes our hearts grow fonder for *Pop Rocks'* favorite wild child.

Sources close to the celebrity stylist say Delaney had grown increasingly frustrated by her limited role on the family's increasingly popular reality show and vowed to do whatever it took to make herself a household name, even if that meant releasing a risqué video of herself with onetime boyfriend Boyd Hampton.

"Delaney was always a good-time girl," sources close to Hampton say. "She was up for anything, and obviously, so was Boyd."

He kept reading, his eyes burning at each word, until the article finished with another quote.

"I guess dressing stars wasn't enough for her anymore," said one client who asked to remain anonymous. "Maybe Delaney decided it was time to be the star, instead."

There were pictures dotted all around the article, seven or eight of them, and every single one was of Elaine. At least, the woman he knew as Elaine, but this woman was a stranger. She was glamorous in a shimmering, backless dress in one photo, sultry in another wearing a black miniskirt cut up to there. Her hair was various shades of light brown or nearly blonde in most, but there was one picture that made his heart feel like it had pierced itself on one of his ribs. It was her with dark hair and little makeup. She was in a cheerleading outfit and had to be a teenager, but that photo looked just like his Elaine. *His* Elaine.

But he didn't have an Elaine. The woman he'd professed his love to not ten hours ago was nothing but a mirage. A propaganda machine, a master manipulator, and he'd fallen for every bit of it. How could he have been so blind? The article said she wanted attention. She'd certainly gotten his. Calling her a *reality* star was an understatement, though. She had real acting potential. She'd managed to convince his entire family, a busload of musicians, and him that she was just a sweet young woman trying to spread her wings. At least Miranda had been forthright about her career motives, but Elaine—Delaney—she was sly. She'd flat-out lied, and she'd used all of them.

Especially him.

For nothing more than publicity and fame. But he should have seen it coming.

———◆———

Delaney was nervous as hell, but the minute Grant got back with that coffee, she was going to sit him down and tell him everything. Everything. Every last detail. She'd only sent him away so she could gather her thoughts for a minute, but she couldn't stand the subterfuge any longer. Hiccup.

Last night she'd handed over her heart, and this morning he was probably going to drop-kick it right back to her, but full disclosure was essential. They were leaving for his aunt's house just as soon as she was ready to go, so it was now or never.

Although *never* wasn't actually an option.

So . . . it was just . . . now.

He took a while getting the coffee. She paced as she waited, thinking of various openers.

Oh, by the way, funny thing about . . . everything. I made most of it up.

Her skin prickled. She was perspiring, and she desperately wanted to rewind, but even if she could, what would she have done differently? If she had known then what she knew now, would she make the same mistakes? She paced some more, wishing he'd hurry.

She'd avoided having that panic attack the other morning, but now might work just as well. Hiccup. Finally, when she heard him at the hotel room door, she jumped so high she was practically a cat clinging to the ceiling with kitten-sharp claws.

Big breath, Delaney.

She was standing in the center of the room, right under the blue-sky-and-clouds mural, when he came inside. Empty-handed.

"Where's the coffee?" she asked.

He pulled out something tucked under his arm. "No coffee, but I got you a magazine."

He dropped it on the floor, right at her feet, but one look at his face and she already knew. She'd hit the tabs again. Her heart skidded to a halt and left her teetering on the edge of a cliff. No, no, no. Not now. Five more minutes. Five more minutes and she would have told him herself.

She bent over to pick up the magazine as he stalked into the room to stand by the window with his back to her, his hands jammed into his pockets. The floor tilted and the walls shook, but it wasn't Memphis having an earthquake. It was *her* world that was falling apart. And maybe Grant's. She hadn't meant to involve other people in her charade, but she had, and the enormity of that surrounded her.

She looked at the glossy cover and there she was. She grimaced at the headline. God only knew what lies they'd printed inside, but even if they'd only printed the truth, it was still pretty bad.

"I was going to tell you—"

"When?" He cut her off, twisting back in her direction, face flushed. "When were you going to tell me? Because we've been together nonstop for about a week now and it seems like this might have come up somewhere between, oh, I don't know. Somewhere between *hello* and *I love you*."

She should have told him sooner. She should have told him sooner. Damn it. She *really* should have told him sooner.

"I know. It's just . . . it's complicated."

Complicated? That sounded pathetic even to her. She was shaking, and cold and clammy, but she had to pull it together. She had to make him understand how this had started with one simple falsehood and yet had somehow exploded into this mushroom cloud of events.

"Complicated," he growled. "Yeah. I can see how confusing it might get trying to remember your own fucking name." His voice rose with the last part, and she was almost glad. Glad to finally be getting this out in the open, to expose the wound she'd created so they might begin to move past it and heal. But how, she had no idea. She couldn't undo anything. She could only try to fix it from this point forward.

"Grant, I'm so sorry. I just—"

He cut her off. "So where do I fit into the general spin of things?"

"The spin?"

"Yeah. Am I the brainless idiot who never recognized you, or the dedicated lover willing to call the cops on his own mother just to keep you entertained?" His eyes glittered with anger, and her heart, the one he'd touched just an hour earlier with the sweetest words, now splintered, cut by his sharp gaze.

"You're neither. That's not what happened. Grant, the media spins things in a hundred different ways and it's hardly ever true. I was trying to protect you from that."

He looked like he'd been jolted with electricity. "Protect me? Protect me by lying to me about who you are?"

"No, protect you by keeping you out of the media storm. That's the whole reason I was hiding out. Ever since that awful video surfaced, the paparazzi have been hounding me and I was just trying to get away."

"Get away. Right. Leaking that video didn't have anything to do with boosting the ratings for your TV show and making you famous. Oh, and by the way, you didn't think to mention you had a TV show? I'm a fucking cinematographer, *Delaney*. I know a thing or two about television."

He said her name like it was a curse, and it stung. Agitation stuck in her throat, making her voice raspy. "Yes, you're a cinematographer, and everything you hate about television is everything that my show represents. I admit it, Grant, that's no excuse for me not telling you, but it is the reason I hesitated. But you have to believe I never leaked that video. I didn't even know it existed until a few weeks ago. I'm not a fame-seeker. I'm the opposite of that, and I just wanted you to get to know the *real* me before you made any judgments."

His bark of laughter was harsh, without an ounce of humor in it. "Oh, OK. In that case, I'll just make my judgments based on what you've shown me yourself. No cameras, no crew. Just me and *the real* you. Oh, and look. You still lied. Even when it was just the two of us. You had a dozen chances to come clean, and you chose not to."

They were standing feet apart, facing each other, but it may as well have been an ocean between them. Or a pit of fiery lava. At least if it was lava, Delaney could fling herself into it and have this all be over with. What a hot mess she'd created.

"You're right. I should have told you sooner. I should have told you right away, but I didn't know you at first. I didn't expect you to be in that house and I had no idea if I could trust you. Then, once I did, I couldn't figure out when or how to explain. I just . . ."

Her voice dwindled away, the excuses and explanations dying on her lips. How could she defend herself when she basically agreed with him?

"This was all just a little elaborate, wasn't it?" he said, finally moving, stalking to the other side of the room. "The whole running away scam? The hiding out? The bag of money? My mother taking it must have made your day! That's why you've been such a good sport about all this, isn't it? You couldn't have scripted a better drama. Did you rent that house from her on purpose just hoping she'd take that money?"

"What? No! Of course not. I didn't script anything. Listen to me, Grant. I broke my show contract and left Beverly Hills because I wanted to be done with all of it, with all the trappings of celebrity and fame. I'm not interested in the spotlight, and that video humiliated me. I thought if I dropped out of sight for a while this would all just go away. But it hasn't because we got in that stupid accident and left the car behind and got the police involved."

"So this is my fault then, for getting us into an accident?"

"No, that's not what I meant, but once the police filed a report and the news media got ahold of it, well, it became impossible to contain. That's why I told you I had to go home sooner than expected. I have to go back to Beverly Hills and deal with all of this, and I didn't want you to have to be any part of that. Grant, I didn't want to lie to you. I hated it, and I swear I was going to tell you everything just as soon as you came back with the coffee."

"Sure you were. Forgive me if I have a little trouble believing that since you have been lying to me, every single day from the first second we met."

"That's not true."

But it was. She had been lying all that time. Maybe Boyd had started her off on this hit-and-run journey, but she'd taken things further than she'd ever intended. The body count was piling up.

"Not true? That's a great phrase coming from you. You're the queen of *not true*, aren't you? Tell me, did you get any of this on camera for your show?" he rasped. "I hope so. I hope you got that part from last night when I said I was in love with you. You'd better save that footage, *Delaney*, because you'll sure never hear me say that again."

Her heart turned to ash. She could practically taste it in her mouth. She stepped toward him but he moved back fast, as if her touch was toxic. He was out of reach, just like the truth had been since the very start. The fight left her. The guilt swooped in to pick away what was left.

"I'm so sorry, Grant. I never meant for any of this to happen," she whispered.

"Yeah, me neither. So let's go get your money, and then we can both pretend it never did."

Chapter 22

THE TAXI RIDE TO GRANT'S aunt Tina's house was silent, but inside Delaney's head were a dozen different voices yelling and screaming. She was desperate for her wallet and phone and cash. She'd relied on Grant for everything over the last few days, and now that he was not there to support her, she was determined to prop herself back up. Once she had her belongings, she'd have some options. Then she could figure out what to do and how to make this right. Because she had to make this right.

That's what one voice was yelling about, but another voice was mostly just moaning and wailing. How could she have ever anticipated things would get to this? How could she have known that her money would go off on a joyride and she'd have to chase it, and that she'd fall in love with Grant in the process? And she had fallen in love. Of this whole insane mess, that was the only thing she was certain of.

So many of the circumstances since she'd left home had been beyond her control, and her reasoning had seemed justifiable, but as she peeked over at Grant's rigid profile, she knew she'd taken a lousy situation and made it exponentially worse. Whatever came next, she was done avoiding the blame for her choices. No matter who did what to whom, the only thing that mattered now was what she did about it here and now.

The driver dropped them off in front of a one-story redbrick ranch that had definitely seen better days. The mailbox dangled from the post, and the bushes in front were scraggly and sad. A fitting ambiance to match the mood between them. Delaney got out on her side, slamming the door behind her. Grant got out on his side, said something to the driver, and then handed him some money.

Cab fare. She'd add that to the list of what she owed Grant Connelly. She could pay him back for the food he'd bought for her, the gas that had filled the tank of that yellow Volkswagen, and even the Elvis pajamas. But what was his time worth? How did she pay him back for that? And his heart? What was his heart worth?

Tina met them at the door wearing faded jeans and a yellow University of Tennessee sweatshirt. She was a brown-haired version of Donna, petite and blue eyed. Delaney recognized her from Tyler's wedding, only she appeared to be significantly more reserved today than she'd been after ten rum and Cokes at the reception.

Tina reached out and clasped Grant's forearm as they entered the house. "Grant, how are you? I'm so sorry about all this. I honestly had no idea what your mother was up to, but we've had a long, serious talk. She's overwrought." She let him in and turned to Delaney. "Oh, my dear girl. What a fiasco for you. Please, come on in."

She led them into a paneled family room, not much different from the one Grant's mother lived in back in Bell Harbor. Everything was a little messy, a little frayed around the edges, kind of like how Delaney felt. Broken down. Used up. Irreparable.

"Please sit down. Can I get anyone some coffee?"

"Where's my mom, Aunt Tina? Delaney doesn't have much time to waste."

Delaney looked at him and wondered where that had come from. Sure, she wanted this over with, but at this point, what was the rush?

Tina looked confused too. "I'm sorry. *Delaney?*"

Delaney looked at Grant, wondering if he wanted to go into the full explanation about her name.

"Elaine," he said tersely, while still looking at his aunt.

Her guilt doubled, as if that was possible. Because of her, he was lying to them. Maybe not in the purest sense of a lie, but he certainly wasn't telling them the truth. It was a slippery slope that she was very familiar with, but not one she wanted to send him down.

Tina nodded. "Elaine. Won't you please sit down?" she asked again. Delaney sank onto the sofa and Grant crossed the floor to sit on the edge of a chair near the fireplace, as far as he could get from her and still be in the same room. She could still feel the anger emanating from him and it scraped at her soul. This wound would be a long time in the healing. For both of them.

"So, no coffee then?" Grant's aunt seemed to be stalling.

"No coffee, Aunt Tina. Thanks, but could you just get my mother out here and give . . . Elaine her bag back?"

Tina sank down next to Delaney. "There's a little situation, and I wanted to tell you myself. Maybe I should make Donna do it, but she's so upset, I know it'll be easier if I just do it."

"Situation?" His word landed like a brick on cement.

Tina nodded and looked down at her folded hands. "It seems your mother spent more than she previously admitted."

Grant visibly blanched and Delaney wondered how much worse this would all get before it finally started to get better. If it would get better.

"How much more?" Grant ground out.

"She told me this morning she spent closer to five hundred."

Delaney exhaled. That was nothing in the scheme of things, but Grant's jaw flexed in reaction.

"Fine," he said. "Now would you get my mother please?"

His aunt looked over at him, twisting her fingers in her lap. "Don't be too hard on her, Grant. She's terribly ashamed. She knows what she did was wrong and caused all sorts of people all sorts of pain."

Tina was talking about his mother, but those words could have been directed at Delaney too. She winced at the irony.

Grant's voice was stilted as he spoke, as if he had to push the words out through his frustration. "I don't even want to get into that right now, Aunt Tina. All I want is that bag so that *she* can get back home to . . . wherever the hell it is that she lives." He tilted his head toward Delaney and said *she* as if he couldn't make himself say her name. Either name. Like the taste of it was so foul on his tongue he couldn't bear it.

"Here I am," Donna said softly from the doorway. Her face was splotchy with recently shed tears, and she had her arms wrapped about the backpack as if it were a life preserver. Delaney felt moisture springing to her own eyes. Tears of relief, and sorrow—because Donna Beckett was a sad little woman with a great big problem.

Grant stood up quickly, but Delaney couldn't. Her legs had turned to Jell-O—warm, jiggly Jell-O—and didn't seem to function.

Tina wiped her hands down the front of her Tennessee sweatshirt, just like Delaney had seen Donna do a dozen times.

"I'll do my best to pay you back," Donna whispered, staring at a spot just next to Delaney, as if she couldn't quite make eye contact.

"Yes, you will," Grant said, but his voice wasn't sharp any longer, or harsh. Just . . . efficient, pragmatic, emotionless. He reached over and took the bag from her, then looked at his aunt.

"Aunt Tina, is there somewhere I could talk to . . . Elaine for a minute. In private?" he asked.

"Uh, of course. There's the guestroom just down there."

Tina pointed to a narrow, paneled hallway and Grant stepped toward it. He ignored his mother and looked back at Delaney, his face still Mount Rushmore stony. His expression hadn't changed since they'd left the hotel. "Come on," he said to her.

The other women exchanged glances but said nothing.

Delaney stood up and followed him reluctantly down the hall on those wobbly Jell-O legs. They went into a small, square bedroom full of old pine furniture and a threadbare lavender bedspread dotted with faded flowers. Grant slammed the door behind them, and she jumped at the boom of it. Then he chucked the backpack onto the bed.

"Dump it out." His voice remained flat and detached, but still, his words surprised her.

"What?"

"Dump it out on the bed. Make sure all your stuff is there." He crossed his arms and stared at the lavender bedspread rather than at her.

She looked at him a minute, watching for any signs of softening, but there were none. She unbuckled the bag and turned it over above the mattress. Her hands quivered, not from the motion of emptying the bag, but from the collateral damage of this whole situation. Stack upon stack of banded bills bounced on the purple-flowered coverlet, along with several loose twenties. She jiggled the bag again, and out came her wallet and her phone. Then she unzipped the side pocket to see that her laptop was right where it was supposed to be.

"Is everything in your wallet?" he said.

She zipped the laptop pocket back up and set the backpack on the bed. She picked up her red leather wallet and unsnapped it. It seemed the same, filled with her license, various debit and credit cards. "It doesn't look like anything is missing." She slid it back into the bag and started to scoop up the money.

"Count it." He ground out those words like a cigarette butt under his heel.

"Excuse me?" Her hands paused in their stuffing of the sack.

"Count it. Make sure your money is all there."

He was doing this just to aggravate her. She could tell. "Your mother said she only spent five hundred dollars. I believe her."

"Well, I don't. She's as much of a liar as you are. Count the fucking money." Now he sounded pissed. And it pissed her off in return. Something deep inside snapped.

"Fuck you, Grant. I'm not going to count the money. I don't care about it. I don't care if she spent five hundred or five thousand or all of it. This whole trip was never about getting my money back. It was about me keeping my *privacy*. I know you think I did all this as some sort of publicity stunt, but nothing could be farther from the truth. I have no idea why Boyd released that awful video, but that's what I've been running from. Not to create ratings. Not to make myself famous. And certainly not to make a fool of anyone. The only fool here is me. I should have stayed put in Beverly Hills and taken my hits instead of running away and dragging anyone else into this mess."

A car honked from the driveway.

He paused for a moment, still staring at the bed and not her, but then he gave an abrupt tilt of his head toward the door. "That's your cab. I told him you'd need a ride back to the hotel in fifteen minutes. Looks like our time is up."

Our time is up. No subtle innuendo there. She knew exactly what he meant. They were done.

"That's it? You think I'm just going to leave with so much unresolved here? Grant—"

His gaze snapped to her, like a slap to her skin. "What's to resolve? We came down here to get your bag. There it is. You have it. My mother will have to figure out a way to pay you back that five hundred dollars, and the six months of rent. Frankly, that's not my problem. You can work that out with her."

She took a step closer. "Could we talk about this, please? I know you're angry and you have every right to be, but I wish you'd give me a chance to explain things better."

He scoffed at that. "I think I'm pretty clear on the chain of events, and I think I've been more than accommodating, *Miss Masterson*. Maybe you're used to people coddling you on your TV show, but I'm not a groupie, and I've done my time. You're on your own now. I'll be riding back to Michigan with my mother."

God, he was angry, so angry, but those sweet, loving moments they'd shared had been real, and somehow she had to make him see that. Remember that. She had to make him listen through his frustration and cynicism. She had to make him hear *her*.

"Grant, do you want to know why I didn't tell you sooner? Why I couldn't?"

He looked down and crossed his arms. His chest rose and fell in a shallow breath and Delaney's heart split in two. His anger was easier to take than this sense of him being wounded.

He shook his head and kept his voice low. "It doesn't matter."

Maybe it didn't matter to him, but it mattered to her, and she knew unequivocally if she held anything back now she would regret it, always.

"I didn't tell you sooner because I loved the way you looked at me. You looked at me as if I was sweet, like I was somebody *worth* caring for, somebody easy to love. Not because you wanted something from me, or from my family. And yes, I lied about the details of my life, but what you've seen in the last few days is everything about me that's real. I wasn't playing. I fell in love with you for a dozen different reasons, but most of all because of how I felt, *how I feel*, when I'm with you. And the truth is, no matter how much this hurts right now, I'm never going to regret this time together because this has been the best week of my life. No one ever saw me the way you did, and no one else ever will."

The muscles in his jaw clenched and she could see him working through his thoughts, and she hoped against hope he'd forgive her, but the taxi honked again, and he shook off the trance.

He walked over to the bedroom door and opened it. "Your cab is waiting."

She stood in place. "I didn't lie about falling in love with you."

He finally looked at her then, his beautiful eyes meeting hers, and regret shackled to her heart.

"I don't care." His voice was a whisper but may as well have been a whip for the way it sliced. "Your cab is here. *Delaney.*"

Chapter 23

"HEARTBREAK HOTEL, SWEETHEART," THE CAB driver said as they pulled into the driveway. Delaney had the presence of mind to marvel at the perfection of the name. Heartbreak Hotel, indeed. Hers was most certainly broken, shattered into pieces and tossed in a Dumpster. And judging by Grant's expression back at his aunt's house, his was frozen solid. He was furious, but worse than that, he was hurt because of what she'd done, and what she had failed to do. Regardless of her reasons, justifiable or not, he had loved her and she'd ruined it.

She paid the driver, climbed out, and went into the hotel lobby. It was more crowded than she'd seen it before. Another flood of revelers to celebrate Elvis and his birthday had arrived, no doubt, although there were no jumpsuits this time. Maybe it was just too early in the day. It wasn't even noon yet.

"There she is!" someone said, and a flashbulb blew up near her face. Delaney blinked and took a step back. Suddenly the room was full of flashing lights, with microphones and iPhones being waved in her face. And people calling her name. Her real name.

"Delaney! Over here! Tell us why you ran away!"

"Delaney, is it true you're caught up in a love triangle between a cameraman and a musician?"

"Delaney, how much money have you made from the sale of your video with Boyd Hampton?"

The flashes, and the shouting, and the arms reaching forward made her head spin. She was drowning in the sea of bad press. She tried to turn to go back outside but her way was blocked by a mangy-looking piece of paparazzi.

"Folks, folks, folks! Give a girl some room!" It was Finch's voice she heard, and then his hand was on her arm and he was pulling her from the crowd. Humphrey was there too, moving in to protect her, blocking people as they tried to follow her toward the elevator, past the Elvis '69 poster.

"Is that him?" someone called out. "Is that the musician? Or the cameraman?"

She was quaking, inside and out, as Finch punched at the elevator button. More questions were shouted out.

"Are you hoping for a spin-off show of your own?"

"Will there be any new videos?"

Finally the elevator doors slid open, and Finch rushed her inside as Humphrey blocked a reporter from forcing his way on.

"Aw, come on now. Don't be pushy." Humphrey's voice was as mellow as ever, and the doors closed with just the three of them inside: her, Finch, and Humphrey.

Finch brushed her hair back from her face. "You OK, sweetness?"

She looked at him. It sounded as if his voice came from deep underwater. There was rushing in her ears. She was hot and cold and prickly all over with nausea rolling through her. She felt the walls close in, and then everything went black.

Delaney came to with a cold washcloth pressed against her forehead and the smell of Sissy's overly sweet perfume stirring up another round of nausea. Delaney opened her eyes, and there they all were in a circle around her, Reggie, Humphrey, Finch, Sammy, Sissy, and Clark. She felt like Dorothy after returning from Oz, but Delaney wasn't in Kansas. She was in the Graceland Suite of the Heartbreak Hotel. She could tell by the lemon-yellow and navy-blue decor. This was a replica of Elvis's TV room.

"Here she comes," Finch said. He was next to her, holding the washcloth in place.

Delaney tried to sit up but he pressed a hand against her shoulder. "Hold on there, sweetness. Give yourself a minute. And give me a minute too because you damn near made me wet myself on that elevator. You scared the livin' bejesus out of me."

"What happened?" she asked faintly.

"The press swarmed you like a hive of angry bees and you fainted. How are you feeling now?"

"Oh, God. The press." She glanced up at Reggie. "They called me Delaney. How did they know I was here?" She closed her eyes as dizziness spun her again, and when she opened them, she realized the rest of them must know now too. They must despise her, although she saw nothing but concern on their faces.

Reggie shook his head, his dark eyes peering intently at her face. "I don't know, but obviously somebody told them."

"Did you come back alone? I didn't see Grant in the lobby," Humphrey added.

More nausea. That whole panic attack thing—she'd kind of been kidding about that before, but now she was damn certain this was what one felt like. Either that or she had food poisoning. And coronary artery disease. And tuberculosis. Or maybe it was just that her life had completely fallen apart in the space of a few hours.

She tried to breathe, deep and slow, and stared back at Reggie. If she kept her eyes in one place, maybe the room would hold still.

"Grant is back at his aunt's house," she said through the breathing. "He's really upset with me. He knows everything." Numbness was slowly replacing the panic, and that was preferable because otherwise she was going to start crying, and crying never did anybody any good. Plus if she was about to face the press, she didn't want her eyes to be all puffy and red. That was just the kind of thing a girl like Delaney Masterson had to worry about.

Finch flipped the damp washcloth over and put it on her forehead again so it felt nice and cool.

"Don't worry about Captain America," Reggie said. "He'll get over it."

She struggled up to a sitting position on the lemon-yellow sofa and let the washcloth fall. "I don't think so. He thinks I did all this as a publicity stunt, and the press being here is just going to convince him he's right. He'll think I called them myself. I need to get out of here."

She put her hand on Finch's shoulder to stabilize herself as she stood, and Clark reached over and took her elbow, steadying her. My God. When had she gotten so fragile? This was not who she was. Or . . . at least it wasn't who she intended to be.

"You want me to walk you back to your own room?" Humphrey asked.

"No, I don't just mean get out of this room. I mean out of this hotel. Out of Memphis."

"Oh, well now you're just talking silly talk, darlin'," Sissy said. "You sit back down and let me get you some soda pop. You're white as Clark's buns, and you still need to catch your breath."

Delaney wanted to argue, but she couldn't, because gravity had dragged her down and she found herself sitting on the lemon-yellow sofa again.

"I'll get you something to drink," Humphrey said, turning and walking into the mini version of Elvis's glass-and-mirror bar.

"Maybe you should just go have a nice little chat with those reporters, and tell them your story. And we'll all get our picture taken," Sissy said, patting her stiff helmet of hair.

Delaney shook her head. "No. No story. No pictures. Those reporters aren't looking for the truth, they're just looking for something they can twist into sensationalized headlines. You heard them, didn't you, Finch? A love triangle? Where the hell did that idea come from?"

Humphrey handed her a glass of something fizzy. "Here. Drink this."

Delaney gulped it down. Apparently fainting made her thirsty. Then she looked around at all of them. All the men had sat back down but Sissy was standing up. Even so, all of them were staring at her as if she was about to sprout moose antlers or turn into a pillar of salt.

"Listen," Delaney said. "I owe each one of you an apology. I'm sorry I lied about who I was. I was just trying to keep things simpler."

Clark pushed his hat back on his head. "Aw, shucks, don't you go give no nevermind about that. We understand. Sissy told me yesterday about all your troubles."

Sissy tapped him, none too gently, with the back of her hand against his shoulder.

"Yesterday?" Delaney looked up at the other woman. "You knew who I was yesterday?"

Sissy's already rouged cheeks deepened to a bright cherry red. "Well of course I knew. I'm not a simpleton. I knew who you was just as soon as we came back here and you tried on some of my shirts. You got that little hummingbird tattoo right there." Sissy tapped her own shoulder. "If I wasn't certain already, that pretty much gave it away."

The tattoo. Great. That meant Sissy had probably seen the video too. Not that any of that mattered at this point. What was done was done.

"Why didn't you tell me?" Delaney asked.

Sissy shrugged, making her enviable breasts jiggle. "I don't know. I guess I figured you was keeping it a secret for a reason, and if I went and blabbed, you'd just run away again. But . . ." she paused and her face rose to a whole new level of red.

"Aw, Sissy." Clark shook his head. "You didn't keep this a secret, did you."

It wasn't a question. It was a statement. Sissy started to cross her arms but that was physically impossible so she just harrumphed and her hands landed on her hips. "Well, I'm sorry, but it's not as if Reggie didn't know too. And her picture was on Facebook for goodness' sake. Maybe I'm not the reason the press found her here."

"Who'd you tell, baby?" Clark asked. "Please don't say your momma, 'cause we all know your momma couldn't keep a secret if the dear Lord Hisself had a hand over her mouth."

Sissy's gaze skittered around the room, not making eye contact with anyone.

"Aw, Sis," Reggie said. "Even I know your momma can't keep a secret. What were you thinking, telling her?"

Sissy started to visibly bristle as she stared down at Reggie. "I was thinking that I was sitting around eating catfish and ribs with *t-h-e-e* Delaney Masterson, and even though my momma has never been impressed by anything I've ever done in all my life, she might be impressed if I told her that the same Delaney Masterson was in my hotel room, and wearing one of my blouses. So there. That's what I was thinking."

Now all the men were frowning at Sissy and Delaney knew that wasn't fair. "Hey, it doesn't matter, you guys. It wasn't anyone's responsibility to keep my secret, and Sissy's right. I was on Facebook. I was playing piano. I've been around in the lobby. Anyone could have seen me and figured it out. Trust me. If the press wants to find you, they find you. So now it is time for me to face them, but on my own terms." Delaney stood up, feeling just slightly stronger than she had a moment ago. "I think it's time for me to go home. I've finally got my wallet and phone and computer. There's nothing keeping me in Memphis."

"What about the cameraman?" Finch asked.

Hot tears sprang to her eyes but she wouldn't let them fall. Not here in front of everyone. But it was a fair question. What about the cameraman? What was she going to do about Grant?

"I think I'm on my own, Finch. He told me he was going back to Michigan with his mother. And since I'm heading to Beverly Hills, well, I guess that's that."

She didn't believe that, though. Not for a second. Her heart wouldn't let her. Grant might have said he didn't care, but she knew he did, and he'd come back. He'd come back to the hotel so they could talk this through and she could make this right. Everything would be fine just as soon as he'd calmed down.

———•———

Delaney Masterson may have underestimated how long it would take for Grant Connelly to calm down. She'd heard nothing from him by late afternoon, and the longer she waited, the more awful she felt. Like *ten-fatal-illnesses-all-at-once* kind of awful. This was dread on top of regret on top of heartache, and it sucked.

When a knock sounded on the door around dinnertime, she let herself hope—but it was only Reggie.

"You look disappointed, honeybun. I'll try not to take that personally. I brought you some spaghetti from the Jungle Room Lounge. I figured you'd be hungry by now, yeah?"

He stepped inside carrying a beige plastic tray with a covered plate on it, along with two beers.

"Thanks." She wasn't hungry, though. Her stomach had more knots in it than a baby hat knit with drumsticks, but she pointed to the table anyway, indicating he could set the tray there. She hoped both the beers were for her. Not because she didn't want Reggie to stick around, but because she needed *at least* two of those right now.

"Any word from your cowboy?" Reggie asked, twisting off the top of one and handing her a bottle.

"No. I left him three messages but he hasn't called back. I don't think he's going to."

Saying it out loud made her heart feel like the iceberg that took down the *Titanic*, sharp, frozen, and accidentally destructive. She hadn't meant for it to happen, but her actions caused disaster.

She and Reggie sat down on the white vinyl sofa, and she pulled her legs up under her. "I even texted him saying I needed to book a flight home and wanted to talk to him before I left Memphis, but . . . nothing."

"Did you book a flight?" Reggie took a sip of the other beer.

Delaney nodded. "Yes. I leave tomorrow at noon. I talked to my sister about an hour ago and told her I'd be home. She said the producers are anxious as hell to tape a special edition of *Pop Rocks* just to address all this crap as soon as I get home. Like a press conference. Getting the police involved in my search has taken this to a whole different level." Her eyes puddled up, again.

She thought she'd cried out every bit of moisture in her body when she talked to Melody, but apparently she still had a little juice left. Out came the tears, twin streams of frustration rolling right down her cheeks, but she swiped them away. Delaney Masterson might be a runner and a hider, but darn it all, she was not a crier. She swiped those stupid, helpless tears away.

"Everything I've done has completely backfired, Reg, and now I'm getting more media attention than ever. I'm beginning to think the purpose of my life is to serve as a cautionary tale to others."

Reggie chuckled and patted her leg in the most brotherly way. "Aw, sugar, don't cry. Maybe you just need to figure out how to put a positive spin on things." He grabbed a tissue from the box sitting on the coffee table and handed it to her.

She snuffled into it. "A positive spin? Haven't you been paying attention? I'm involved in a sex scandal, the police believe I faked my own disappearance, and the man I love thinks I'm a liar and a fake."

His dark eyes widened as he looked over at her. "*Man you love?* You've come a long way since yesterday, yeah? I thought he was just the landlord."

Delaney threw the damp tissue on the table. "We had a *really* good night last night."

Reggie chuckled harder. "I should say so. Look, the bigger they are, the harder they fall, and your man is the type to fall hard. He'll come around. Like I told you, he's got that same sappy love-look in his eyes just like you."

She sighed. "You didn't see him when he stormed in here and threw this magazine at my feet." She pointed to where it now sat on the coffee table.

Reggie leaned over and picked it up. It made her sick to look at, but she'd read it anyway, just so she'd know what kind of lies Grant had been exposed to. A new knot twisted in her gut. "The article was pretty awful. All those *sources close to* quotes basically mean the reporters make up whatever they want. They accused me of everything shy of being pregnant with an alien baby." She took a big gulp of beer. "And apparently there is some suggestion of a love triangle. Does anyone know you're here? You could end up in the papers."

He tossed the magazine back on the table. "I would love to be your fictional other man. You know what they say. No press is bad press."

She set her bottle down next to her glossy picture. "I would argue that the person who said that wasn't trying to outrun a sex scandal."

Reggie cocked his head. "Maybe not, but it seems to me that running from this is like trying to outrun a bear."

"How so?"

His shoulders rose and fell. "It can't be done, so your safest bet is to just stand still."

"Stand still? How does that help me?"

"If you stand still, a bear will only eat you if he's hungry."

Something must be lost in translation here. His hillbilly advice was not going to help this California girl. "Great, except reporters aren't bears. They're more like . . . piranhas or sharks, or . . . oh, I don't know. Whatever kind of animal shreds you to pieces just for the fun of it."

"OK, sharks then. You know how to outswim a shark?"

"No."

"That's because you can't, but you can punch them in the nose. You can go on the offensive and startle them. Maybe that's what you need to do in this situation."

"Go on the offensive?" Apparently the animal kingdom analogies had morphed into sports talk.

"Yeah. Now, Lord knows, darlin', I've never been accused of overthinking a situation, but I do know that facing stuff head-on is better than running. Stand your ground." He put his feet up on the coffee table and crossed his legs at the ankles. "I know this is none of my business, but if you were my girl and some guy released a video like that jackass did, I'd go after him every which way. Sue him, have him arrested, sic some Rottweilers on his ass, or something. Seems like this was all his doing."

Delaney's cheeks heated up. "I did some doing."

"Did you have the expectation of privacy?" His expression was serious.

"What?" Her expression was surely one of surprise.

Reggie chuckled and took a sip of beer. "OK, so we watch a lot of *Law & Order* on the tour bus, but I'm not fooling. Check with your lawyer 'cause that guy did a terrible thing and he certainly broke the law. I mean, you know I love me the honeys, and I've had some wild times on that bus, but I would never, ever record a woman without her consent. A real man would never do that. I see you running from this situation, but he's the one who should be ashamed, don't you think?"

She'd never really thought about it that way before. She was so busy feeling victimized, but Boyd *was* the one who should be ashamed. Boyd had violated her trust. He'd exploited their relationship for fame and financial gain without caring how she'd be humiliated. It really was reprehensible.

Reggie took another sip of beer. "You know what else? I think maybe you should tell people about the baby hats."

"The baby hats? Why?"

"Yeah, the baby hats. You're worried over what folks think of you, and you've got everybody's attention right now, so take this chance to tell them about all the nice stuff you do, like making hats for all those poor little bald kids. If you offer up some happy shit, maybe those reporters will stop looking for the nasty stuff. I'm telling you, honeybun, this is all about how you spin it from here on out. You're a celebrity and you can't do much about that, but people love a comeback story. So tell them how you ran away to find yourself, or some new-wave thing like that. You're from California. They'll buy that. Tell everybody how you've grown from this hardship or whatever. Shucks, tell them anything you want to, but take charge of it. Be the sheepdog and not the sheep."

"So we're back to animal examples again? What if no one believes me?"

He scowled at the ceiling then looked back at her. "If they don't believe you, then fuck 'em. Look, sugar, you can't control what people think or what they do. You can only control how you react to it. Bottom line is you need to decide who it is you're living this life for. You or them?"

Delaney reached over and picked up her beer, taking another gulp.

"That's kind of smart, Reg. You might be on to something."

His chest puffed up as he moved his feet and sat forward on the sofa. "My vast wisdom is a well-kept secret. But listen, I hate to leave you all by your lonesome, but me and the boys agreed to play here for two more nights. You want to come down to the lounge?"

Was it that late already? Evening now and still no word from Grant. "No, I think I'll keep a low profile tonight. I'll just hang around here and eat my spaghetti. Alone."

"Maybe your fella will still show up," he said.

"I don't think so. I don't think he's coming back."

He reached over and squeezed her shoulder. "I'm sorry, sugar. I'd hit on you if I thought it would make you feel better."

It took all her strength to smile at that. "Thanks, Reg. I appreciate it. I'll pass, but do you think you could go with me to the airport tomorrow? I need to leave around nine thirty in the morning, and honestly, I'm not quite ready to take on any scene at the airport. I'll be OK by the time I get to Los Angeles, though. Home-field advantage and all."

He stood up. "Absolutely. It would be my pleasure. Speaking of pleasure, you sure you don't want me to come back later tonight and tuck you in? You might need some comforting." He cocked an eyebrow suggestively but she could tell he was teasing. He still looked mostly sympathetic, and the knowledge that even Reggie was realizing Grant was history made her feel worse than before.

She did need comforting, but she needed it from Grant. She needed him to call, and to come back to the hotel. She needed him to kiss away these tears and tell her he understood. She needed him to say he forgave her and he loved her.

She needed all that, but she wasn't going to get any of it.

All she was going to get tonight was a plate of cold spaghetti.

Chapter 24

GRANT, PLEASE CALL ME. I HAVE TO FLY TO LA TOMORROW MORNING BUT I REALLY, REALLY NEED TO TALK TO YOU. I'LL BE AT THE HOTEL UNTIL 9AM. I'M SO SORRY.

The woman formerly known as Elaine Masters had sent him that text last night, but he'd turned off his phone and didn't see it until this morning. He'd deleted her three phone messages without listening to them too. In fact, he'd turned off his phone specifically to avoid her, knowing that the temptation to call back would be too great. And if he'd called her back, they would have talked in circles for a while, with her apologizing and trying to explain why she'd lied, and him feeling no better than he did right now. All things considered, her sorrow was irrelevant. It didn't change the fact that he'd offered up his heart to a mirage. A woman made of smoke and mirrors. And that made him feel like a fool.

It must have been the novelty of her that had made him act so recklessly. The novelty of all of it, having a woman in his house, the sweet-smelling soap and the lacy panties in his laundry. He'd have to be a zombie to not fall prey to her allure, and he'd gotten to play the heroic knight to her damsel in distress. It was fun. Exhilarating, even, but he'd let himself get caught up in the hype.

The frenzy. He of all people should have realized that the things that *seem* real, often are not.

He'd thought he was wiser than that, but he was an idiot. A love-sick idiot. And his brother was an idiot too, with all his *when-you-know-you-just-know* crap. Nobody knew when love was real. If it was ever real. Hadn't his own mother shown him that with her collection of husbands?

His mother. There was another whole set of issues. If this was what Tyler had put up with during all those years Grant was off traveling, well, he owed his brother a case of scotch. Now Grant was sitting in Tina's kitchen drinking coffee as dark and bitter as his mood. No amount of sugar could sweeten it. Donna sat across the table from him, and Tina was there too. They'd eaten breakfast and now his mother was toying with her red-and-white coffee cup and staring off into space.

"You need to come back home with me, Mom," he said finally, setting down his own coffee cup.

Donna looked over at him and nodded. "I know. I'm ready. I spoke with Carl last night after you went to bed and he's happy to hear I'll be home soon." She paused and looked into her cup. "I didn't mean I was going to *leave him*, leave him. I only wanted to leave him for a little while."

"Maybe you should be more careful how you word your notes then."

Her shrug was noncommittal, as shrugs are apt to be. "Maybe."

His head already ached from a sleepless night and far too many thoughts of . . . Lane. His brain had taken to calling her that. Lane. Because Delaney was just too foreign, and Elaine . . . well, Elaine wasn't her name.

The pressure in his head expanded until at last he said to his mother, "And we have to talk about this stealing business."

Donna's eyes welled up with tears. "I know. I was doing so well but the wedding just threw me, and then you coming home, and all the relatives and chaos. And then Tina and I were coming here, and I saw that brown leather bag full of money and just, well, like I told you, it went so nicely with my coat."

He wanted to be angry. He was on the verge of that, but it wouldn't help matters any to scold her. As calmly as he could manage, he said, "You do *get* that it's not OK to take stuff, right? You do understand that there is never a valid reason for stealing?"

Her chin tilted defiantly. "Haven't you ever seen *Les Mis*? They stole bread because they were starving. Would you have them starve?"

He looked at Tina for help.

"Donna," she said in a far more patient tone than the one he used. "Stealing food because you are starving is quite a bit different than taking someone's money just because you come across it. You know that."

His mother pulled a wadded tissue from the sleeve of her green sweatshirt and dabbed at her nose. She really was quite a sad little thing at the moment, and Grant felt the first tremors of pity ripple over him. He'd been gone for so long, dismissing her problem as just a fondness for gambling and a splash of kleptomania, but deep down, he'd known it was more than that. It's partly why he'd stayed away, and because of that, he'd been no help to her at all. No help to the family either. He'd been too busy off having his adventures, living his life. Leaving things to Tyler to handle. Maybe if Grant had kept in better contact, visited more often, she'd be in better shape now. Yes, her problem was *her* problem, but that didn't mean he shouldn't step up now and help in whatever ways he could.

"I'm sorry about this, Mom," he heard himself say.

"You're sorry?" she asked.

"I'm sorry if my disconnecting from the family made things harder for you. I should have checked in more after Dad died. I blamed a lot of things on Hank, but I don't really have an excuse for not coming back once he was gone."

Her lips trembled. "I know it was hard for you, that whole situation. I made a mistake marrying Hank. I did the wrong thing, but I thought it was the right thing. I thought he'd take care of us but he didn't."

Tina reached over and patted his mother's arm. "You were doing your best, Donna."

Donna nodded but looked at Grant. "I know it must seem like I got remarried because I'd forgotten about your father, but the truth is, I just didn't know how to be without him. I loved him so much and missed him so much, I just didn't know what to do with myself. I was so brokenhearted. I still am. Carl's a good man, but he doesn't compare to your dad."

She blinked back a tear and a wave of compassion flooded his senses. He'd been angry at her for so long for betraying his father's memory, but the heartbreak part of it he finally understood. If she'd felt about his father the way Grant felt about Lane, then it all made more sense—because the idea of facing the future without her was a devastating notion.

He nodded his head. "Mom, I know I've missed a lot of opportunities to be a part of this family, but when we get back home, I'll try to make up for that. I mean, I'll still have to travel. I have to work, but I promise I'll get home more often. And Tyler said you were working with a counselor about some of this stuff, right? Maybe we should dial that up a notch, huh? How about I give her a call and fill her in on what's been going on?"

His mother nodded. "I think that's a good idea."

"Good. In the meantime, how about if I book us some plane tickets to get us back home tomorrow or the next day? I'm not sure I can handle that drive again and neither one of us actually has a car."

Donna looked at Tina. "I was hoping our visit could be a little longer, but all things considered, maybe it's time I went home."

Tina nodded and her relief was evident. "All things considered, I think you should."

The Jungle Room Lounge was quiet that afternoon when Grant walked in, but Finch and Humphrey were sitting at the bar. He wasn't sure what to say, wasn't sure if he was still angry or sad or just heartbroken over this whole mess. He wasn't even sure why he was there since he knew Lane was gone.

He sat down on the stool next to Finch.

"What's up, Cameraman?" Finch was disappointed in him. It was obvious in his tone.

"Not much." Grant signaled to the waitress and asked for a beer. "How many more nights are you guys playing here?" he asked as she filled up a mug from the tap.

"Tonight's the last night. We head back to Nashville tomorrow. You know Delaney is gone, right?"

His heart flinched a little. He nodded and was glad the waitress was fast with that beer. As soon as she set it down, he picked it up. "Yeah. She sent me a text. Said she was on her way to LA. Good for her."

"You don't really think she leaked that video herself, do you?" Humphrey asked him, eyebrows pinched together and his usual grin noticeably absent. These guys were pissed at him. She was the one who'd lied. How did he get to be the bad guy?

"I don't know what I think. She sure wouldn't be the first woman I'd known who worked an angle. My last girlfriend dumped me for Blake Rockstone because he promised to make her a TV star."

Even as he said it, the words felt hollow. Calling Miranda his girlfriend sounded ridiculous after what he'd shared with Lane. There was no similarity to the intensity of those feelings. It was like comparing a flashlight to the sun.

Finch shook his head slowly and stared down into his beer. "She didn't call those reporters, Grant. That woman didn't want anything to do with that."

"For sure," Humphrey said, his tone clipped. "Thank goodness Finch and I were there to pull her out of the crowd before things got worse."

Grant choked a little on his drink. "Pulled her out of—what are you talking about?"

Finch and Humphrey exchanged glances, then Finch turned to Grant.

"I guess you wouldn't know, would you, since you sent her back to the hotel alone. Sweetness got back here yesterday and the lobby was swarming with reporters. They pretty much mobbed her, but Humph and I happened to be in the right place at the right time and whisked her away," Finch said.

"Actually," Humphrey added, "we were sitting right here drinking a beverage just like we are now."

Finch nodded. "Yes, sir, and we heard the ruckus and went out to see what the fuss was all about and there she was, in the center of it all, white as chalk."

"Those reporters were aggressive too. Shouting rude questions. It's no wonder she passed out," Humphrey said.

Grant's glass hit the bar harder than he'd intended. "She what?"

"Passed out," Finch said. "Fainted dead away. Scared the crap out of me. Little bitty thing but, damn, she's heavy when she's out cold. Can I get a whiskey?" he asked the waitress, as if the memory required a little self-medicating.

Grant drank down his entire beer and signaled for another. She'd fainted? Because of reporters? That didn't seem like a woman seeking attention and publicity. He felt a plunging sense of remorse just then, and a fervent desire to retrieve those phone messages he'd deleted without listening to.

"Then what happened?" he asked.

"We all went up to the suite and Humphrey got her a soda pop," Finch said.

Humphrey nodded sagely, listening. Concurring.

Grant's head spun from this news, and probably from chugging that beer.

Lane had fainted, and he wasn't there. What if Finch and Humphrey hadn't been there either? What if something worse had happened? His mind spiraled through a list of possibilities, but he tried to shake it off, that sense of obligation. She wasn't his problem, but he felt it anyway, that need to watch out for her.

It might take a while for that sensation to wear off, but it needed to, because he wouldn't be there for the rest of it either. It's not as if her trials with the media were over. She was going back to Los Angeles where things would only get worse.

"When did her plane leave?" he asked, his throat feeling parched in spite of the drink he'd swilled down.

The waitress set down a shot glass in front of Finch and he twirled it slowly in front of him. "Not sure what time. They snuck out the back way this morning because a few pesky reporters had camped out in front."

"They?"

"Yeah, Reggie took her to the airport this morning. We expect him back anytime now," Humphrey answered.

Finch's eyes narrowed as he looked over at Grant. "Now, don't be getting that jealous face going, sweetness. In spite of how he acts, Reggie is not after your girl."

Apparently it would take a while for that sensation to wear off too. He had no claim to her or anything she did. She was, for all intents and purposes, a stranger.

"She's not my girl," he said quietly. "I don't know who she is. I'm not even sure what we had going."

Humphrey hung his head low. "Looked damn fine to me, whatever it was."

Grant shook his head, as if he was trying to deny it as much to himself as to them—because he was. "I didn't even know her name. I thought she was a soap maker from Miami."

"A soap maker?" Finch finally chuckled.

"Yeah. I guess if I couldn't see through that story, well, maybe I deserved what I got."

Finch nudged the shot glass of whiskey toward Grant with his fingertips. "Here, Cameraman. I think you need this more than I do."

Chapter 25

LANDING AT LAX WAS LIKE reentering the earth's atmosphere. For one thing, it was warm, and Delaney Masterson hadn't been truly warm since she'd driven that yellow Volkswagen past the California state line heading toward Michigan. She shoved up the sleeves of the bubblegum-pink sweater Sissy had given her and wished again that she'd had some time at the Memphis airport this morning to buy something a little less vibrant to wear. It was hard to sneak through a crowd in neon-highlighter pink. Sissy had given her some jeans to wear too. They were too tight and too short, but Delaney's other jeans were in desperate need of washing. She couldn't stand to wear them one more day.

She made her way through the airport terminal hallway, head down, Louis Vuitton backpack over her shoulder, University of Memphis baseball hat pulled low, wearing a pair of oversized sunglasses that she'd picked up from the Heartbreak Hotel gift shop before leaving.

Her good-byes at the hotel with Clark, Sissy, Sammy, Humphrey, and Finch had left her a little sad, as if she were leaving family behind to take a long voyage to another country. They'd each done the *oh, we should keep in touch* thing, and she sincerely hoped they would. They'd become her friends over the last few days and shared an experience that no one else would quite understand.

Reggie had even been a little teary eyed as he'd wished her well before sending her through the security line at the Memphis airport. Or he might have just been hungover. Hard to tell.

"Good luck, honeybun," he'd whispered in her ear as he gave her a fast hug. "You ever need anything, you know who to call, right? Finch. Call Finch. Don't call me." Then he'd laughed and hugged her again.

"Thank you, Reggie. For everything. And don't forget. Come out to California someday and I'll introduce you to my dad. You two can jam. I promise."

"It's a date." He'd smiled, then turned and walked away before she could say anything else. Of all the Paradise Brothers, she'd miss Reggie most of all.

But nothing compared to how much she missed Grant. That was a gaping hole right through her chest. She could practically feel the wind passing through it, but she didn't have time for that distress right now. One thing at a time, and right now her focus had to be on getting back to her family and figuring out the rest of her life.

She'd spent her airplane ride planning and pondering and plotting her next steps. Whatever came next, she wanted to be in charge of it. No more letting herself be buffeted about by other peoples' actions. Being without her phone and wallet and money had made her feel vulnerable, but it had clarified things for her too. The whole experience had given her a chance to realize just how little she actually needed.

At the end of the LAX terminal a cluster of people stood waiting for disembarking passengers. Delaney was nearly face-to-face with her sister before Melody gasped.

"Lane? Oh my God. Is that you?"

"Incognito," Delaney said and kept on walking. There were always photographers at LAX, and she hoped to get to the car before they spotted her.

But Melody turned and trotted along beside her, and Delaney only made it two more steps before her emotions got the best of her and she pulled her sister in for a big, full hug.

Home. She was home. It wasn't perfect here, and she wasn't perfect either, and the next couple of weeks might be ass-sucking awful, but at least she was home. "I'm never running away from home again," she said breathlessly.

"Good." Melody was emphatic, her arms tight. "You scared the crap out of everyone. Roxanne read some article that said you'd joined a hillbilly cult or something."

Delaney loosened her grasp and they started walking toward the exit again. "Hillbilly cult? What would make her say that?"

"I don't know. Just something she saw online. Who are the Paradise Brothers?"

Delaney chuckled. "Just some friends." Apparently friends who had scored a little notoriety from this. Reggie would be pleased.

They kept walking, past baggage claim and ticket counters.

"What are you wearing?" Melody asked as they reached the doors and headed out into the California sunshine. "Is that . . . is that polyester?"

Delaney glanced down. "Um, I don't know. Probably."

"It looks flammable. It's an awful color. Are those . . . oh my God. Are those Wranglers?" She may as well have been saying *oh my God, do you have cancer?*

Delaney stopped and faced her sister. "Do you have any idea what I've been through in the last several days, Mel? Do you realize how insignificant what I'm wearing is given the circumstances?"

Melody patted her shoulder. "No, I don't have any idea what you've been through because you've refused to tell me anything. But you sound like you've been brainwashed, and if that's led to you wearing this, then it must have been harrowing."

———

"Lane, oh my darling," her mother cried just as soon as Delaney was in the front door of their Beverly Hills home. She pulled her in for a tight hug, her jewelry jingling over a spandex workout top. "Thank God, you're finally home. We've been worried sick."

"I know, Mom. I'm sorry. My phone got stolen and then there was the car accident. It was all crazy."

Her sister Roxanne joined in on the hug. "Hey, welcome home. We missed you."

"Lane, is that you?" Her tall, lanky dad came into the room wearing something from the Steven Tyler collection, and she moved from her mother's hug into his. His hair was back in a ponytail that every single one of them wanted him to cut off. "Hi, Daddy."

He kissed the top of her head. "Well, we are sure glad to have you home. I was about ready to call out the National Guard. What the hell have you been up to?"

"Just trying to take a little break from reality. Turns out reality follows you."

"Well, come and sit down and tell us everything." Her dad pulled her over to the sofa but the others moved with them en masse, as if no one wanted to let her out of their sight, and it warmed Delaney through. The press might be out there ready to pounce, but her family loved her, and that's what mattered most.

She filled them in on most of the details, wanting to be as honest as possible. If she'd learned anything from this experience, it was that dishonesty just wasn't worth the trouble it caused, and it ate away at your soul, leaving a big black stain. But one thing she wasn't completely forthright about was how much she missed Grant. It wasn't so much a secret, but it was *private*. Another thing Delaney had figured out during her soul-searching plane ride was that she had a right to that. Privacy. Just because she shared parts of her life, she didn't have to share all of it.

She held it together pretty well with her family, and she was feeling a little proud of herself for that. No pity. No whining. She owned up to her part in everything that had happened, and she was determined to face what came next. But when she was getting ready for bed that night and pulled out the *I love Elvis* shirt Grant had given her to sleep in, she gave in to all her sadness. She'd earned that too, this right to feel devastated. Whatever they'd had, it had been beautiful and special and she wanted it back. She wanted him back. True love wasn't about the amount of time you spent with someone, it was about the quality of the time. She just needed for him to figure that out too.

———◆———

"Good morning, Lane. Sure is nice seeing you sitting there again," her dad said the next morning as he poured a cup of coffee. She was at the kitchen table sorting through a few weeks' worth of junk mail that had arrived in her absence. She'd have to remember if she ever ran away again to forward her mail. It was going to take her hours just to deal with all of this.

He came and sat down. It was just the two of them. They were the early risers and she'd always loved that they had this little pocket of time together before the rest of the family was buzzing around. It was also before the cameras showed up.

"Are they going to be filming today?" she asked.

He nodded. "That was the plan. You know they actually want to do some extra interview time with you too. Are you ready for that?"

No, she'd never be ready for that. "Sure. I'll do my best."

He sighed, and for just that moment, he looked his age. He looked almost paternal. Almost. "You don't have to, you know."

"I don't have to do my best?" she teased.

He smiled the famous Jesse Masterson smile. The one that had made all women of a certain age melt and remember their high school days, but to Delaney, it was just her dad's smile.

"You should always try to do your best, sweetheart, but what I mean is, you don't have to do this interview. You don't even have to do the show if you don't want to. Honestly, I feel just awful that the stress of all these cameras made you drive off into Timfucktu, Michigan." He took a slug of coffee and set the cup down hard.

"Dad, it wasn't so much these cameras as it was Boyd's camera. That's what sent me over the edge." Few things in life could be more humiliating than talking to your father about your sex video, even if your dad was a longtime rock 'n' roller with a checkered history of his own. But he still had that paternal face going, and for the moment she felt very much like his little girl.

"You just say the word and the lawyers will go after him. Tony says the case is strong, especially if they can prove Boyd benefited financially."

"Word." She smiled.

"What?"

"I'm saying the word. Let's tell Tony to go for it. I'm not much for revenge, but Boyd broke the law and that's not OK. Yes, I was a consenting adult, but I never consented to being videotaped, so I have to think about what kind of message it sends if I don't defend myself."

Her dad nodded, contemplating her words, his hands wrapped around his mug of coffee. "That's true. I guess you do."

"You know, I spent the last few weeks being terribly embarrassed about this, and honestly, I still am, but the worst thing I could do was to hide. I don't want people thinking I'm a coward, but even more than that, I don't want people thinking I had any part of this. I have to speak out and remind everyone that Boyd is the one who did something wrong."

Her dad stroked his chin with his thumb and index finger as if he was letting this soak in. "That's pretty courageous of you, Lane, and you know the family is behind you one hundred percent."

"I know you are. I appreciate that. I'm sorry I ran away and freaked everybody out."

"Well, you did what you had to do, I guess."

"I could have handled it much better, though, and there's something else you should know."

"What's that?"

"I'll keep doing the *Pop Rocks* show because I want to honor my contract, but we have to tell the producers no more footage of me looking ditzy. That's not who I am, and it's not the persona I want people to see. I do nice things, and I do worthwhile things, so I want viewers to know that and not just think I spend all my time getting my nails done and gossiping about other celebrities."

He leaned back in his chair, tilting it on two legs. "Delaney Louise Masterson, you're like a whole different person this morning."

Delaney smiled because that felt like a compliment. "I've tried being a different person, and it turns out I liked it, only it wasn't so much about being different as it was about being authentic. I think I got so caught up in creating a show *about* my life, I forgot about actually *living* a life. Remember how you and I used to volunteer at that music studio? I want to do that again. We had fun, but better than that, it was a really valuable thing that we did for those kids. We made a difference in their lives just by sharing time with them and teaching them a little music. I want to do more stuff like that, things with some substance, stuff that actually adds value to humanity. Honestly, I don't think the world really needs another celebrity stylist, plus I'm not really cut out for it."

Her dad's eyes widened as she spoke, the coffee cup hovering forgotten near his lips.

"What the hell happened to you out there in the real world?"

"I'm not sure."

He brought the chair down to four legs again. "Well, whatever it is, I like it. I'm proud of you."

"Proud of me for running away?"

"Proud of you for taking the time you needed and then coming home stronger. It takes a lot of guts to face this music but it sure sounds like you're taking charge of things now."

"Maybe. A friend recently told me it's better to be the sheep-dog than the sheep."

Chapter 26

GRANT CONNELLY STOOD IN LINE at Gibson's grocery store the day after returning to Bell Harbor and realized something he'd never even considered before. It's entirely surreal to see your face on the cover of a magazine. But there he was, right on the front of some glossy celebrity gossip sheet.

It was a picture of him and Lane, all snuggled up on the piano bench in the Jungle Room Lounge. How the hell had a picture like that found its way into the news? He pulled the magazine from the rack, left his cart off to the side, and wandered dazedly over to the little coffee shop inside the grocery store. Sitting down at a table, he opened the pages to find half a dozen pictures of the two of them, all lousy quality photographs, obviously taken by an amateur opportunist with a cell phone, but just as obviously them.

The headline of the corresponding article read MISSING IN ACTION?

While we're very glad to report that *Pop Rocks* star Delaney Masterson is no longer missing, it's clear she's still getting some action. Hiding out at the Heartbreak Hotel in Memphis, Tennessee, recently with cinematographer boyfriend Grant Connelly, the 27-year-old celebrity stylist looks anything but heartbroken. Sources close to the pair say the canoodling was impossible to miss.

"They were kissing and laughing and totally into each other," reported the confidential source.

Connelly, 31, a coproducer and director of photography for the popular action-adventure show *One Man, One Planet* was recently fired, but lucky for him, if he's looking for a "job," he's found the right girl. Although sources report she seems to be splitting her time between Connelly and Paradise Brothers front man Reggie Bryce, 29. It was Bryce who escorted Masterson to the Memphis airport days later, leaving us to wonder who she might be flying mile-high with next.

What a steaming pile of horseshit.

No wonder Delaney tried to hide away from this kind of crap. For one thing, he hadn't been fired, but that lie wasn't even worth being upset about compared to the slanderous innuendos made about Lane jumping from man to man. It just wasn't true.

He knew that now. A little distance from the situation had helped Grant understand that the honky-tonk huckster had never been an issue. Not because Reggie was such a stand-up guy, but because Grant knew Lane.

The feeling knocked him forward.

He knew Lane.

That idea had clung to him ever since leaving Memphis yesterday, but seeing this article drove the point home. He did know her. Whatever she called herself, he'd seen everything that was real about her. Everything that mattered. It still hurt that she'd lied, and it was humiliating too, but having had some time to think about things, he wondered if maybe he'd been unfair. She wasn't Miranda, and after hearing Finch and Humphrey talk about her reaction to the paparazzi, he knew fame hadn't been her goal after all. The magazines had lied.

The truth was, maybe some of the details about her life weren't as important as he'd originally thought, or as nearly important as how he'd *felt*. He'd followed his instincts with her, and it had all felt right. It was just too bad he couldn't decide what his instincts were telling him now.

He looked down at the photos again. There was one of them facing each other, smiling and leaning close. His hand was on her leg. Her hand was curled around the side of his neck, as if she was pulling him close to whisper some naughty secret. He remembered that moment. He couldn't think of what she'd said just then, but he remembered the feel of her lips as she'd pressed a kiss just below his ear seconds later.

Whump went his heart, as if the thing was trying to get his brain's attention. This was how she made him feel. Breathless. Dizzy. Overheated. He missed her. More than he'd ever imagined it was possible to miss a woman. More than he'd ever known it was possible to *love* a woman. He did love her, still, whether her name was Elaine or Delaney or Mary or Sue. He just wasn't sure if it was real.

He'd wanted to call her a hundred times since she'd ridden away in the taxi after leaving his aunt's house, but pride was a buzzkill stopping him each time. Then he'd been busy making travel arrangements and getting his mother home. They'd arrived back in Bell Harbor late last night, and Carl, God love him, had welcomed her back with open arms and a sloe gin fizz, so at least that had gone well.

Now Grant was on his way to Tyler's house to have dinner with him and Evie. He'd only stopped at the grocery store to pick up a bottle of wine, so he couldn't call Lane now. It wouldn't be a fast conversation, and he wasn't even sure what he'd say. Until he had things figured out . . . well, he just couldn't call her right now.

He pulled up at his brother's house fifteen minutes later with two bottles of wine and one tabloid magazine—because he needed some advice. Tyler seemed to have a much better handle on this whole relationship thing than he did. Maybe his brother could tell him what the hell to do.

"Just call her, you jackass. If she doesn't hang up on you, then keep talking."

That had been his brother's not-so-helpful advice.

"That's it?" Grant said as he uncorked the first bottle of wine. "You just got back from your honeymoon and that's the best, most romantic advice you can offer? What the hell am I supposed to say to her? Hi, total stranger. I'm still really angry that you lied to me about everything, but I can't stop thinking about you."

"No," Evie said, walking into the kitchen where the brothers were discussing Grant's current predicament. "Skip the part about being angry. She already knows you're angry, but definitely tell her you can't stop thinking about her. Women love hearing that."

She ran a hand along Tyler's waist as she walked by. They'd been doing that all night, that seemingly unconscious touching. It was like sharing a meal with static cling.

It was also more than a little awkward discussing this topic in front of his new sister-in-law. They hardly knew each other, but if Evie could shed some light on what he should do, he'd listen. Tyler was proving to be much less useful than he'd hoped.

Grant turned to Evie instead. "So, I tell her I'm thinking about her, and then what?"

"Tell her why."

"Why . . . what?"

Evie's smile was patient. "Why you can't stop thinking about her."

"Oh, but I'm not . . . I'm not sure why I can't stop thinking about her." He felt like someone had asked him to do a very complicated story problem in math class. It was making him sweat.

"OK, then, what things are you thinking about? What are you remembering?"

Vision upon erotic vision crashed into his brain all at once, each one involving Lane, and each one sending heat to his face. The X rating must have been obvious.

His brother started laughing.

Evie blushed. "Oh. Well, tell her that then."

"Listen," Tyler said a moment later, "I don't know what you should say, or honestly even what you should do, but it seems pretty obvious you have feelings for this woman and the only foolish thing would be to not give it another chance. Sometimes life gives you a do-over, so make the most of it. Call her. And don't be a douche bag."

———

MY SISTER WOULD KILL ME IF SHE KNEW I WAS SENDING U A TEXT, BUT U SHOULD WATCH TONIGHT'S SPECIAL EPISODE OF POP ROCKS. STARTS IN 15. JUST SAYIN. MELODY MASTERSON

Dinner was over and the second bottle of wine was almost finished when that text showed up on Grant's phone. He stared at it for a full minute, wondering if he'd had too much to drink and read it wrong. Maybe his brain was imagining things.

"Bad news?" Tyler finally asked.

"I'm not sure. It's from Lane's sister."

Evie's eyes lit up. She'd had on lots of makeup at the wedding, but tonight without any she looked more sweet than elegant. She was still completely out of his brother's league, but after spending this evening together, talking and laughing and getting better acquainted, he could see she and Tyler really were ideal for each other. It made Grant happy for them, but reminded him of just what he was missing.

"A text? What's it say?" she asked.

"It says I should watch *Pop Rocks* tonight, in fifteen minutes." He couldn't decide how he felt about that. His instinct wires were crossing again. Falling in love had made him a second-guesser.

Evie sat forward. "Really? Want to watch it here?" It was obvious she was now fully invested in the outcome of this relationship.

"I don't know if I want to watch it at all." But he knew he would. Even if it was like watching a car crash, he knew he wouldn't be able to look away, and he'd have to watch it here because he still had yet to hook up any sort of television at his house.

Tyler stood up. "We might need more wine."

Fifteen minutes passed in a blink and Grant realized he should've gone home just as soon as the opening credits began. Sitting here watching *his Elaine* traipse about in some palatial Beverly Hills home was going to make his head explode. Would her hair be blonde again? Would she even sound the same? Did she know the picture of the two of them together at the Heartbreak Hotel had been splashed all over a tabloid magazine? Was she hurt, mad, vengeful, relieved? Inquiring minds wanted to know.

Then there she was, on the screen. Her hair was still dark but straighter. He liked the waves better but this wasn't too drastic. She had on a plain white blouse and jeans, and was sitting cross-legged in a flowered armchair in an average-looking living room. And she was barefoot. For some reason that melted his defenses just a little bit more. Maybe some part of him had worried she'd be that Delaney from the first magazine, with the slinky dress or the tight miniskirt. Not that she hadn't looked smokin' in those outfits, but barefoot in jeans, that was Elaine. That was the one he'd fallen for.

A bleached-blonde interviewer sat across from Delaney in another chair. She made some inane introductions, explaining that this was a special segment leading into tonight's regular episode.

Tyler and Evie fell silent as the show progressed, or maybe they'd gotten up and left the room, or maybe they were having wild monkey sex right behind the couch. He really had no idea, because his eyes, ears, and heart were focused on the screen as all his senses tried to communicate with Delaney through the airwaves.

The interviewer smiled, showing off perfectly white teeth. "Delaney, I know your family is happy to have you back safe and sound. Can you share with the viewers what you've been doing for the last few weeks?"

Would she mention him? The house, the car, the tour bus, the hotel? The stolen backpack? The love? Any of it?

Lane smiled and gave a little laugh to cover up her hiccup. He might not have even noticed the hiccup if he didn't know her so well.

"The last few weeks have been . . . memorable for a lot of reasons. I'd like to focus on what I've learned rather than the specifics of where I was or what I was doing. First of all, I've realized that even though I share part of my life with the public, that doesn't mean I don't have a right to privacy. Everyone has a right to privacy, especially in the bedroom."

Grant took a glug of wine as Lane continued.

"As most viewers are aware, a video of me surfaced recently that was recorded and distributed without my knowledge or consent.

That's not only hurtful to me and my family, it's also illegal and I intend to have the person responsible prosecuted to the full extent of the law."

Another glug. He might need the bottle.

"So you will be pursuing legal action against Boyd Hampton?" the interviewer asked.

"Absolutely."

"That must be an awful burden to carry around, knowing that the video exists. How do you feel about that?"

"I admit it bothers me. It's embarrassing, but the thing I've learned from this experience is that you should never let anyone else determine how you feel about yourself. If someone takes advantage of you, speak up."

If someone takes advantage? Is that what had really happened? Remorse swept over him. The only thing he'd seen or heard was that single magazine article suggesting she released the video herself, and he'd hesitated to give her the benefit of the doubt. She'd told him as much, but he hadn't believed her, and that made him nearly as big of a jerk as the guy who'd made that video in the first place. Nearly.

Lane shifted in the chair, dropping one foot down to the floor, casual, comfortable, in spite of the topic. The camera loved her. She was a natural as she went on talking. "I've finally realized there is no shame in defending yourself. There's no shame in owning up to your mistakes either. I've made plenty. I'm probably not finished."

She smiled brightly and the interviewer laughed. "We all make mistakes, right?"

Lane nodded. "Some of us just like to go big. For instance, running away from this situation was a mistake. I should have faced it straight on. Turns out you can't outswim a shark so your best bet is just to punch it right in the nose."

The interviewer chuckled again. "Interesting analogy."

Lane chuckled along with her. "I think the bottom line is that whatever life hands you, deal with it. You can't hide. Whoever you are, whatever you've done, whatever the circumstances, own it. Be yourself, don't try to hide, don't try to be someone or something you're not. Image is a pretty big deal around here in Los Angeles, probably in most other places too, but when it comes down to it, it's the person we are at the core that really matters. All the rest is just details."

Details. All the rest was just details. That's what she'd tried to tell him about her name. And she was right. He knew who she was at the core.

The interviewer nodded, her head tilting sideways a bit as if she was pondering this very controversial point. "That's true about image, but as a celebrity stylist, I would think you'd consider image to be pretty important too."

Lane nodded back. "It's human nature to want to look your best. There's nothing wrong with that as long as that's not your only focus. I've enjoyed being a stylist, but now I'm excited about turning my attention to some other projects that I'm really passionate about."

"Such as?"

Such as? What other projects? What was she talking about?

"I have a few charity projects I'm interested in, but you'll learn more about those as the season goes forward."

"So you've decided to stay with the show, then?" the interviewer asked. "There were rumors you'd decided to leave."

Lane giggle-hiccupped. That one was more obvious. "There are rumors I'm having an alien baby too. I can pretty much promise that nothing you read in a magazine is verifiable."

"So what about the rumors concerning you and a certain cameraman, or you and a certain musician?"

Grant leaned forward on the couch.

Lane brushed her bangs to the side. "As I said, nothing you read in a magazine is verifiable, but this might be a good time to mention I'm making it my official policy to not publicly discuss who I may or may not be involved with. That part of my life will stay private."

The interviewer practically wagged a finger at her. "Your fans will be disappointed to hear that."

Delaney's smile looked tight for the first time, but only for a second. "My fans will probably be much happier with their lives if they go out and find their own romances, and not waste time speculating about mine." Her voice was pleasant but the point was clear.

"Even so, I have to ask," the interviewer pressed, "with all that you've been through recently, being betrayed by an old boyfriend, being disparaged by some of the tabloids, Delaney Masterson, do you still believe in love?"

Her smile turned genuine and Grant's heart paused. She pressed her thumb against her lip for a second before dropping her hand into her lap. "Absolutely. Life is messy, it's complicated, and sometimes we let down the people we love the most. And sometimes they let us down, but you can't give up. Every day is a chance to get it right. So, yes, absolutely. I believe in love. You know what Elvis said. Sometimes you can't help falling."

Grant nodded at the screen. She was telling the truth. Sometimes you can't help falling.

Chapter 27

"COME ON, MELODY. HURRY UP," Delaney called to her sister from the kitchen. "If we get to yoga late we'll get stuck in the front of the room where all the mirrors are."

Sun shone in from every window as Melody hopped down the hall with one hand on the wall while trying to pull her shoe on with the other. "I like being in the front by all the mirrors. How else can I see myself?"

"Hurry up." Delaney screwed on the top to her water bottle just as Melody tipped over and fell on the floor.

"This is actually yoga right here," Mel called out, giggling. "Me trying to put on my damn shoe."

Delaney laughed at the heap that was her sister. She was glad to be home. Life in the Masterson household had returned to its loosely structured chaos, and the outpouring of support she'd received from friends and fans in the four days since her interview aired was helping to boost her spirits. But the Grant-sized canyon running its way through her heart was just as craggy, sharp, and deep.

She'd thought for sure he'd try to call her by now, but nothing. It had been over a week since she'd left Memphis, but no calls. No texts. Nothing. Then she'd seen a picture of the two of them on the cover of a magazine and wondered if he realized he'd become part of the story. He wouldn't be pleased by that. He probably thought she leaked those pictures herself. So maybe she should call and tell him she hadn't, but what would be the point?

She wanted him back. Desperately so, but she hadn't yet figured out how to make that happen. She'd even thought about calling and pretending to care about the rent money, even though she *didn't* care about it. If anything, she was glad for that last link connecting them. But pretending had an awful ring to it these days. No more pretending for her.

Melody scrambled up from the floor after finally managing to put on her shoe, but then she bent over to peek out the front window. She walked over and moved aside the curtain.

"Oh my God, would you stop dawdling? You're like a little kid." Delaney picked up her keys and headed to the front door. "I'm leaving without you."

"Why is there a hottie standing next to a yellow Volkswagen in our driveway?" Melody asked.

Delaney skidded to a halt, her shoes squeaking on the floor tiles. "What?"

"Hottie. Volkswagen. Driveway," Melody said, pointing out the window and kneeling on the sofa that was in front of it to get a better view. She moved the curtain farther to the side. "Damn. Superhot. Like, supernaturally hot."

It couldn't be. It couldn't be. It couldn't be.

Delaney plunked her keys and the water bottle down on the coffee table and knelt on the couch next to her sister to look outside.

And there he was.

Grant, in her driveway, next to her piece of shit Volkswagen. He was standing there in jeans and a white T-shirt, with his phone in his hand.

Delaney's ringtone chimed from the kitchen, and she nearly twisted her ankle trying to scramble from the couch back to the counter in record time. She did manage to knock Melody on the floor in the process, a feat that had been mostly accidental. Those Masterson girls were nothing if not graceful. Delaney scooped up her phone and stared at the screen.

The number was Grant's, of course. Of course, it was Grant's. She could see him through the window. She could just open the door, but . . . she took a big breath. In. Out. Then she answered, trying to keep her voice mellow, which was no easy task.

"Hello?"

"Lane?"

"Yes?"

His pause was just long enough to rattle her senses. Was he happy to be there? Was he still mad? She needed him to talk. She needed him to set the tone.

"It's Grant."

"I know. You're in my driveway."

"I am? Thank God. I couldn't figure out if this was the right house or not. The address matches your luggage tag but the place looks completely different on TV."

She turned around and looked out the kitchen window to stare at him. God, he looked good. He looked perfect.

"That's because on TV they use a shot of a different house so we don't get crazy stalker fans hanging out in our front yard."

Why? Why was *this* what they were talking about? She watched him nodding his head.

"Oh. Oh, that makes sense. I guess."

"Yeah."

She wanted to say something else, anything else. She'd been waiting for his call since the moment that taxi had driven her away from his aunt's house. Now it was more than a week later, and in spite of all her rehearsing, she couldn't think of any of the stuff she'd meant to tell him.

He cleared his throat. "So, um, I can't stop thinking about you," he finally said, and her heart slammed so hard inside her chest she may have just broken a rib. It felt like she'd broken a rib. She might need an X-ray.

"You can't?"

"No. In fact, I've been thinking about you a lot. Pretty much all day, and . . . definitely all night." He leaned against the side of the yellow car.

"Really?" It was hard to breathe. She might need a pulmonologist too. Her lungs were struggling as much as her heart.

Grant sounded as breathless as she felt, and she was glad. Glad he missed her. Glad he'd been thinking about her. And very, very glad that he was standing in her driveway.

He rubbed his fingertips across his forehead. "Yeah, really. Do you suppose I could come in there or you could, I don't know, come out here? Maybe? I managed to get your car back from the police, and I brought the suitcase that you left back in Bell Harbor."

"You did?"

She could see he'd brought the car but it was still a surprise. A sweet, sweet surprise. But darn it! All that stuff she'd rehearsed to say, and *still* she couldn't remember a word of it. She walked from the kitchen to the front door and glanced at Melody.

Melody fanned her face with both hands and mouthed the words, "So hot!"

Delaney nodded and yanked open the door. She set her phone down on the little table in the entryway and stepped outside. "You didn't need to drive that lousy car all the way to California," she said, walking down the brick sidewalk that connected the front porch to the driveway. She was dressed for yoga. Maybe he'd notice. He seemed to have liked the yoga. This was to her advantage. She stopped walking when she was a few feet away from him.

Grant lowered the phone and slid it into his front pocket, his eyes roving over her until they locked on her own, hot, intense. His were green in this light. She loved it when they looked so green.

"Well, I wanted to bring you your suitcase anyway. So . . . you know."

She crossed her arms, not certain what to do with her hands because mostly what she wanted to do was twist up her fists in that white T-shirt and pull his mouth down to hers. But it seemed like they should talk a little more first.

"That was . . . um . . . that's really thoughtful of you. It's still a pretty long drive."

"Well, I was heading this way anyhow. I have some LA producer types interested in financing my show so I'm meeting with them over the next couple of days."

Her heart tripped and fell. Is that why he was here? But his gaze drifted toward her mouth and she knew he wanted to kiss her just as badly as she wanted to be kissed. He should just do it then. She inched a little closer.

"Your show? The one about the charities?"

He nodded. "Yes. I made a few calls and got the green light. Good news, huh?"

She nodded. "Yes. I'm happy for you."

He reached up and rubbed the back of his neck. "There's a problem though. A big, big problem."

She pressed a thumbnail to her lip. If being involved with her had somehow led to difficulties for him and his new show, she'd feel terrible. "What kind of problem?"

A shy but hopeful smile crooked one side of his mouth. "I

need a host. A beautiful, adventurous host. Any chance you're looking for a job?"

She heated up from the center outward and felt her own smile spreading slowly. "Um, I'd have to think about that. Are you sure you'd want me? I have sort of a lousy reputation with the public, you know."

His hands reached out and grazed her hips, pulling her into the space between his feet.

"The public adores you, and anyway I don't care about what the media says. I don't buy into that sort of hype. I know who you are. I know about the stuff that matters."

His fingers squeezed and he continued talking, which was a good thing because words were beyond her capability just then. "Lane, I'm sorry I gave you such a hard time back in Memphis. I was an ass. I was angry because . . . well, because I was so crazy about you and then when I found out about *some* of the lies, I just thought that maybe *everything* had been a lie. And I wanted what we had to be real."

She closed that final distance because she couldn't bear not to. She wrapped her arms around his shoulders. His arms went tight around her waist and they were face-to-face. Blissfully face-to-face. Right where she wanted to be. She leaned back to gaze at him.

"It was real. I should have told you everything right from that very first night, but it all happened so fast. The truth is I'm not a very practiced liar, and the whole situation spun out of control before I could figure out what to do. It was stupid of me and I'm so sorry you got caught up in it."

He nodded. "I know. I get it, now. I do. The press was always pretty decent to me and my show but I've seen how they twist things when it comes to you. I should have realized that sooner. I should have given you more time to explain. I guess I was embarrassed because I felt like I'd been tricked, but then I saw your interview and I realized how you must have felt about, well, about what happened to you. I see how you got caught up in all of it and it wasn't fair. I'm really sorry about that, Lane. And I never would have sent you back to the hotel if I'd known the press was there waiting. You do know that, don't you? I feel terrible about that."

"That wasn't your fault." It wasn't his fault he smelled so good either. She couldn't possibly stay mad at him when he smelled this good.

"I still feel terrible," he said.

"Well, I still feel terrible about lying to you in the first place. So where does that leave us? Both feeling terrible?" She looked up at his face and wondered if she'd ever get tired of seeing it. His eyes, his smile, his subtle dimples.

"I have a much better idea," he said, smiling down at her, and she had her answer. She knew for sure, she'd never get tired of any of that.

"What's your idea?" she asked, pressing against him, feeling the heat from his body and nearly melting from it.

"We start over. Tell me about yourself. Tell me the stuff that's real."

She sighed, a big happy sigh, and the world seemed to right itself after being off-kilter for far too long. "Well, for starters, I'm Delaney Masterson and I live here."

Grant's gaze dropped to her lips. "That's a good start. What else?"

"My parents are both famous, I'm regrettably infamous, and I swear to you that everything that happened between us in bed, everything I said about my feelings, that all was true. Every moment, every word. Do you believe me?"

His hands moved up from her hips to cup her face, and he looked into her eyes so long she wondered if he'd forgotten the question.

"I do believe you. Let's promise from here on out, no secrets. No lies. Always tell me the truth and I'll do the same. Even if it's not comfortable. It's the only way I know how to do this and be able to trust that it's real."

She loved him so much.

SoMuchSoMuchSoMuch.

"Yes, OK. We'll always be honest. Absolutely honest. I promise. In that case, can I ask you a question?" she whispered.

He nodded. "Anything."

Her heart thudded in her chest, crazy fast. "Do you think it's possible you could ever fall in love with Delaney Masterson?"

His eyes sparkled, and he leaned forward until his lips were very nearly touching hers.

"I already have. I just didn't know it."

And then he kissed her.

EPILOGUE

"ARE YOU SURE YOU KNOW what you're doing?" Tyler asked. He was leaning against the doorframe of the dressing room at St. Aloysius Church of the Immaculate Conception while Grant stood in front of the mirror. Scotty and Carl were there too, and looking good. The men of this family cleaned up nicely when they were all in tuxes. Which they were. Donna was there as well, looking happy and vibrant in a dark purple dress that Lane had picked out just for her, saying it was the perfect complement to his mother's ivory complexion.

Grant smiled confidently back at his brother. "I know exactly what I'm doing, Ty. Getting married is the smartest decision I've ever made. I'm certain of that. And anyway, weren't you the one who told me when you know, you just know?"

Tyler chuckled. "Probably, you dumbass, but what I meant was, do you think you can manage to tie that bow tie on your own, because it looks like you're trying to strangle yourself."

"Here, let me help," Carl said, stepping forward. "I'm pretty good at these. I used to be quite dapper, back in the day."

"You're still dapper, sweetheart," Donna said.

Grant relinquished his grip on the tie and turned to let Carl give it a try. The guy wasn't nearly as useless as Grant had once thought. In fact, over the last several months, the old sloe gin pusher had really come through. He was taking excellent care of Donna and she was doing remarkably well. No stealing, no gambling. No meltdowns at the Bob Evans. Grant liked to think his being home more often had something to do with that, but he knew deep down, the real reason his mother was better was because she was working hard. She'd come a long way since stealing Lane's bag back in January.

Now it was May and the Bell Harbor snow had finally melted. Spring was in the air. Flowers were blooming. Birds were chirping, and Grant Connelly was getting married.

"There," Carl said, giving the tie one last tug. He patted Grant on the shoulder. "You look good, kid."

Donna sniffled, but her eyes were bright. She dabbed a tissue to her nose. "You do look good, so handsome. All you boys are so handsome. I'm so blessed. And before we know it, Scotty will be getting married."

Scotty took a step backward. "Don't start with that, Mom. Let's just get through this wedding first, OK? Without the waterworks?"

"I can't help it." Her smile was tremulous. "I'm just so happy."

Grant stepped closer and gave her a fast hug. "I'm glad, Mom. I really am."

The door flew open and Fontaine burst into the room like a bottle rocket. His dark hair was slicked back and his goatee artfully carved. He clapped his hands. "Lickety-split, Connelly people. What's taking you all so long? If you don't hurry up, I will be forced to notify the pa-pa-paparazzi and your secret wedding won't be so secret after all."

Grant turned toward the wedding planner and smiled again. He had a feeling he'd be doing a lot of that today. Smiling. In fact, it seemed like that's all he'd done for the past six weeks, ever since proposing to Lane on the peak of Mount Otemanu in Bora Bora. Asking her to marry him had been a spontaneous gesture, but there was no doubt in his mind it was the right decision. Every instinct told him so. She made him happy in a way no one else ever had, and no one else ever could. He intended to spend the rest of his life trying to return that favor. Starting now.

"I'm ready, Fontaine," Grant said.

Tyler handed him the tuxedo jacket and he put it on.

"Oh, aren't you fabulous?" Fontaine said with a sigh. "You look like a superhero."

Grant grinned into the mirror and tweaked his bow tie. "Do I?"

Fontaine nodded. "Absolutely. So come on, Matrimony Man. Time to fly off to your next adventure."

"I always knew you'd make a beautiful bride." Delaney's mother blinked away a perfectly timed tear. Even without cameras present, she knew how to work a moment. "This would have made an amazing episode of *Pop Rocks*, wouldn't it have?"

Delaney chuckled and shook her head. Her hair was styled back from her face and was still her natural brown shade. Grant liked it that way, and she'd never gotten around to redoing her blonde highlights. She'd been too busy traveling around the world and falling deeply, madly in love.

She looked into the mirror and adjusted her simple but elegant veil. It was the perfect complement to her white satin dress. She may have left her life as a stylist behind, but she still knew when something looked good. And this looked good. Or maybe she just thought so because everything seemed to make her happy these days.

Even pressure from her mom to turn this wedding into a public spectacle didn't bother her. "Really, Mom? It's my wedding day and you're still thinking about ratings?"

"She's always thinking about ratings." Melody was sitting on a beige velvet chair in the church's bridal dressing room where the Masterson family waited. "But she's right about the bride thing. You do look amazing. If you ever decide to go back to being a stylist, you should do weddings. And I could do bridal makeup. We could have our own show." Melody was teasing. Mostly.

Roxanne did a little twirl in the mirror, making her swishy, plum-colored dress even swishier. "You should do weddings, Lane. These bridesmaid dresses are not half bad."

"Thanks, Rox. That means a lot, coming from you. It's nearly a compliment."

"I'm not always thinking about ratings," Nicole continued on as if her daughters hadn't tried to change the subject. "I just think our fans would be thrilled to see you so happy. But honestly, having a secret wedding in Bell Harbor is going to make for fabulous headlines. It's quite brilliant, really. You do have a flair for the dramatic, darling." She leaned over and air-kissed Delaney's cheek.

"This marriage isn't a publicity stunt, Nic." Delaney's father stepped forward and took his daughter by the shoulders. He smiled down at her, the famous Masterson smile, and she felt her eyes start to puddle up. He'd cut off that ponytail of his at last and looked pretty stylin' in his tux. Her father was finally moving into the next phase of his life, just as she was moving on into hers.

"It's the real deal, right, kid?" he asked. "You're doing this for all the right reasons?"

Delaney nodded, and sniffled. "It is, and I am."

"Good for you. I'm so proud of you."

Fontaine popped his head inside the room after a quick rap on the door. "OK, Masterson folk, the Connelly people are all in their places. Mommy of the bride, the usher is waiting to take you to your seat. Chop, chop. Let's get these beautiful people married, shall we?"

Delaney's mother hugged her close. "Oh, Lane, it seems like I should have some profound words of wisdom to share with my daughter on her wedding day, but all I can think of to say is how much I love you."

"That's perfect, Mom. It's all you need to say." Delaney's heart was bursting with joy, and if her mother said more, they'd all start to cry and ruin Melody's meticulous makeup jobs. Paparazzi or no paparazzi, she didn't want to get married with mascara running down her face.

"All right, ladies. Enough mush." Fontaine hustled her mother from the room, then Roxanne and Melody followed. Melody turned and winked before disappearing into the hallway.

Delaney's father held out his arm, his face full of pride. "Are you ready for this?" he murmured. "You could make a break for it, you know."

Delaney smiled and shook her head. "No running away for me, Pop. I'm happy. And I'm finally heading in just the right direction."

"Good, because I think I hear them playing our song."

———◆———

The headline read, RUNAWAY BRIDE?

Former *Pop Rocks* wild child Delaney Masterson may have snuck down the aisle with hunky boyfriend cinematographer Grant Connelly in a supersecret surprise wedding attended only by their families and a handful of their closest pals, but it looks as if there's no settling down on the horizon for these two lovebirds. The dynamic husband-and-wife duo are off to places unknown to begin filming their new series, *Sweet Charity*, a show featuring international organizations doing charitable works all around the globe. Produced, directed, and filmed by Connelly and hosted by Masterson, each week a different charity will be featured and viewers can go online to make donations or volunteer to get involved. Word has it we can expect a lot of guest celebrities to stop by and hawk their favorite charities, and we're certain that one-time Beverly Hills stylist and fashionista expert Masterson can show them how to make khaki look sexy!

"Hey, Finch!" shouted Reggie from the boogie-woogie room of the Paradise Brothers' tour bus, "You're not going to believe this! Honeybun went and got herself married."

AUTHOR'S NOTE

I'd like to thank the staff at the Heartbreak Hotel for their gracious hospitality and note that any errors or variations in describing the hotel are mine alone. I spent time in the Burning Love Suite and the Graceland Suite, and both rooms were pure Elvisy goodness. The Graceland Suite even has a doorbell. How fun is that? I did take a few liberties with the description of the Jungle Room Lounge because it has no stage. I made that part up, but I get to do that because it's my job. I'd also like to note that, while weather in the South is often moderate, I wrote this book during the winter of the polar vortex when even things in Memphis were cold. Still, I took a few liberties with the weather as well.

On a final note, the main characters of this book are motivated by a desire to contribute to the greater good. If you are similarly motivated, here are some of my favorite charities. Thank you for considering them.

The Wounded Warrior Project: http://www.woundedwarrior project.org/

Reach Out WorldWide: https://www.roww.org/

Heifer International: http://www.heifer.org/

UNICEF: http://www.unicef.org/

ACKNOWLEDGMENTS

First and foremost, thanks to my wonderful and tireless team at Montlake Publishing. Your support is surpassed only by your generosity and zeal, and I am grateful. To Hai-Yen, Helen, Melody, Susan, Thom, Jessica, and Kelli, you guys are the best. Beyond the best. You are the superbestest. Ginormous thanks to Nalini Akolekar for your confidence, guidance, unwavering support, and an extraspecial thanks for loving Carl as much as I do.

Thanks to Kimberly Kincaid, Alyssa Alexander, and Jennifer McQuiston. You guys know why!

Thanks to Darcy Woods for your impeccable and enviable mastery of snark, and for sending me a celebratory red balloon when I really needed one. Thanks to Kieran Kramer for those early reads and your fabulous insight.

Thanks to Jane Pierangeli and Samhita Rhodes for reading, reading, reading (sometimes from halfway around the world—or wherever Switzerland is) and for offering up such fabulous suggestions. Can't wait to collaborate again!

Thanks to Shelley and Stacy Smith for inventing an imaginary product that should seriously become a real product.

Thanks to the Eskimo Brothers for their sassy lyrics and honky-tonk style, because when I said, "I'm a romance writer and you guys have totally given me an idea for a book," I wasn't kidding. Thanks to Molly Mesnick who graciously agreed to answer my questions about life as a TV reality star. I'm glad you got your "real life" happily ever after.

And finally, thanks to my husband, who has always supported me, but who truly went above and beyond this time to make sure life didn't fall apart for the rest of the household while I was otherwise occupied, and to my wonderful children, who cheer me up and cheer me on. I'm so proud of you. Without you, none of the rest would matter.

ABOUT THE AUTHOR

photo© Allie Gadziewski, 2012

Tracy Brogan is an award-winning, best-selling novelist who writes fun and funny stories about ordinary people finding extraordinary love, and also lush historical romance full of royal intrigue, damsels causing distress, and the occasional man in a kilt. She has been nominated by Romance Writers of America® for a prestigious RITA Award for her debut novel, *Crazy Little Thing*, and was nominated by RWA for two Golden Heart Awards. She's a Booksellers Best Award recipient, along with two Golden Quill Awards in both contemporary and historical romance. Unapologetically devoted to romance, Tracy lives in Michigan with her often-bemused husband, their gloriously above-average children, and their two intellectually challenged dogs. Tracy loves to hear from readers, so please visit her website at tracybrogan.com or e-mail her at TracyBrogan@att.net.